What the public said about Ian's first novel, 'Crossing The Water':

'an atmospheric and heartfelt tale'

'a captivating book, which demonstrates passion and intellect in every chapter'

'the feelings of the characters and their responses to their lives and relationships were both subtle and at times shocking, but always fully believable'

'evocative descriptions litter the text, bringing disparate landscapes vividly to readers'

'lean, realist prose that lends itself well to storytelling... elements of thriller, romance, tragedy and humour, all sewn together with strong historical accuracy'

The Cardinal's Hat

Makri Press
ISBN number 978-0-9928485-4-5

Foreword

In 2002 I was shown around Istanbul by my Turkish friends Ayse and Cengiz. I fell in love with the sheer splendour of the city and its timeless feel, but was simultaneously shocked at my own ignorance about it.

This, I discovered, had been Constantinople: not only the greatest city of the medieval era, but also the capital of the 'Christianised' Roman Empire from 330AD (when Constantine established it as his 'New Rome') until 1453! The eastern half of the Roman Empire had remained intact, a dominant power in the eastern Mediterranean and western Asia (and arguably, the greatest Christian Empire of the era) until 1204.

Then, in a spectacular and catastrophic own goal (and a black comedy of epic proportions) city and Empire were partially destroyed and their treasures looted... by an army of crusaders. (See 'The Fourth Crusade' by Donald Queller and Thomas Madden.) Yet this bizarre episode has been so successfully 'buried' that two literary agents returned this novel on the grounds that they did not deal with fantasy! Sadly, the story that follows has a solid backbone of historical truth...

As I mused on this hidden history over the intervening years, I became aware of voices clamouring in my imagination, demanding that their stories be told...

A Good Wine

The girl moves silently into the corridor, cradling a wooden bowl and spoon against her chest with one hand, balancing an oil lamp in the other. On her left, bright shafts of sunlight penetrate stone arches and embroidered curtains, warming her calves, but she turns her head, her eyes avoiding the glare. As she steps from the cool of white marble onto silk rugs, they seem to caress the soles of her feet. Her eyes are drawn to the mosaic that covers the walled side of the corridor, her focus flickering along the design as she moves, looking for the birds amidst the leafy branches.

In the centre of this design a heavy drape hangs, masking an entrance to the underworld. She pauses there and inhales deeply, trying to fix the comforting aromas of incense and perfume, the smells of the main house, within her lungs. Then she pirouettes, pushing the drape to one side with her hip, and slips through the aperture behind it, her slight body brushing against the cool stone within. As the drape falls back into place, the world of light and luxury vanishes.

She raises the lamp, peering forward and down into the gloom, sniffing at the stale, damp, musty air. Stone steps, roughly hewn, descend into the rock under the house. She sighs, grits her teeth, and feels her way carefully down, reluctantly pursuing a small void of increasing darkness. Where the steps end, the narrow corridor divides – a sharply cut, narrow passage curves to the left and a rougher, wider corridor opens off to the right. She turns left; a dozen steps later, a wooden door flickers into view. A few steps more, and her lamplight glints on metal hinges, outlining a spider's careful tapestry above her head. She pauses here – a whiff of human decay and despair seems to slither out from under the rough wooden door, assaulting her throat. Her bare feet sense the coldness of the rock; her toes curl.

She shivers, sets the bowl of cold soup down and reaches to grasp the iron bolt – then frowns when she sees it is already released. Her heart stops. Did she forget, this morning? She closes her eyes and prays to God that no one has been down here, so that she may escape a beating. She sucks in another deep breath, and pushes the door open. A rancid stench, not quite solid, rolls over her. It causes her to flinch, increasing the violence of her urge to step away, to flee to the light above.

Against the far wall, covered by a single rough woollen blanket, a shapeless figure lies prone on a small cot. The old man's body lies still and silent, but he is clearly awake. Two eyes glitter as she approaches and then, as recognition dawns, they regard her with curiosity. He speaks softly, his voice a little slurred, devoid of his usual precision. 'Ah, so you have come at last... my little treasure. Has Timon sent you... to be my last request?'

The girl shakes her head at his nonsense. She feels far too exhausted for this today and sighs as she places the lamp on the ledge above the cot. *At least he seems here in this world today*, she thinks. 'I've brought your food...'

She stops, puzzled, noticing a jug and bowl upon the floor in the corner. She shrugs, sets down her own bowl and pulls back the blanket; now she sees that the old man's hands are bound together, the same rope looped around his waist to immobilise him. She drops the blanket, wringing one hand with the other, biting her lip. *Has he tried to escape again, and been caught? If so, I will surely be whipped again.* Her face remains a mask, but her shoulders contract, and she whimpers.

Amidst his matted, patchy hair and whiskers, his eyes watch her, studying her reaction. He nods slowly, and gives her a half-crooked grin. 'Don't worry, little donkey. Timon brought this wine here for me. You'll not be punished... at least, not for this...'

She nods and breathes a deep sigh of relief, only to cough the foul air out. Can she believe him? *This is just how he used to sound, before they put him in the cellar. But now, he cannot promise me anything. Can he?* She steps forward to examine his face at close quarters, searching for signs of deceit. Eventually, she shrugs and pulls his light, bony body upright, balancing him against the wall. He smiles again and when he speaks, she hears a tone of authority mixed with resignation.

'Let me explain, my little treasure. You know what I am now: an old, helpless husk. But once I was Basil of Makri, a Roman, a merchant who traded with wealth beyond the dreams of most men – and also with lives and souls, even of those whom I loved. I survived fire, war, storms and pirates. At least, once I was such a man... now, through lack of foresight, I find myself a prisoner here in my own home. I trusted my family too much – and they have repaid me by shutting me away. Is this not true?' His eyes fix upon the jug, and his voice urges her, 'Give me a little more of Dionysus's liquid amnesia... I must dissolve within its magic...'

She does as he bids, though her mind is still racing. *No one has dared bring him wine since they locked him down here, in this miserable storeroom – so why would Timon, of all people, now?* She pours wine from the jug into the bowl. It smells rich, not even watered.

He snorts with amusement as he watches her face. 'Ha! You do well to sniff it, my little treasure, before you taste. It is good wine, granted. But the potion within it is not for you, unless you wish to sleep like the dead. Timon tells me it is a sleeping draught.' He shrugs. 'I have no reason to disbelieve him. But he hasn't given me enough – as you know well, his malice far exceeds his forethought. The fool tied my hands first, and only then realised he would have to feed the wine to me. And you can also testify how little patience he has. Come, let me sup.'

She hesitates for a moment, then lifts the bowl to his lips. Basil slurps and sucks, naked greed on his face, wine spilling out around his chin. She waits until he finishes, lowers the bowl, and wipes his chin with the blanket. He tips his head back, licks his lips, and rolls his tongue around his mouth, searching for the last remnants of the wine, before gulping some air. While he struggles to catch his breath again, she studies him, searching for some further clue. She watches him half-close his eyes and emit three deep, shuddering sighs.

'Listen to me, little treasure.' His voice comes in short gasps, breathing and talking to the girl at the same time. 'Timon will return soon, to finish me off. This... this is his way. The wine is a kindness, a blessing. It makes it easier... for both of us. He'll return later with a silk rope, or suchlike: something that leaves no mark.' He meets her eyes briefly and shakes his head, staring at the floor. 'I will spend my time in eternity feeling grateful to you if my last vision of this world is not the pleasure on his face. I would rather dream my way into the next world, even if my dreams do sometimes fill with ridiculous visions and spirits...'

She stares at his face as he sits there for a long moment, locked within his private thoughts. He sniffs and looks up, appealing to her with his red-rimmed eyes.

'Give me more.'

The girl obeys. This time he guzzles more slowly, deliberately, savouring his own last supper. With each swallow now, she watches liquid pulse gently from the corners of his mouth. His actions seem slower, less coordinated, as the deep red wine and the potion within it seep through his veins, filling him with a pensive weariness, drifting in like fog. As she tips the bowl for him to drain, the last few drops bleed from his mouth and dribble down his scrawny throat, following paths formed by wrinkles and blue veins. She tries to beat down the horror and fear that is rising within her. This time, she cannot wipe his mouth. She is frozen.

He catches his breath, and lifts his head to look at her. 'Listen to me very carefully, my little slave. You must not remain in this house. You know too much. And if they think that you may talk, they will silence you too.' His eyelids are drooping now, but he sighs and continues. 'You... you gave me kindness when no one else would. The only way I can repay you is with this advice. When you leave here, don't try to take the main roads – that is how runaways are caught. You must hide yourself where no-one will look. Go over the pass above the town... onto the peninsula, to the village near the ruins of Karmylessos. Look for a family in that village. Any family

4

with old ones: the older the better. Tell the old ones you were a friend to Basil of Makri, the husband of Eirene. In that village, they will all shelter you. And ask the old ones to show you the path to the ancient shrine... to the goddess of fortune, Tyche. Someone will know the way...'

He closes his eyes for a second. Then his head twitches, twice, until the eyes half open and meet her own. 'Go to the shrine. At the mouth of the cave, under a layer of flat stones, you will find an ancient well. Look within it. You will find gold there, enough to start your life again. My wife hid it there, many years ago. You have been my last treasure, so you shall have my first...' He sighs, closes his eyes again. Then he slumps back, mumbling, 'Be careful, though. Respect Tyche, or she will play a trick upon you. As she did to me, many times...'

She sits, stunned and paralysed, feeling her stomach churn while she watches his body surrender to sleep. Her mind races, comparing his words to everything she already knows about this house, this family. Can she trust him? His slack, inert form begins to slide sideways and down. She moves to catch him and pulls his body across the cot. She forces herself to think, to plan. 'A curse upon this house,' she mutters... then shakes her head, remembering that this particular house has no need of curses.

That thought spurs her, and she shakes herself like a dog. She wipes his body and the drinking bowl clean, replaces the blanket, and checks that she will leave the room much as it was before she entered. Only when she shuts and bolts the door, does her body permit her to make haste, to flee. At the top of the steps, she pushes the heavy curtain aside and rushes into the blinding light, sucking life into her lungs at last.

She almost blunders into the cadaverous figure waiting there.

'Did he refuse his food?'

Timon's dark eyes examine her and the bowl of soup she carries, just as a cat observes a bird. He has a pillow tucked under one arm. She cannot speak.

'Well?'

'No... no... he was asleep. I could not rouse him.' The words spill out without thought; she floods with relief at what she hears herself saying.

'Well, perhaps I shall go and see him now. You may leave. Go and help in the kitchen.'

She swallows, ridding her mouth of the taste of rising bile, for a moment at least. 'Yes. Thank you, master."

*   *   *

Arrival In The Underworld

Like Lazarus, I drift back reluctantly into my body. My arms and legs ache and throb as if they have been crushed within the tomb, their strength so diminished I can barely move, my hands and feet curling into useless balls as they twitch and spasm. That rasping sound must be my own breath. Gradually, I realise why darkness pervades my bedchamber, why night has murdered day. After beating my old body senseless, Leo has had me cast down; below the level of the slaves, into this small, locked cellar with no air or light. Am I not right? I lie in my own shit and piss. It must stink so badly in here that my fastidious daughter's ghost would take one sniff and die a second death... for pity's sake, Leo, why did you not leave me in the tomb?

Yet, still they bring me food. The older slaves who knew me as their master slop it into me carelessly, roughly pushing the spoon through my lips, leaving me to search for scraps of food scattered in my bed later, when my stomach aches with emptiness. And some of them add different kinds of foulness to my food: animal droppings mixed in like raisins, judging by the taste. No doubt they find this hilarious, knowing they now have me in their power. The younger ones, like my donkey, that little treasure who did not know me as a cruel master, take more care, treating me like a sick child. Once a day a bucket of water arrives with rags; hands appear out of the darkness (sometimes roughly, sometimes gently) to wash me. Occasionally, when Leo and his family leave the house, my little treasure takes me up to the bathing rooms and cleans me properly. I suspect I owe this mercy to Leo's wife and her Christian charity. Once, I would have thought this a weakness. Now that my own strength has drained away and I have so little other pleasure, I must be grateful. I have no books: my inner world, too, has been stolen from me. Even if I had, this stale cellar is as black as pitch. So, within this living tomb, I constantly cross the border between sleep and wakefulness. Memories and fantasies are my only comfort; they merge into my dreams so that I find it hard to tell whether I am awake or not...

Something disturbs my thoughts. At first I think this new interruption is a dream, and perhaps it could be, since it has the brightness and sharpness of another world. The youngest slave, my little donkey, is lifting me up. She shows me a book, and whispers, 'I will leave a candle to read it by. The book is from Sophia.' Which Sophia? It must be the child, Leo's daughter, for the other is long gone. Her hair brushes my face as she leans over me and I smell the heavenly scent of a young woman. Ah, this must be a dream. Yet the book is real; I can feel it in my hands. I watch while she places the candle on a ledge above me and lights it, before leaving me alone.

My hands and fingers are as numb as clubs, but I manage to turn the pages. I discover a play by Menander; a dire attempt at comedy, but in my situation bad theatre is better than none at all. Carpe diem; I read for an hour or two, only to fall asleep and waste the rest of the candle – perhaps I can get another, and finish it. My body aches like fire when I wake, while my mind races around this darkened room, remembering that scent of a young woman, and more. A door opens, and the memory of my own Sophia enters my prison.

Such graceful steps her image takes, around my bed. She stands and smiles down at me, as if waiting for me to rise and walk with her. She seems far too young; she must be a ghost, come to haunt me by bringing back memories of that blessed and cursed time... And yet she seems real, I can smell her; she touches me, brushing my forehead with her fingers. What a blissful sensation. Is it really her? Strange how I still think of her as my Sophia, though I suspect she was only briefly mine in her heart. Let me tell you how I came to meet her, and perhaps you may understand my infatuation.

As a child, I lived in the shadow of my older brother Justin. Reckless, brave and strong, no other boy dared to stand in Justin's way. Danger attracted him like a magnet: I often watched him climb rocky heights to dive from them and swim down, trying to catch fish with a spear. I thought him a little crazy, but Justin survived and thrived, and our parents encouraged him. Centuries of war against barbarian invaders had made our society value such boys, vital in the army that defends the Empire. Justin left us all behind, entering imperial service as a tall, muscular, young soldier. Army discipline channelled his energy usefully; the game of war suited him. While I grew to maturity, Justin fought on the Empire's borders and rose through the ranks, sending money to our parents every month to buy a better house. My parents constantly discussed Justin's prospects: perhaps he will become a general, perhaps after his service in the army he will be rewarded with land and status. Perhaps, they hoped, he might even govern a town.

They had lower expectations for me – just to follow my father, a fisherman. With his help, I bought a small boat. But even at sixteen, I had a sharp mind beneath my mop of dark hair. I did not fish for long; instead, I began to barter goods along the coast of Lycia. Outside the major fortified towns and cities, our population scattered itself widely, in small settlements. Goods had to be exchanged. Traditionally, merchants possessed little status and influence; trade attracted heavy taxes. When the Empire needed extra revenue, merchants bled first. But I could sense a wind of change...

Once, the heartland of our Empire lay inland. But now the Seljuk Turks had spilled across much of the Anatolian plain. They ruled this territory as 'the Sultanate of Rome'. Such impudence! They had stolen the Empire's name, as well as its land... thus our coastline had become a frontier area – and this new frontier bubbled like a pregnant melting pot, as merchants and traders, pilgrims, slaves and mercenaries of every race and religion passed through. They all had needs, or goods to trade. Meanwhile, the people grew cynical about our leaders and their laws. In various treaties, our Emperors made foreign merchants exempt from taxes. This infuriated Roman merchants, who began to find their own ways to avoid paying tax. Fortune occasionally favours the brave; more often, she favours those brave enough to constrain their scruples. Pots of gold waited, like hopeful brides, for men willing to take a few judicious risks.

I learned to load and unload most of my goods in small bays, avoiding the main harbours where the tax collectors lurked. But every so often I took a small boat into the main harbour at Makri to keep up appearances. On one particular day, the tax collector greeted me with his usual hopeful smile. This turned into a scowl when I showed him my cargo, a few sacks of new olives. Careful to play the part of a dutiful, slightly stupid fisherman, I offered him a few small coins and asked if it was enough. The collector took them all and stomped away along the jetty, muttering and looking up to heaven as I grinned behind his back. Then I noticed a tall, dark skinned man of middle age, smiling broadly at my little theatre. He wore fine silk robes, plain white in colour, with a small beard, and a white skullcap on top of his head. He nodded at me and I made a little bow while he stifled his laughter.

Once the tax collector was out of earshot, the stranger strode over and asked me if I lived in Makri. At first his upright, haughty bearing, made me wonder if he had some official position. But he spoke to me far too politely for an official. He asked me questions about the local towns, the distances to other ports, the local tides and currents. Each time I prepared to ask who he was, he asked me another question about local prices, the weather, and so forth; such was his dizzying pace that I never did find out his identity. That evening, my father told me the same man had made enquiries about me, in the town. I felt alarm, worrying that I might have told him too much. Had my far too-eager tongue landed me in trouble?

The next morning, I heard a knock at the outer door. I opened it and jumped a little when I saw the stranger again. He stood alone, looking expectant; perhaps a little nervous, too. My own fear subsided a little. 'Who are you?' I blurted out.

The stranger blinked and for a second, his brow furrowed. Then he nodded to himself, slowly. 'Ah. I must apologise for not introducing myself yesterday. My name is Luke of Antioch. I am like you, a merchant. I wish to discuss business with you.'

I felt my body relax, my curiosity rising about this well-dressed stranger. 'Well, in that case you must take bread and wine with me. This is my parent's house and they will welcome you. Come in.'

After the formalities, Luke put his cup down, straightened his body, and stared at me with his dark piercing eyes. 'I have a warehouse in Constantinople and I am looking to expand my business. I need a local man to help me distribute luxury goods in this area and provide me with cargoes of food to take back to the city. Someone who can meet my cargo ship in a quiet bay – somewhere safe, where we can unload the most valuable cargo away from the tax collector's eyes.' He looked at me calmly, waiting for my reaction.

I grinned. 'I can do that, certainly. But it might be wiser to have several smaller boats, the size of large fishing boats, entering these waters, rather than one large cargo ship. From a distance, the smaller boats pass as fishing boats, arousing no suspicion or gossip. They also move faster under oars, reducing the risk of piracy, and manoeuvre easier in small harbours. Add a few nets for decoration and you also create a good hiding place for small amounts of luxury goods. I already have one like this but can easily build more and find local men to sail them.'

Luke fingered his beard, studying my face intently while he listened. Then, he took off his skullcap, revealing a monk's tonsure, and folded and refolded the skullcap while he considered. At last he replaced the cap and nodded. 'That makes sense. It also means a smaller outlay per cargo and a more constant flow of goods and profit. Shall we be partners, then, Basil of Makri? I shall buy and sell the goods in the capital; and you will do the same here?'

I tried to hide my elation by simply nodding back. *Tyche, I am yours.*

'And together, we will grow our own little fleet?'

I nodded again. *Forever, Tyche, forever.*

Arrival In The Underworld

Luke took my hand between his own and shook it, three times. 'Agreed, then. We shall be partners, you and I.' After hammering out more details, he left; I pinched myself, twice.

With Luke's help, my little business quickly grew from two boats into seven. Luke organised the trade in the capital, sending silk, incense, and spices. I sold these throughout Lycia and sent Luke the best of our local honey, olive oil, grain, and wine. Before this meeting I had taken a few small, tottering steps on my road to fortune, but this chance encounter, this unexpected good fortune, changed my life forever. Luke had opened up one new world for me; and he would open another when I met his beautiful daughter, Sophia.

* * *

My next visitation emerges abruptly out of the darkness, smelling of death, his shoes squelching out muddy water from hell's river. I recognise his shambling gait; it's that fool Bernard of Chevreuse, whom my brother found on the road to Nicaea, who rescued two children to try to save his soul. He sits by my bed, waiting, while I pretend to sleep. Perhaps if I sleep, he will dissolve back into the air and return to where he belongs.

Alas, he seems solid enough. I feel my arm being shaken, persistently, by a strong, bony hand and I open half of one eye to glance at him: he sits in a plain woollen tunic, with a cross of red sewn upon it, large as life. I shut my eye, willing for sleep to carry me away. Then I feel him grip the flesh of my side, under the rib, and pinch it, hard. That hurts. I knock his arm away, curse aloud and tell him to go back to hell.

He laughs softly. 'I can wait a little for that. Right now you must listen, Basil of Makri. I have a need to confess to you, to explain to you how I came to your land.'

I open my eyes. He too is old now; he has lost his front teeth and stinks like a goat. 'I am not a damned priest,' I say, 'go and confess elsewhere, let me sleep.'

'You will listen to my story, Basil, if you wish to rest. It's not a bad tale; when my soldiering was done I made my living by it, going from tavern to tavern, entertaining others for my supper and some coin. You knew me as a soldier, yet most of my life I was a storyteller.'

Despite myself, I cannot ignore him. Slowly, I slide into his chronicle like a boat down a greasy slipway. I live his journey along with him, on his trek to Venice, that city of thieves...

*   *   *

The Pilgrim's Tale

You must imagine me in a tavern, Basil, an expectant crowd gathered around me. I brought my pilgrimage to life with my costume and my sword: with the cross on my chest, I let them feel the blade of a true soldier of the cross, promising to tell them how its cutting edge had bitten. Then I showed them my dagger, a curved Cuman blade, from the eastern edge of the world. They would feel its weight and quality, and wonder at how a pagan tribe could fashion such metal...

When my story begins I was young; I had hair on my head. A faith most plain also possessed me: I truly believed in the goodness and rightness of our church and its leaders, especially our Holy Father in Rome. In the summer of 1198, the new Pope, Innocent III, proclaimed a pilgrimage to recover Jerusalem and the Holy Land. In my village of Chevreuse, thirty leagues from Paris by the river Yvette, men and women chattered of little else. We young men boasted of what we would do – and I, the best archer, crowed far too loud. Yet in truth, we did not really believe this mighty drama would touch our ordinary lives, and we soon forgot. But then, early the following year, the parish priest began to call each and every Sunday for contributions to the plate, to pay for the costs of the pilgrims. I was just establishing my own smallholding; a free man, though I could ill afford to give money. This played upon my mind as a man of faith; I was touched, at first, by guilt.

Yet my life kept its course, and courting the beautiful Catherine kept my mind and body fully occupied that winter. Oh yes, my friends, this bold young archer knew where he desired to shoot his arrows. She was a maid, so she made me wait. But as a keen and skilled archer I uncovered her target, and she caressed my arrow. I could not miss, coming so close to her. No maid (as my Catherine had now become with me) could have made me happier. We came together very joyfully that winter, many times. We pledged ourselves to each other, during the spring of 1200.

On Easter Sunday that year, I walked to Orsay to

hear the preacher Fulk of Neuilly. Curiosity and excitement crowded the streets that day. People whispered his name with awe; only Saint Paul himself could preach alike. I had heard Fulk once before, at the great Cathedral of Notre Dame, when I had made my pilgrimage there to ask for God's grace and mercy for my livelihood, on becoming a man. On that occasion, he raged against usurers and fornicators, ending his sermon by pointing out corrupt priests with their concubines in the congregation. Picture this heavenly justice, my friends, as the mob drove those lazy parasites out into the street. Now picture earthly justice, as the crowd furiously pelted them from head to toe with mud, and worse, from the sewers. After this entertainment, a crowd of penitents surrounded Fulk, and many prostitutes gave up their trade that day. This kind of miracle made him famous.

At Orsay, it seemed as if he commanded the light itself. He began by telling us the life of Jesus. The story of Our Saviour in the Holy Land came alive in our minds; we felt as if we walked alongside Him, watched Him perform His miracles, and felt His Holy grace in our hearts. After filling us with grace and light, Fulk then plunged us into darkness. He described the infidels descending like parasites upon the Holy Land, robbing and murdering pilgrims in the churches, and desecrating the sacred places where our good Lord revealed His teaching; pissing and shitting wherever our Lord had walked and knelt upon the ground in human form.

'Such darkness has no place in our world,' Fulk told us. 'It is our Christian duty to undertake a pilgrimage to the Holy Land, and restore the light to the world. This is God's will, made plain to us by our Holy Father, the Pope. You are the fortunate generation chosen to undertake this pilgrimage of grace. Those who set out now to rid the Holy Land of darkness will be blessed both in this world and the next. Those who take the cross today will receive payments to assist their travel, and the repayments of all loans will be suspended during the pilgrimage. Here on this earth, many of these infidels own great wealth, stolen from others. You pilgrims may take these riches from them as part of your work, with God's grace and blessing, to earn the great respect of your communities. Heaven awaits you, for you pilgrims will receive absolution for all your sins; your souls, including those unfortunate few who do not return from the Holy Land, will go directly to heaven at your appointed time...'

The flood and force of Fulk's sermon swept us away; scarce a man in that church did not take a piece of cloth away with him, later to be sewn onto his tunic, that day. This red cross, the pilgrim's mark, spells out the promise that each man gave to God. Even some of the old, the sick and the lame stumbled forward, which gifted Fulk a broad smile, but he blessed us all.

Many of these 'brave' men hid their cloth away later and forgot what they had promised. But those of us who took our word seriously had to consider what this promise meant. This drama had me in its net; I had to tell my Catherine. She turned her face to the wall and cried for a long time. Then she whispered, 'You must do what is in your heart. But I will marry you anyway, before you go.' In the church, pennies dribbled slowly into the plate. Later that year, a gathering of nobles and knights pledged support for the pilgrimage. These men, including the mighty warrior, Count Thibaut of Champagne, would be our leaders... but when?

Catherine and I put the question aside and got on with our lives. The following year, we also heard little – only that agreement had been reached for the pilgrims to travel with the fleet of the Venetians in the summer of 1202. A long winter followed, and despite the uncertainty of what lay in store, a happy one. I practised my archery, while my Catherine made for me both targets and quiver. All my arrows hit her targets... again and again, and yes, once more in the morning...

Looking back these surely were the flower of all my days and nights, and that long winter feels all too short. I also see now that heaven sent me warnings of the huge difficulties to come. First came news of a death – the great Thibaut. For a long time after, no one wished to succeed him as leader. How could such an expedition lack a leader? Eventually, we heard that a Prince of Lombard, Boniface of Montsarrat, had taken Thibaut's place. We knew nothing of him, and men do not trust what they do not know.

In the spring, I asked for the money promised by the church in the spring to pay for my arms, the journey, and food. The priest told me, 'Place your mark here.'

'What for?', I asked.

'This will be considered a loan if you do not return with letters from one of the Bishops in the Holy Land, as proof of your work.'

When I protested, this usurer priest snapped back. 'Every pilgrim has this task. You need not worry. If you die at some point on the journey, then the debt will be cancelled. The church will help your wife.'

My doubts kept sleep at bay, but I prayed to the Lord for the strength to help His work. Shortly before I was due to leave my Catherine fell with child. She insisted this gave her joy, as she would have company until my return. My brother advised me that this alone furnished good reason not to go, and I thought long and hard. Could this be a sign that the Lord did not need me? But other pilgrims were fathers too and I did not want to be known as that coward who turned tail at the last. I had my pride and I kept it. When a young fool keeps his pride, he forgets that pride is a sin, and little comfort on a cold winter night.

I delayed my departure, but I could not avoid it. As I got up to dress that last morning, Catherine slipped a linen undershirt over my head. She had dyed it green, and embroidered a cross within a shield, using scarlet thread, upon front and back. 'Wear this in battle', she whispered. 'It will keep you safe. And take this to help you remember me.' She slipped a keepsake on a leather cord around my neck. It was a silver coin, with the image of a queen stamped upon it, long hair spilling around her face, like Catherine. I stumbled away, half-blinded by tears, thanking God for our time together, and praying that Catherine would find great joy as a mother. Now, I do not understand. How did heaven allow me to wrench myself apart from her?

That April of 1202, I ripped apart from my home. Swallowing my anguish, forcing myself not to look back, I started my journey along the pilgrim's trail, south and east to the great mountains, through the Mont Cenis pass, and down into Lombardy. Four of us (*les Chevrotins*, from the town of goats) travelled, and later fought, together. Our sergeant Martin had the wisdom that came with long years as a professional soldier – a man to be respected – tough, clever and good humoured. Jacques was a little bull of a man: he had youth and boundless energy, was coarse and easily provoked. A natural soldier, he loved nothing better than a fight. His giant cousin Robert had piercing blue eyes, and strange patches of baldness amongst the white hair that stuck out in all directions from the scabby skin on his scalp. He had the strength of an ox, but the same intelligence. When we were children I had often seen Robert tethered like an animal outside his family's hut, covered with bruises. At some point he escaped to live with his aunt, Jacques' mother, and Robert became Jacques' shadow.

We sang often as we marched. People wished us well, and many gifted us food and shelter. We took our time exploring the grand cities and cathedrals along the way. Sometimes Jacques told Robert to go with us as he preferred to dally with one of the peasant girls who, so impressed with our valour, would wave as we passed. If they draped rings of flowers around our necks, Jacques would wink and say, 'Come, my pretty, I will show you a much better place to hang your flowers...the like of which you have never seen...'

Although Jacques looked like a pig, he was hung like a donkey. And as some girls may say to each other, in private, it is not always the pretty worm that attracts the bird, but the fat one. Jacques had no care about misusing these girls – he believed that all his sins would be forgiven, whatever he did. So his worm was seen by many a bird; many got far more than they bargained for, since this monster was most difficult, if not impossible, to swallow. Jacques boasted that some girls would scream in fear at the sight. He laughed about their pain, glorying in it. Not even the sight and stink of Hell's gate would have made our Jacques think twice.

We arrived in Venice at the end of June to join a mighty army camped on the island of Saint Nicholas, opposite the main city. The rest of us gaped at the endless rows of tents, while Martin grunted, spat, and scratched his head: 'Smaller than I expected.'

Here, we had left the real world behind and entered a dream. The city of Venice rises from the sea, a place of water, boats, palaces and churches upon islands of stone, the like of which I have never seen before or since. There, we waited. Our island encampment, warmed by the sun, with the sea to fish and swim, seemed a place of magic at first. But the heat of midsummer and the stink of the latrines slowly grew intolerable, even within the shade of our tent. Worse still, they rationed our fresh water. Our island camp became a trap: only the nobles could afford a boat to escape. Every day, smiling Venetian traders appeared, trying to sell us strange and costly food. If we complained, they shrugged. 'Our harvests have been poor.'

It was Robert who rescued us from starvation. He would cover himself with dark sailcloth and squat on the rocks by the shore like a statue, for hours. Suddenly the water would jump; Robert would stand, pulling in our supper, impaled up on an arrow.

The atmosphere of hope and expectation that welcomed us decayed and rotted with the piles of rubbish. Small or not, this army caused the latrine pits to overflow. Who here knows the stench of the sewers of Paris? Ours stunk far, far worse. We also heard dark rumours: 'Fulk has died, it is true... such a terrible omen... this must be God's punishment, for our continuing delay...' As the summer wore on, boredom and frustration bred like rats. Tempers frayed, and brawls became commonplace. Our camp held not one army, but a hundred. Each evening, men grouped along the shore together by region, from France, Flanders, Saxony and Lombardy: by their allegiance to their local noble, or like us, in small groups from one town or another.

Reasons for the delay had to be found, and these bred arguments and disagreements. Simon de Montfort's man insisted, 'The Venetians want to attack Egypt, not the Holy Land – the gold calls out to them. Knowing this, some of our army has embarked from other ports, to go directly to Jerusalem.' Some men left Venice, on hearing this. A Flemish soldier whispered that the infidels themselves had bribed the Venetians to delay us, or maybe even bribed the nobles to divert the crusade. A Saxon announced, 'The Venetians have demanded extra payments. Our leaders are trying to bargain with them.'

Martin whispered, 'That's possible. A Venetian trader told me they had built far too many ships: if so, our army will not have enough men and money to pay them.'

At the end of each evening, confused and angry men raised their voices until a fight spilled out into the night. Each morning, the priests reassured us that the Pope wished us all to proceed directly to the Holy Land. In our tent, I sat and gazed at my keepsake for hours on end, remembering the smell and taste of Catherine's skin, wondering how large her belly had now become.

In August Boniface of Montsarrat arrived at last and the Barons collected the money for the transport. We each paid the sum agreed, and watched the war chests carried over to the Ducal palace of the Venetians. Still nothing happened. Events proved Martin right. The priests came round asking for more; men began to drift away, those who had not taken loans, those lucky few who could afford to say farewell to what they had paid. For once, Jacques spoke for all of us. 'We have no more, we are poor men; let the nobles pay more, but we cannot, or we will starve.'

The priests told him, 'But you will gain riches from the infidel.'

Jacques shrugged. 'We cannot give what we do not have.'

Our leaders argued while we loitered, growing ever more furious with these Venetians: these sailors who did not sail, these cheats and swindlers. They robbed us whenever we bought a loaf of bread, leaving us counting the pennies remaining. On the Sunday of the Nativity of the Virgin, I joined the other pilgrims crossing the water to the great cathedral of San Marcos to pray for guidance. What should we do? September had arrived – and if we did not leave soon, winter would trap us and close the mountain passes. Like many others, I wished I had left earlier, or stayed at home.

I watched the great cathedral slowly filling with pilgrims and Venetians mixing together, uneasily. I knelt, feeling for the keepsake inside my tunic. After mass, the blind old Duke of the Venetians, Dandolo, took centre stage. He spoke to his people with great emotion, and though I knew not his language, he spoke slowly and with great dramatic effect. At the end of it, he knelt before our leader Boniface, who carefully placed a pilgrim's cross upon his bald old crown. At this, a huge roar of approval burst from all present, with much embracing and tears of joy. The other Venetians all went forward to receive the cross. At last we would be leaving; we celebrated long into that night, and many Venetians crossed the water to bring us wine and ale as a sign of our repaired friendship and unity.

Three weeks later, our fleet sailed. Two hundred magnificent ships – enormous transports of troop and horse, all flying giant banners and crosses – each ship ringed with the shields of its soldiers, upon a sparkling blue sea. I can still hear the thumping of our drums, while thousands of pilgrim soldiers roared out their songs and beat the rhythm with their feet upon the decks. Sixty war galleys escorted our fleet; at its head was our flagship, the Venetian Duke's personal galley, adorned with crimson silk. Our hearts burst with pride, just to be part of this great parade.

Yet, even now, one ill omen silenced our cheers. We had scarcely left the port when one of our largest ships fell through the water without warning. It left hardly a splash, just four men and bubbles on the surface as Neptune belched: the only sign of a hundred lost men. And back on our own little ship, more rumours spread...

'The envoy of the Holy Father has returned to Rome...'

'It's true, yes, and Boniface has also left the fleet. Perhaps he has gone to Rome too...'

'I swear to you, we are not going to the Holy Land, but to fight for the Venetians – they demand payment for the debt still owed...'

So, my friend, it was not only the motion of the waves that made me sick to my stomach, on that voyage...

*   *   *

Heaven On Earth

Lulled by my own memories of the sea, I drift away from Bernard into sleep. As a young man I spent most of my time in boats of one kind or another, the smell of the sea in my nostrils. These memories carry me into a dream, remembering how we would sleep upon the deck under the stars, a cool breeze upon our bodies during the heat of summer. This memory must trigger another, for I can hardly believe my good fortune: Sophia is in my arms again, and our bodies are young. We are drifting alone on one of my cargo boats, lying together upon a bed comprising rolls of my finest silk. Even as I wallow in these sensations, in the back of my mind I have a distinct and uneasy sense that the goddess Tyche is reminding me of the good fortune she sent my way. But Sophia seems to know my thoughts, for she whispers in my ear, 'I see that Tyche has raised more than your hopes, Basil'. Her hand moves down to demonstrate her argument. So even my unhinged forebodings cannot spoil our precious moments together ... yes, I discover that I can touch her, and smell her skin, and stroke her hair. She too seems to be savouring the moment, blissfully unaware of futures now past. She is real, everything is possible. Time stands still.

I wake in the darkness, alone again. What a wonderful, priceless dream.

I remember that Luke of Antioch once remarked, 'Memories and knowledge are more precious than gold.'

At the time I replied, 'Only to those who have both.' (Like most young men, I placed little importance upon books then.) Now that I lie trapped in this room, I would trade all my former riches for more to read. My body may be broken and crippled, but my poor mind, though addled and confused, can still fly from place to place, from page to page.

My little donkey, the youngest slave, sometimes brings me a candle and a different book. I call her my treasure, since this is what she brings me. Sophia's father, Luke of Antioch, collected all these books, which later became my library. I grew hungry for his wit and wisdom during the years that I worked with him. I grew more curious about him after I had seen him within his library. It contained works in Greek, Hebrew and Arabic; he could read them all. I came to suspect that he originally came from Persia, not Antioch. He certainly knew much about science and philosophy, and all the cultures of the east.

He became my teacher during our conversations, educating me with stories about classical poetry, mythology and history. He taught me mathematics during our business dealings and geography on our travels together. One particular day he said, 'You know, the knowledge of the ancient world almost died out during the excesses of early Christian zeal and pagan book burning. The Syrian Christians of Antioch hid and preserved most of it. Only later did our Imperial civil service revive this wisdom, in order to have educated and intelligent officials.' He shook his head. 'So much might otherwise have been lost, for all time.' I suspect this was why Luke claimed Antioch as his birthplace: in his heart, he lived for knowledge, not trade.

After two summers of our partnership, Luke told me I should accompany him on his next return to Constantinople, to see the other end of our business. I sensed a hope that I could help with all of the work, which matched my own keenness to learn. I think he wished to be a scholar: since he had no son, he hoped I would free more of his time. His hope became my opportunity.

On our way we passed several cities, all of which made Makri look like a village. But all of these seemed nothing at my first sight of the capital: from miles away, it stretched as far as the eye could see, covering the hills. Golden and painted roofs glittered in the morning sun. I swallowed and asked, 'Where do the walls and buildings end? How big is it?'

Luke grunted. 'Nearly a million people live either within the walls, or nearby.'

As we grew closer, the crowded sea around us rocked so many boats of all sizes that I could not count them. Neither could I count all the towers along the walls surrounding the city.

We moved around and under one great stretch of wall on the seaward side until we rounded a point, entering a wide opening into a lagoon-like harbour: the Golden Horn. A second stretch of wall loomed above the harbour on this side of the city. Surely no ladder could ever reach the top?

'The landward walls are even higher,' Luke murmured, catching my eye.

We manoeuvred into this harbour and somehow found a berth. I gaped at the variety of goods being loaded and unloaded along the vast quaysides. Merchants from all corners of the world milled about – some in exotic coloured silks and turbans, some with bodies and faces completely wrapped, some virtually naked. The smells were intoxicating, the colours a riot of hues and tones. I felt a little out of my depth.

'Business can wait,' Luke smiled. 'Come, I'll show you the city.'

I have seen many wonders in my life, but the sights and sounds that day (two years before the Latins ruined the city) rank among the highest. I followed Luke as we joined a throng of faces surging around richly decorated buildings on pavements of patterned mosaics: libraries, churches, palaces, public baths... all covered with works of art, commonplace, for everyone to view, in the streets. I thought of my mother, and her home-made pots.

'Where does all this wealth come from?' I asked. 'The street sellers dress better than most people in Makri.'

Luke threw his arms wide and grinned at me. 'The wealth of trade, Basil: remember, we too create it.' He smiled and called a salesman over to buy fruit juice. My mouth was parched, but I choked when I tasted it. It was a warm autumn day, yet the juice was as cold as snow in midwinter. I was too shocked to comment, or ask how this was possible.

Antiquities and decorations from all parts of the empire adorned the public buildings near the city centre. 'Up there,' Luke gestured. The sun dazzled my eyes, glinting off a giant Justinian watching over the city on top of a marble column, riding his horse. 'Look,' Luke continued, 'he's holding a golden globe of the Empire in his hand, warding off the threat from the east.' He took me into the Hippodrome: it was not a race day, but we watched chariots practising, racing around two long lines of animal statues and three giant intertwined bronze serpents. I felt like a small earthworm.

After this, Luke led me down a narrow street to a small, insignificant doorway, and knocked: 'As a practical man, Basil, you might enjoy what my friend Marcus can show us.' Inside, Marcus embraced him like a brother and then, without comment, led us down some stairs. Down and down we went, torches lighting slippery steps, down into the bowels of the earth.

'How much further?'

Luke looked back, his eyes glittering, and his voice boomed out. 'Do you imagine we can find the underworld so easily?'

We turned a corner. Hollowed out of the rock deep under the city, with massive columns supporting the roof, I found myself looking at a huge, deep underground lake, hundreds of paces across. Marcus turned, head held high, and smiled at me. 'Whatever else might happen in a siege, this city will not run out of water'. Indeed, the inhabitants could always drown themselves.

Luke saved the best for last: the great golden dome of the cathedral of Saint Sophia. I had never seen a building on that scale: it seemed far too large to be built by human hands. My heart pounded with excitement as we approached. And when I stood within it and looked around and upwards, panic overwhelmed me. I felt terrified that it would fall down upon me at any second. I had to make myself look down at the cool, patterned marble floors. Gradually I calmed down; a little prayer helped my nerves. I let my eyes take in the walls, the giant pictures of the saints and emperors, in gold and brightly coloured mosaics. The altars dripped with gold and jewels. Solid silver columns supported silver canopies: everywhere were silver lamps. Finally, I dared to look up again. The dome seemed to stretch up to heaven itself, from where an image of Christ gazed down upon us. I was still a peasant boy at heart, but thank the Lord I did not piss my pants.

As we left through the great doors, our eyes dazzled as we emerged into the sun, a tall, beautiful angel called out and flung herself upon Luke, embracing him. I felt a rush of envy and desire. I realised that her dark eyes, hair and skin matched his, and that she carried herself in the same proud way. I watched her warmth and affection pour from her to her father. My other thought was clear: this is the kind of woman I want.

'Basil,' Luke let go of her and turned to me, 'here is my daughter, Sophia.'

How apt to meet her here; she had the same name, that means holy wisdom, as the church. I smiled and nodded, entranced. My world had changed again. Even at that moment, I knew I had to have her.

Later in my life, I loved Eirene in a different way. I approached Eirene from a distance, like a ship on the horizon that gradually takes a shape and appears. The closer I got, the more intriguing Eirene was. With Sophia, a young man who had grown up without knowing the warmth of the sun suddenly stepped into the light. I felt such warmth, in her presence, but not only upon my skin. I felt it inside my very soul.

*   *   *

Out of the darkness the dim light of an oil lamp appears. The slave girl sets my bowl of food down by the bed, and helps me to sit up. My dream of Sophia recedes, but what remains of my manhood still stands erect to her memory. The little slave catches sight of it, and giggles. 'Oh my,' she whispers. 'There is some life in the old goat yet, isn't there? What can we do with you?' And, much to my surprise, she takes hold of it with her small hand. 'I will do this, but only this,' she says, moving her hand a little, and squeezing playfully, 'and only if you keep still, and very quiet.' She looks at me and raises her eyebrows.

My eagerness is such that I both nod and splutter, 'Yes, yes,' simultaneously.

I may be an old goat, but I am very willing to be led and sacrificed to Aphrodite. I nearly die with pleasure. Oh, the joy of feeling like a man again. No matter that she uses only a hand, taking pity on me and amusing herself. She is only learning how to keep men happy, quietly developing a skill. I am not shocked and will not call her names. To me, she remains a quaint innocent; her act is a great kindness, freely given. Because my own hands are almost useless now, I have to rely on her charity as it couples with my own imagination. Perhaps I will tell my little treasure about Tyche's well; but not yet, or she might leave me...

After my first journey with Luke to the capital of the Empire, my own hands had much work to do (whenever I thought of Sophia). My first visit lasted a week – Luke showed me where he bought and sold his goods, and introduced me to other traders he knew and trusted. I stayed in Luke's home; a heaven sent opportunity to get to know Sophia. I did not make any foolish efforts to impress her as I knew she must have had a far better education than I. Sometimes my peasant boy self would feel too nervous to speak in her presence. So I decided to ask questions of her, too, and give her every chance to speak her mind. I showed that I could listen, thinking this might be the way to impress an educated young woman. Perhaps my infant wit was not entirely as stupid as I felt at the time. I tried to show my appreciation for their kindness in a quiet way, by appearing competent but modest...I shut my eyes, and remember one particular day...

* * *

Sophia laid out our breakfast upon the table, a simple meal of bread, fruit and a light broth. Watching her, Luke rubbed his hands and smiled. 'I wonder, what will our visitor like to see today? But first, we should eat.'

I hesitated, waiting to see how my hosts would begin their own meal. "I've been astonished with everything so far. It's like another world.'

Luke winked at me. 'Well, Basil, now you know how the leaders of the barbarian nations react when they come here. They feel overwhelmed by the marvels here, by all the sights of this great capital. When the Emperor treats them well, they feel like a child with his father. Many of them feel intimidated, and they go away thinking they cannot ever compete with such power and riches. That ploy has often helped our Empire to stay intact.'

I nodded. My mentor had an uncanny ability to describe my own feelings back to me, while ascribing them to others.

Sophia looked up, and wrinkled her nose. 'Not all of them, father. Some decide they will try and grab it for themselves.'

I blushed.

Luke smiled an acknowledgement, but continued on his theme. 'That cathedral of Aghia Sophia is not only impressive, but it also puzzles everyone. It has stood for over six hundred years now, but none of our current architects know how they managed to build it. All they know now is that they could not do it again. So people say it must have been inspired by God.'

Sophia lifted a hand, as if she wished to speak, but Luke ignored her.

'And of course, our Bishops also think of our whole Empire as the Empire of God. This great Roman Empire chosen by God to spread the word of Christ across the world, even after the barbarians overran Rome itself... you know this?'

I nodded. Sophia tried to interrupt again, but Luke waved his hand to silence her.

'The Empire of God... such confidence!' Luke watched while Sophia put her hands on her hips and stuck her tongue out, frowning at him. Then he turned to me, and his voice dropped to a stage whisper. 'Some theologians get so carried away with this idea they believe that this city of Constantine may be the capital of the kingdom of heaven, manifested here and now on earth.' He shook his head, tapped it to indicate madness, and grinned.

'Father!' Sophia tried once again to capture her father's attention, but he turned his back to her, teasing her by ignoring her completely. She cried out in frustration, shook her fists in mock rage and moved behind him, beating his back with her fists in a sham attack. Luke looked at me, then up to the heavens, and turned to face her. 'What's this?' In one movement he rose and picked her up, as if she were much younger. 'See what happens, Basil, if you spare the rod and spoil the child?'

This time, her cry was louder. 'Oh, put me down, stop lecturing us, and listen. Why don't you take Basil to see the slums, and prove to him he's not yet in heaven?'

Luke raised one eyebrow. 'That's not a bad idea. Do you wish to come too?'

Sophia shook her head, frowning, and pegged her nose. 'Never: but if you do go, you should both put on some old clothes.'

Later, as we walked through the streets, Luke entertained me with irreverent stories of how various religious groups view others. He told me how Christians were perceived by Jews – as a very odd cult indeed – bringing this to life with a parody of an unthinking new convert, filling his voice with naive enthusiasm. 'We Christians are not an ancient wisdom, we are totally new. But we use the same scriptures as you Jews, which you have studied carefully for a thousand years. The thing is, though, you Jews simply don't understand them properly. Whereas we, of course, having just read them yesterday, understood their true meaning immediately...'

He paused as a monk passed by, and winked at me.

'Your God used to be concerned only with the Jews,' Luke continued, 'we know that, but not anymore. And He recently decided to incarnate himself, so He made a virgin pregnant...' Luke scratched his head, now using a puzzled tone of voice. 'A married woman too... that may sound a bit mean to her husband, but since the man obviously hadn't touched his wife, this particular husband probably didn't mind too much...'

He shrugged, reverted to a tone of enthusiasm again. 'The Son of God then grew up to become a preacher of great wisdom. Unfortunately he died a horrible death at the hands of the Romans...' He glanced all around, as if suddenly afraid of eavesdroppers. His voice dropped to a stage whisper again, '...though don't make a big fuss about this if your master is a Roman.' He put a finger to his lips, his eyes round, and continued. 'Because they killed the son of God, the world must be about to end. But don't worry, if you believe in our teachings, you will be saved and go to heaven when it does, unlike everyone else. This all makes perfect sense, doesn't it?'

I grinned. Unlike Sophia, I had not heard any of this before. I found listening to Luke a pleasure, a real education, to hear such a balance of irreverence and wit.

'Did you know,' Luke continued, 'that at first, Christianity only appealed to the powerless? To slaves, the oppressed, and women, it promised freedom, even though in the next world. And to others who were terrified of demons, capricious gods, and evil spirits Christianity promised safety; protection and an afterlife in heaven, away from these threats forever. Better still, it demanded no expensive sacrifices; just to have faith. So heaven becomes easy to reach for us all, which is the essence of its appeal.'

As I grinned again, Luke shrugged and added, 'I can be pious too. The basic teachings of Jesus, the words that are written down as his own, make an excellent guide to life. Perhaps hard to live up to... but he describes a good way of life, one that leads to contentment. That's the essence of it: forget all those dense arguments about the nature of God that concern the bishops.'

I frowned. 'So you think we should choose what to believe?'

'Of course we should. We do this anyway, but often blindly. We are led to many of our beliefs by others who have blindfolded us by the strength of their persuasion. Rid yourself of that blindfold and make your own choices. And not just in religion, in everything. Choose your own life, one that suits you; but you know this already, don't you?'

'I suppose I do, or I would be a fisherman.'

'Exactly: you can choose what you think as well as what you do. Cultures and religions are just pages in the book of history. Christianity, or any other religion, must be embedded in a healthy culture, as clothes need to be worn by a healthy body.'

'That sounds a little crazy...'

'Does it? Remember the early Christians, how they burned the books? Our culture was not so healthy then...'

We lapsed into a thoughtful silence. In years to come, I would look back on this conversation as the day my mind unchained itself from my upbringing. My own variation on this theme would be: those who believe in nothing but their own religion look to others like an Emperor dressed in rags, strutting around with an air of superiority, but blind to the perceptions of others.

The slums of the city lay on the western side, on low ground between the wall of Justinian and the wall of Constantine. As we approached, the numbers of beggars and cripples in the streets increased. A smell of excrement and rotten swill began to pervade the air, even above the acrid fumes of the tanneries that we passed through. Ordered streets give way to ramshackle collections of wooden huts draped with lines of hanging animal skins. Through gaps, I glimpsed a sea of tents and ramshackle shelters, piled on top of one another. It seemed to be in constant motion, like a pile of maggots. After a moment of shock, I realised that I was watching a stream of people picking their way to and fro between the shelters.

Luke handed me a bag of strong herbs. 'Breathe through this. It'll help. If anyone asks, we are looking for a friend, a labourer.'

Around us, deformed and limbless humanity held out bowls in desperate appeals. Luke turned and set off, apparently randomly, into the mass of shelters. As we picked our way through, windows opened into different lives. A woman in rags, five or six hollow-faced children huddled about her, shared out stale bread. Six or seven dust-streaked men snored, splayed on bedrolls in a makeshift tent. In one doorway, the buzz of flies and the smell of shit and vomit pushed me back; a shapeless mound groaned in the darkness.

I tugged at Luke's arm. 'Where do they all come from?'

He stopped and turned, speaking quietly. 'Most are from the countryside, looking for work. Added to that are the outcasts; cripples, beggars, old whores, drunkards and thieves.'

The stench became overpowering as Luke headed for a line of spaces between the shelters. I heard a crowd murmuring, like a buzz of anticipation. He climbed up to the lip of what looked like a wide, shallow trench, and silently gestured downwards. I looked over into the dried up bed of a stream. The noise came from a sea of flies, swarming over the filth scattered everywhere. Every so often, a figure moved in and out, squatting down at the edge to add a contribution, or tipping a jar to dump the contents.

'I've seen enough. This is no heaven.'

Luke raised an eyebrow. 'But the churches give out free bread. Sometimes, the Emperor sends wine too. It keeps the riots at bay.'

'That's no reason to live here.'

'No, but the rents are cheaper.'

I gasped and then regretted it, coughing an exhalation. 'They pay to live here?'

'Oh yes. The men who own these fields are some of the richest in the city. Every few months, they have to come and burn everything, to prevent disease; more often if the wind is in the wrong direction, towards the palace. Everyone has to leave the place for two days, and then it all starts again.'

'So this part of heaven burns?'

Luke grinned. 'Indeed.'

When we returned, Sophia was waiting outside the door. She made us change our shoes out in the street, and then handed us clean robes.

'Now, father, you should take Basil to use our beautiful public baths. Perhaps I shall come with you both, this time?' She put her fingers to her lips as if deep in thought, and turned to face me, looking into my eyes. 'Would you like that, Basil?'

I did not know what to say. It was a wonderful prospect which set my blood racing to all my parts – but in Makri, the public baths were strictly segregated. Was mixed bathing really allowed here? I hoped so, and wanted to say yes...

Luke rescued me. 'She's joking, Basil. Even in New Rome, bathing is not mixed. Unless, of course, you are wealthy enough to have your own baths and liberal, like-minded friends...'

I blushed, and noticed Sophia studying my reaction. Her teasing was flirtatious, I realised; perhaps she did like me. She also had a quality of giving her attention fully, unreservedly. I told myself I must try to do the same for her, and not allow Luke to have all my attention...

The next day, Luke left me alone in his library for an hour. After perusing the titles of all the books, I noticed a box pushed under a bench; I pulled it out. Inside, I found a prayer mat of a Persian design, a book in Arabic that I suspected was the Koran, plus a number of letters and documents in foreign scripts, and miniature paintings that looked like personal mementos. One was a portrait of a woman, resembling an older version of Sophia in eastern costume. Luke had already told me that he settled in Constantinople because his wife was buried here; she had died giving birth to his daughter. This must be her, I thought. Perhaps Luke had escaped conflict or persecution in Persia as a young man and made his way to the safety of the Empire with his wife, adopting the guise of a Christian from Antioch?

When my first visit ended, Sophia kissed me warmly on each cheek. I felt a flood of relief; I, the poor boy from the country, had managed not to make a complete fool of myself, so far. And I sensed that Luke both liked and trusted me. Even a foolish peasant could work this out: my best chance to gain Sophia's affection lay in working hard as Luke's apprentice and partner.

Once back in Makri, I made plans to leave my

parents' home using my share of the money I had earned. I bought a good piece of land for my own house: outside the crumbling, ramshackle walls, but overlooking the harbour. Long ago, Makri had been a Lycian city, named after Telmessos, the son of Apollo. The Lycian defences had never been renewed. In the unlikely event of trouble, I knew that a fast horse to the mountains offered the safest way to escape. But why waste energy planning too much? Luke and Sophia would probably never wish to leave the safety of their great city, and besides, did I really have a chance with Sophia? How generous could Tyche be, to a dumb peasant? I resolved to be patient, and make my fortune first.

*　　*　　*

I hear footsteps approach, disturbing my rest. A heavy body sits on the end of my bed, and something metal strikes the stone floor: a sword. I silently curse, for I know it is Bernard. He returns to remind me of his journey, of the approaching nemesis for our great city, for Luke and all the other citizens of New Rome, the city of Constantine. I can smell his rank odour mixed with the acrid tang of wood smoke. Has he come from hell, I wonder, or is that the smell of the taverns? He grasps my arm again: I flinch, and open my eyes.

"Go away", I cry, in a pathetic, whinging tone.

He chuckles, realising that I am awake, and begins to talk...

*　　*　　*

God's Own Eyes

So, my friend: now you must accompany me across that wide ocean. Our great fleet of ships set sail, but only after much argument and many bad omens. We carried a weight of men, but a much heavier load of foreboding.

We left the lagoons of Venice behind and moved out from the shore, surrounded by deep water as far as the eye could see, heading south towards the Sea of Rome. We pitched up and down and rolled sideways like a cork in the waves, until our guts spilled out. Robert leaned over the side next to me, praying for his life, while Jacques cursed. I hung on grimly to a rope, staring into the distance. I shut my eyes, and then heard Martin's voice, laughing, telling us this sickness would pass, and offering us a piece of cheese.

I turned around. 'Go away, before I spew all over you.'

Martin cut off a piece for himself, and chewed it, regarding us intently. The smell of it made me gag, but I could see that something played upon his mind. Sure enough, Martin added, 'The Venetian captain tells me we're heading for Zadar.'

'Soon, I hope. Where is this place?'

Martin shrugged, 'Never heard of it before.'

Something in his manner made me ask, 'It's nowhere near Jerusalem, I suppose?'

The lines on his face twisted into a grin, and he nodded. 'You are too sharp by half. No, though it lies on our route, a Venetian colony which has rebelled. In order to defer the debt to Venice, our leaders have agreed to force it to surrender.'

Jacques looked up, interested.

'But here is the rub,' Martin continued, 'these are Christian people, allies of the king of Hungary.

'So what?' Jacques spat, clearing his mouth. 'A little fighting would get us in shape. If we take money from these rebels we pay our debts for the passage to the Holy Land.'

I found my tongue. 'To attack fellow Christians is a sin. We have no quarrel with them.'

'Aye, indeed,' Martin nodded, 'I wonder what the priests will say. But these Venetians spent a king's ransom building this fleet, and must be paid. If this becomes the only way to do God's work, our Bishops may not be so full of charity.' He winked at me.

We landed and made our camp outside the walls. As the people of Zadar raised Christian flags and displayed signs of the cross all around their city walls, our priests, repeated the same speech to each of us. 'God wills us to keep our pilgrimage together, and thus continue to the Holy Land. With our prayers this city will surely surrender, so that no blood will be spilled. But a siege may be necessary to make this happen. The Holy Father in Rome will grant absolution, for he sanctioned our journey and certainly wishes it to continue...'

Even among the common soldiers, voices cried, 'Why should we attack fellow Christians? A mortal sin cannot be excused by any priest.' Heated arguments broke out. Other men called the doubters cowards. This dispute went on for days.

Back in our tent, Martin was sharpening his blades, checking bowstrings and arrows, testing straps on his body protection. We archers wore a tough leather cuirass and apron, plus a metal cap. We watched, copied his actions, and listened. 'We look after each other first, lads, remember that above all else. And when the city falls, we have the right to sack it for three days, without restraint.' Jacques grinned, while Robert looked puzzled; I felt a lump of fear turning in my gut. We constructed a large screen of wood and hide to protect us; I felt inside my tunic again, touched my keepsake.

The people of Zadar had little hope if we attacked; they simply withdrew into their city and watched from the walls. But we common soldiers were not the only ones divided. One morning, the city gate swung open and six envoys emerged on fine horses, carrying flags of the cross. We joined a curious crowd and followed the envoys to the camp of the Venetian Duke.

'Watch out there! Make way!' The drumming of hooves scattered us like corn when a group of nobles led by de Montfort galloped through. His loud and haughty voice carried on the wind. 'My Lords, I assure you that we firmly oppose an attack on fellow Christians, and we argue strongly against it.' The jaws of the envoys dropped. They looked from one to the other, and whispered among themselves for several minutes. Then their leader bowed to Montfort, and they all calmly rode back towards their city. Just as they disappeared from view, Boniface, other barons, and the Duke himself emerged from the largest tent. They looked around them, puzzled.

Martin nudged me with his elbow. 'This should be fun.'

Boniface looked over, spotted de Montfort and frowned. He shouted, 'Where are the emissaries?'

De Montfort shrugged and grinned. 'Our Christian friends have gone back into their city.'

Boniface's face turned crimson. 'What have you said to them, Montfort?'

De Montfort grinned again, savouring the moment. 'Simply that they have nothing to fear from good Christians.'

Boniface turned purple with rage. 'Curse you, Montfort, you damned coward...you son of a traitor's whore...' The Venetian faction also started shouting, pointing and waving fists. They formed a chorus around Boniface, turning the air blue with noble curses as hands reached down to grip their swords. Those shouting loudest drew their swords in anticipation, but in the end only sharp tongues cut the air.

Montfort had the last word. As he rode off, he turned, stood in his saddle and shouted, 'If you attack this city, you worm-eating backsliders, the devil will fuck all your arses in hell...but then, I'm sure you'll enjoy every minute...'

What would you have done, Basil? Can a sin be necessary?

The next day, dozens of brawls erupted among the men-at-arms within our rank and file, much to the astonishment, then amusement, of Zadarans watching from the wall. But those poor Zadarans did not laugh for long... far from helping them, de Montfort had sealed their fate. If they had surrendered that day, our army would have entered the city in friendship. Instead, they foolishly fought off our front rank for five days, ever hoping that de Montfort would persuade the others to give up. Meanwhile, the Venetians fed only those who fought; and even those who had no stomach for a fight had to fill their bellies. And during those five days, men saw comrades wounded or killed. Our mood hardened; most men determined to fight, just to end this unpleasantness. So when the city finally surrendered, a host of starving and angry men poured into it, looking for food, drink, money, and women.

Jacques had pushed to the front of this horde, Robert beside him. Martin and I waited and walked in calmly after the rush died down. I wandered alongside him through a carnival of distraction; around us echoed cries of anger, pain, fear and despair, roaring and cackling laughter, the sound of doors and windows banging shut, or being smashed open. Carrying our sacks, we strode on through this cacophony until Martin found us a storehouse, and we stuffed our sacks with food. Local men were sitting in the street outside their houses, hands over their heads, or their ears. Occasionally, a figure lay crumpled in a bloody pile or sat hunched, clutching a wound, moaning. Another, gentler noise seemed to follow us, creeping around us wherever we went. I listened carefully, and at last understood what I was hearing; the soft cries of women submitting to force. Was that Catherine's voice? I felt the bile rising in my throat. I pushed her keepsake against my heart, murmuring a prayer to stop my ears.

Martin led me away from the chaos, deeper into the narrower, quieter side streets. 'We want a small house, but well kept.' Eventually, he chose one. 'This will do.' He banged and kicked on the door, threatening to break it with his sword. The owner, a small, fat man, shaking with fear, opened the door. In sign language, Martin made him understand that if he gave us money, we would protect him and his family. The man glanced quickly behind him, at his wife and two young daughters. Nearby, a woman screamed, and then a man. The owner nodded and paid us willingly, feeding us their best food while we sat in their doorway, refusing others entry. After a day and a night, the pillaging stopped. Jacques and Robert staggered along, bellies bulging, senseless with wine. They fell into the family's bed, drunk and exhausted. We listened to their snores for a while, but we could not stay in the same room. They pumped air like a pair of bellows, and these farts would have killed a hog at twenty paces, I swear it.

Martin and I knew our Christian duty: we had to save their two young girls from Jacques, our donkey friend. In sign language, Martin made the family understand that they must take whatever they could carry and leave that night. We escorted them to the city gate at midnight where they joined an exodus of locals. They kissed our hands and vanished into the night, while we returned to occupy their home.

Many pilgrims woke the next morning and did not wish to remember what they had done. Robert looked like a scalded cat, when Martin asked him, 'What did you two get up to, then?' He glanced away, and stayed silent.

'Must have been bad,' said Martin. 'Let's hope you don't go to hell.'

'Nonsense,' Jacques interrupted, 'the priests gave us permission.'

Martin smiled and raised his gaze upward to the heavens. 'Ah, but did you not notice? They chose their words carefully. They said we surely *will* be forgiven; not that we *have been*.'

Martin had selected our winter quarters well. The men at arms of the nobles threw out many common soldiers who had taken over finer houses, now required by their masters. Other men had to hand over valuables they could not conceal, adding to an angry mood. In the streets, black bloodstains reminded us of the divisions within our own ranks.

Four days later, we stood idle, brooding, while Venetians stacked goods and valuables for shipment back to their own city. Martin muttered, 'Too busy to bring us the food we've paid for, but not too busy to take someone else's.'

Jacques could bear this no longer. He strutted over to one of the piles and started to open baskets, looking for food. A tall Venetian shouted something. Jacques ignored him. The man strode across and tried to pull him away; a bad mistake. In one movement, Jacques butted his face and kicked him between the legs. Down he went. More Venetians quickly appeared, surrounding Jacques. He put another down, but then two caught him by his arms. As we moved to help, a bearded Venetian pulled out a dagger, threatening to stab Jacques, while others kicked him. Suddenly, all hell descended upon them as Robert's sword split the skull of the Venetian with the dagger and a group of German soldiers waded in to help us. The other Venetians disappeared under a forest of kicks and punches. Our brawl rapidly spread up and down the streets of the city; some men took to arms, and the fighting lasted all day. A monk told me of twenty pilgrims wounded and three killed, but the Venetians, outnumbered everywhere, suffered the worst of it – they had a hundred badly hurt, or killed.

This chaos announced exactly how the eyes of the Lord regarded us. The Venetians retreated to the port to lick their wounds, while Boniface left the city on some mission to repair the alliance, which hung by a weak and flimsy thread through the month of December. Martin felt sure that our pilgrim army would burst apart in the spring.

But the devil had a needle, and Boniface provided the thread. He reappeared in mid-December, accompanied by envoys from the king of the Germans. By this time, Martin had found us a tavern where wine and rumour flowed in equal measure. He and I sat drinking one night, listening to the bodyguard of a nobleman's son; Martin plied him with drink to loosen his tongue. 'Something is afoot,' the bodyguard told us, 'Montfort's men say we have all been excommunicated, though my Lord says only the Venetians. His father thinks that the other barons are plotting to conquer more land for themselves, with the Venetians.'

'Did he say how, or where?'

The man looked at his jug. Martin refilled it. 'Well, my Lord has a German friend.' He tapped his nose. 'Boniface's nephew is the brother-in-law of the German King. This nephew happens to be a Prince; his father was once Emperor in Constantinople, but deposed by his own brother. My master suspects the barons plot to put him or his father back onto the throne in return for gold and land. The Venetians would then collect the money owed them...'

Martin interrupted, 'This supposes, of course, that we can all fly like birds over the walls there...' He flapped his arms and his new friend began to laugh so hard, he choked on his wine. Martin explained to me, 'Constantinople is not Zadar; its walls have never fallen, even to armies many times the size of ours.'

'Indeed,' our friend continued, 'it would be a miracle, to take that great city. But don't scoff too much. One of de Montfort's men also mentioned this to me; he was right about Zadar.'

'What about the Holy Land?' I insisted.

The bodyguard shook his head and chuckled. 'You never were going to the Holy Land. Look at the fleet. You don't need galleys in the Holy Land. They always planned to take us to Egypt, for the gold.' He could afford to laugh. He had taken no part in the attack on Zadar; his soul was not in doubt.

Rumours spun my head, and others, all winter. I filled those long, cold silences and dark nights by imagining Catherine with her child, imagining her holding a boy, feeding a baby girl. I hoped for a girl who would look like her. Eventually the priests did confirm that the Pope had forgiven us; though they continued to insist the Holy Land was our next port of call. This reassured some, but I had begun to think that the Holy Father's wishes changed direction with the wind.

In the spring, we watched our army bleed as men packed up and left, including de Montfort and all his supporters. Thousands of men and priests crept away, some to make their way home, others to find another way to the Holy Land.

'What do you think?' I asked Martin. 'This may be our last chance to leave.' I couldn't do it alone.

He thought for a while. 'It doesn't feel good, this army, I know that.' Then he patted his sword. 'But for our small group, it's safer to stay. The locals will attack men they catch travelling out of Zadar on foot. And how would we feed ourselves on our way back? We would return as poor as a church mouse, with nothing to pay the debt.'

In April, we moved back into camp outside the walls and watched the Venetians destroy Zadar. The walls and buildings of pure white stone, glittering in the sun by a sparkling blue sea, were all torn down. Only bare and empty churches, stripped of their decoration, were left among desolate, flattened ruins. We boarded the ships and looked back as we prepared to sail.

Picture this sight, and try to feel as we did, when we looked upon those churches. Empty windows stared back at us from the bell towers; in our hearts we felt that God's own eyes watched us from those windows. I touched the embroidery upon my shirt, and sighed.

* * *

Justin's Warning

Bernard's voice ceases, and I drift into a deep sleep; in my dreams I slip back into my young body again, wrapping the past around me like a blanket.

My second visit to Constantinople came in June of 1203. Shortly before I set out, my parents heard from my brother; Justin had obtained a plum posting with the capital garrison, defending the city walls. I wrote back to him immediately, to let him know I was coming. I sent a second message to his legion when I arrived; he replied straightaway, asking to meet the next evening at a particular wine house.

Justin had last seen me as a young boy, not a fully grown man. So when I walked up to his table, he looked puzzled for a moment when I stopped in front of him...

'It's me, Justin,' I said, waving a hand in front of his face, 'your brother.'

He blinked. 'Is that you, Basil... really? By Christ, where is that thin stick of a boy that I remember?' He jumped up, and instantly I realised I was still a foot shorter than him. Then he nearly crushed the life out of me with his bear hug, lifting me off my feet to show he was still the eldest, and the strongest. 'My God, but you have grown up into a handsome devil. That's what fooled me. You must have our mother's looks. And by your clothes, you are doing well, too. Tell me about this business of yours...' His infectious grin spread over both our faces, as his optimism and good humour washed over me. He had not changed in that way. He had patiently taught me many skills; I had always felt jealous of his strength, but also pleased that he protected me with it. Now we had both left our youth behind, we had a lot to catch up on.

'Would you like to know how I got my first good fortune as a trader?'

He nodded. 'I would. Tyche's first gift, as we soldiers would say.'

'Indeed. One summer evening, I overheard a burst of giggling from our kitchen, where our mother sat gossiping with one of her friends, an attractive widow.

They spoke half in whispers, half in excited sighs.' I adopted two falsetto voices, and acted out the scene:

'*He fills a gap in my life, truly...*'

'*I'm sure he does, but how well does he fill it?*'

Another round of giggles...

'*Very well, very well indeed, and often, I can assure you...*'

'*...and not with the Holy Spirit, either...*'

Justin chuckled. 'That sounds interesting.'

'It was, indeed. The widow was boasting of a clandestine affair. Bless our dear mother, you know how she never criticises others. Better still, she has such a great gift for extracting confidences, along with an insatiable curiosity. I could hardly believe what I heard... guess who the widow's lover was?'

Justin shrugged.

'Only Antoninus, the Abbot of our local monastery.'

Justin choked on his wine.

'I could not resist. I was not completely innocent, but I was also young and curious. So I followed the widow carefully to their meeting place: a hay meadow near an abandoned farm. I waited for a while to let them get started, until I could hear them moaning, and crept as close as I could. I could see Antoninus was in very deep, with her feet waving around his ears... so I climbed a fig tree to get a better look. But then disaster struck, or so I thought. The branch I was standing upon collapsed, pitching me into the meadow.'

Justin roared with laughter. 'The fallen angel appears...'

'I'm not sure who was more embarrassed, him or me. I feigned astonishment, muttering that I'd been picking figs, and added my apologies... but I was careful to address him as 'My dear Abbott', to show that I knew who he was...

'What did they do?'

'She giggled and covered her face. He looked confused, reluctant to get off her... I wasn't sure what to do next, so I just backed away and started walking back the way I had come. After a few seconds he called out to wait, and then chased after me.'

'What on earth for?'

'To save his reputation; he wanted to prevent any gossip. At that moment, I glimpsed my opportunity. I reassured him that I could be very discreet, and asked him if I could trade some of the Abbey's goods on his behalf...'

Justin nodded, looking at me with narrowed eyes. 'Tyche's gift.'

'Yes. I gained a right to supply his monastery with incense, and also to buy their produce, good quality olive oil, fruit and grain. Silence has a price, after all.'

'Ah, Basil,' he said, 'I wish I could have traded some of my strength for your wit. I was always jealous of that.' He winked as he said it; I could tell he meant it. The idea that he might be jealous of me was intriguing. He scratched the crown of his head, and then felt around his temples, where his hair had already receded a little. 'And I would like some of your hair.' To prove his point, he pulled a little tuft of mine out...

Justin told me stories of the northern frontier, including the strange customs and diet of the barbarian mercenaries he had fought alongside: a wife traded for wine here, dogs roasted with honey there...

If there was a flaw in his character, it was his suspicion of strangers and foreigners. When I told him how Luke of Antioch had made me his partner, Justin started to warn me that Luke might cheat me. I told him about Sophia, thinking this might help him understand, but this seemed to make him even more suspicious.

'Good God, don't go near the women in this city – they cannot be trusted, believe me. They blow with the wind, not faithful like our Lycian girls. She will be nothing but trouble, and may simply be part of the deception...'

At this I grew a little hot, banging my fist on the table. 'Listen, Luke lent me most of the money for my boats, so it's far more likely that I would cheat him, if the truth were told. Except that I am far too fond of both of them.'

Justin gave me a strange look, but he let it drop. I asked him about the army here in the city, to change the subject.

He scratched his head and called for more wine, before finding his good humour again. 'It's a bit like the wine of the Latins. It looks a lot better than it really is.'

'What do you mean?'

'We have 50,000 regular troops here, and that would look impressive on a battlefield. But many are either badly trained peasants, or foreign soldiers of fortune. The peasants have courage, but little else. The foreigners can fight well when it suits them, when they feel sure to win, but they might all vanish if things get difficult. After all, they don't defend their own homes. There's one notable exception; the Emperor's Varangian guard, all big Norsemen and Anglo-Saxons, who would fight the devil himself. They swing a double bladed axe like our farmers swing a scythe, and I've seen them cut men down like making hay.'

He looked around and lowered his voice. 'The real problem's our leadership. We've had no strong emperors since the Comnenus family; just one palace coup after another. This last lot's the worst of all. They sit on their arses counting their gold. In the north, province after province has rebelled and they do nothing. Worse still, they appoint useless cronies of the imperial family as generals, none of them fighting men. Generals who don't even know the troops they're supposed to command. But, if you think that's bad, then ask me about the navy.' He sat back and looked at me, waiting.

'What about the navy?'

'There isn't one. The admiral commanding it sold most of the ships to build himself a palace. Fifty years ago we had five hundred galleys. Now we have twenty.'

My mouth dropped open. I knew our rulers were corrupt, but this?

'The fools think they can always bribe the Pisan navy or the Genoese to help. But what if they don't come? We could be blockaded; and while our walls can be defended forever, we might get a little hungry, don't you think?' He grunts his disgust. 'This lack of ships will be the ruin of the Empire, believe me. We have given away the sea trade that made us great. It's madness.'

He leaned back in his chair, waving his finger at me and mocking the mannerisms and voice of our father, 'How many times do I have tell you? I'm warning you, boys, soon you will both be in big, big trouble...' We fell about, laughing.

But fate was laughing at us, because Justin had just become an oracle...

*   *   *

My little treasure gently shakes me. She feeds me broth, and afterwards helps me to the bathing house, telling me that Leo's family have gone out. I tell her that I lived through the sack of Constantinople, though she does not seem to understand what I mean. She lets me soak, then scrubs my useless old limbs carefully and rinses me down while I distract myself by talking, trying to ignore my body and think of hers. When she is finished she takes me back, gives me water in a cup, and rubs my back. For this hour, I dwell in Olympia. Then she says she cannot stay any longer. I fervently hope she will return, later. She tells me she is sorry; she has no candle today. So I am left in the dark, and my mind lets loose my memories again...

Justin and I had made no arrangement to meet again, but the next morning a soldier with a message greeted me – a request to go with him, to meet Justin. Was he playing a joke? Or was he in some trouble? I agreed, and followed the soldier across the city towards the wall that looked out across the Sea of Marmara to find Justin waiting at the entrance to one of the large defensive towers along the wall. He grinned from ear to ear, shifting his weight from one foot to the other, like a boy with a new toy. I wondered if he had been promoted again.

He embraced me with his customary bear hug and whispered, 'Come, follow me. You just have to see this.' He set off inside the tower at a run, up the endless steps to the top.

'What's up?' But Justin was in too much of a hurry.

I followed at my own pace. Emerging at the top, I found my brother on the seaward side of the tower, shielding his eyes and staring out across the ocean. After the darkness inside the tower, the brightness of the ocean was blinding.

'What am I looking for?' I asked, as my eyes slowly began to lose their blindness.

'Just look. Can't you see?'

And then I saw. In the distance I noticed a large ship, the sides covered with shields, and flags fluttering in the breeze. Behind it, another. And another, and my God... I could not count them all... where did they end? I gasped, and Justin grunted.

'They're so large... enormous, Justin, compared to my boats.'

Then I noticed other long, narrow ships, low in the water, with oars dipping in and out, moving around the large ships. 'Are those war galleys?' I asked, and immediately felt foolish – though I had never seen one before.

Justin nodded, his expression grim. 'Venetians.'

I stared at him in horror. 'What are they doing here?'

'They've brought a crusader army. We thought they might be coming this way.'

'What on earth for? The Holy Land is the other direction.'

He turned to meet my eye. 'I think they know that. Rumour has it they've brought Alexios, the son of the last Emperor Isaac, and hope to put him on the throne in return for gold. He's related to their leader, Boniface.'

'Can they do that?'

Justin gave a hollow laugh and turned back to the ocean. 'Count the ships, Basil, and then I'll tell you.'

We both counted the ships for over an hour while the fleet slowly sailed past the city and anchored in the distance, on the far side of the Bosphorus channel. We agreed on a count of two hundred, and Justin told me, 'That means about ten thousand soldiers, including maybe two thousand armoured cavalry, plus the Venetian sailors. Not so many in number, but if they do fight, these men will fight fiercely. They will be professional soldiers or fanatics, or both. These men are descended from the barbarians who conquered Rome itself. War is second nature to them, and they use their religion as a weapon.'

'What do you mean?'

'The priests in their army tell the soldiers to fight, and make them believe God will always give them victory. So they fight with confidence, whatever the odds.' Justin frowned and scratched the back of his head. 'There's a dark side to that, too. They think God wants them to kill infidels. But when they took Jerusalem, they could not tell the Moslems apart from the local Christians – or indeed the Jews. So, just to be sure, they slaughtered everyone. And I mean everyone. The streets ran with the blood.'

I shivered, despite the warm sun. 'You sound worried.'

Justin looked up sharply. 'I shouldn't be. The imperial army is far bigger. But if I'm honest, most of our troops are no match for these, man for man. That shouldn't matter so much, if we had good generals...' He shakes his head. 'These walls have never fallen yet. But I've got a bad feeling about all this. We have no fleet, so they can blockade us forever if they wish. Worst of all, as I told you, we're led by idiots. That's our real weakness. If you want to be absolutely sure your friends are safe, take them to Makri now. And get your boats out of the harbour here while you still can. If they do blockade us, we will be stuck inside and you'll be lucky if they still float when it's all finished.'

Was this my brother speaking? I had never heard anything so pessimistic from him, ever, before this. His words struck me with great force, as I realised that something important hid behind Justin's furrowed brow. I thanked him and hurried back to Luke's house, deep in thought. In the streets around us, life went on. But I knew secrets that others did not. I had been given a warning. Thank God I had wit enough to use it.

Luke and Sophia had heard nothing about the

crusader fleet. At first, they listened to my story with interest. But when I told them my brother has advised us to leave, Luke and Sophia both laughed at the very idea. Luke shook his head and then scratched his ear, looking down at me, as if I were a child who had forgotten to wipe his nose. 'These city walls are impregnable. We have always known that this city is the safest place in the world, and what has changed? This fleet may be friendly. Even if it isn't, this tiny army doesn't compare to all the others who failed to breach these walls.'

Luke of Antioch had never met Justin. He probably assumed that my brother was some country bumpkin, just arrived. I began to open my mouth, then realised there was no persuading him out of his complacency. Not yet; better to save my arguments for another time. But I would move my ships...

* * *

A sudden draught of cool night air creeps under the door, blowing upon my skin. Whose movement disturbs my rest? Whose rancid breath blows upon my face? I open my eyes. Bernard looks older, thinner, and has lost more of his teeth. He laughs when I tell him he stinks, and retorts, 'It is only good, honest sweat, Basil. And in any case, you are not so perfumed as you once were.' I cannot question his veracity. I call him a barbarian, and then we laugh together.

'What happened to you, after you left Makri?'

He stares at the floor and grimaces. 'After three years on the road I reached my home – only to find my land stolen, and my wife and child in their graves. Such was the welcome afforded to the few pilgrims who did return; and even so, I could never have settled back into my former life. So I fought here and there, until I could fight no more. Then I wandered the taverns, telling my tale, to warn how ordinary men have their lives perverted by the ambitions of barons and kings...'

'And emperors...'

He grins; 'Or barons who wish to become emperors...'

He begins the tale of Boniface's army once

again...and as he describes how the devil whispers in the ears of priests, I realise that I know what he means, far too well...

*   *   *

Nobles On Their knees

A fair wind blew down from heaven, taking us to the island of Corfu, a place of heat and dust and olive groves, after ten days. There, we made camp, played dice, and grew bored, waiting for our leaders to catch up with us.

On the second Sunday, after mass, a priest stood up as if to give us joyful news. 'Our friend, the Greek Prince Alexios, the son of Emperor Isaac of Constantinople, has joined our pilgrimage, with the blessing of our Holy Father. The Church in Constantinople will unite with that of Rome, under our Pope. Our army will also be supplied and reinforced there as soon as the Prince and his father Isaac, treacherously deposed by his own brother, regain their throne... the people of Constantinople will surely welcome Alexios, so we will certainly not have to fight...'

Hoots of derision and laughter greeted this statement. 'Like Zadar, you mean?' someone shouts. A long silence followed.

'God wills it', spluttered the red-faced priest, 'and this is a necessity, in order to pay the Venetians, before we can sail on to the Holy Land.'

Deep rumbles of anger began to fill the silence. Pilgrims knew Constantinople as a place of pilgrimage, second only to Jerusalem, containing many precious, unique relics such as the Holy Cross itself. Soldiers knew it as an impregnable fortress, its triple walls never breached. To attack fellow Christians in that place would be both suicide, and a sacrilege. For the first time in my life, I saw men stand up, turn their backs upon a priest, and walk out of a church in disgust. What would Fulk have said of this hypocrisy? What would Catherine think?

Two days later, we were dozing quietly in the shade of our tent when shouts of laughter awakened us. We emerged into the heat of the day, blinking. 'What's happening?'

'Look. The Greek garrison are firing catapults.'

A cheer went up, followed by laughter, as a large rock splashed into the water, spraying a nearby ship. As we waited for the next one, a knight rode up. 'Hey, you lot. That's Boniface's ship... he's brought that Greek

Prince with him. We'll have to put a stop to that. Get your weapons.' A chorus of grumbles greeted him, but we obeyed, smirking behind his back.

Martin winked at me. 'Popular, it seems, our Prince...'

The garrison surrendered as soon as we approached, but this mock battle brought our dissatisfaction to the surface. Men grumbled aloud, refusing to go with Boniface and the Venetians any further. 'Let them go to hell alone,' I heard one man say. 'I will not accompany them.'

As if on a whim, Boniface addressed us. 'My soldiers, my army... this is the Prince Alexios, whom we will restore to his rightful throne...'

Boniface had badly misjudged the mood. Men began to shout objections and insults and, if slops had been thrown in his face, Boniface could not have looked more shocked.

After a long, puzzled pause, the Prince Alexios fell to his knees and tried to flatter us. 'What a mighty army you are, what strong brave soldiers you must be, to come so far...'

Perhaps he thought of himself as a noble Prince. To us, he looked like a foolish, callow youth and sounded like a girl.

Martin muttered, 'God save us from our leaders and their poor acting.'

The Prince's whining, begging flattery provided the spark for our fire. Hundreds of voices shouted insults at him, and told Boniface that he could go alone to Constantinople. Boniface looked on aghast as half the army, including Martin and myself, but not Jacques and Robert, decamped to the other side of the valley. Our army had finally broken apart, though one problem remained; our half had nowhere to go.

For six days, men trotted back and forward across the valley to speak to each other and debate. Most of them told us, 'We are simple, practical men. How can we get off this island, without help from the Venetians?' Few, except the nobles and their men, offered positive reasons to agree to the plan, but what was the alternative? Go home in debt? Stay, on this dusty island? On the third day, a grim-faced Jacques arrived, trying to cajole Martin into changing his mind.

'Don't be stupid. We have to stick together. Come back and join us now.' Martin stared into space, ignoring him, while Robert looked at me, pleading with his eyes.

I felt obliged to fill the silence. 'We're not the stupid ones. I came here to do God's will, not Boniface's.'

Jacques glared at me, and then back at Martin, who shrugged, avoiding his gaze. Jacques sauntered towards me and thrust his face into mine. 'Don't call me stupid, you saintly fucking shit.'

'I didn't ...'

Then everything went black; I never saw what hit me.

When I woke up, Martin put a cup of water into my shaking hands. 'Watch yourself with that one. If he's in a bad mood, humour him or keep your mouth shut. Don't give him an excuse. That's what he wants.'

The Venetians fed only those in Boniface's camp and our meagre supplies of food soon ran out. During the blackness of the fifth night, I woke. Somebody was moving nearby, and something dropped onto the ground between Martin and myself. A bird... an animal? I shook myself awake and waited a few seconds; I heard nothing more. I stretched my fingers out into the blackness, moving my arm from side to side. I felt sackcloth, a small parcel, tied with cord. As I grasped it, the contents slipped and moved. I sat up, and gently lifted it into my lap. Something wet and cold slithered out. A fish, with what felt like hard biscuits.

'Martin, wake up.' I heard a grunt. 'Robert has brought us something to fill our bellies.' Despite this little miracle, I watched Martin's resolve wear down the following day.

I ask you, Basil – what would you have done? You do not know? A wise answer...

On the seventh morning a cry of alarm brought us out. Across the valley, Boniface and all the other nobles had mounted their horses. Slowly and deliberately they advanced, their men following, towards our camp. We hastily gathered our weapons while our own horsemen nervously mounted up, afraid of an attack. The rest of us moved out shoulder to shoulder, to meet them. My fingers explored beneath my tunic. I felt nothing; oh, sweet Jesus, I'd left it behind. I had no protection. I tried to breathe slowly, to swallow my panic. As the nobles drew near, we watched them silently dismount and approach the last hundred paces on foot.

Around me men whispered: 'What now?' ... 'Careful, it may be a trick.'

The nobles stopped about twenty paces short, looking one way and then another as if trying to read our faces. Then Boniface raised an arm, and together they all fell on their knees.

'Fellow pilgrims. Please, we beg you, do not abandon our pilgrimage and destroy our army.' The other nobles spoke in Flemish, German, and French, each repeating these words again and again in a chorus. To my astonishment, tears streamed down many of their faces. 'We swear that the army will only stay a month in Constantinople, at most. We will not attack, but only force a palace coup, with no bloodshed. Please do not abandon us.'

The sight of great nobles on their knees, begging for aid, made proud men ashamed. Others felt relief, released from the threat of fighting our own brothers. The rest of us, hungry and exhausted men like Martin and I, had simply lost our will to resist. We resigned ourselves to our fate. With all our conscience worn away, we sailed for the city of Constantine on 24 May 1203.

We entered the straits of St George three weeks later. On the eve of St John the Baptist, we cast anchor in sight of the city of Constantine. Crowds of gaping men covered the deck. This city, the New Rome, twenty times the size of Paris, covered the hills all around. The golden domes on the palaces and churches gleamed brightly in the sun. But what drew our eyes most? The walls, my friend, the walls. Even from five leagues distance, those enormous walls made us shudder. We were like children, gazing up a cliff. Back in Chevreuse, I thought, my little child would also be amidst a world of giants, crawling along the floor, looking upwards.

*　　*　　*

After our fleet arrived at Constantinople, we made port at a town across the Bosphorus channel. The nobles stole the best houses while we put up our tents and sent out foragers for food. There we waited eight days. On the ninth evening we came upon our bodyguard friend again, sitting outside a tavern by the harbour. He waved us over to join him, asking, 'Do you want to hear my latest adventure?'

We nodded, eager to hear. 'I've just been on a little voyage. You know why we've been waiting here?'

Martin shrugged, 'No idea.'

The bodyguard tapped his nose. 'The barons have been expecting to hear from supporters of our Prince.' He cupped his ear as if listening. 'You hear anything?'

I shook my head.

He roared with laughter. 'No and neither did they... only this resounding silence. Our leaders decided that the city must be in ignorance. To remedy this, I sailed across today with my lord, the other barons and that prince in a small fleet; not enough to show our force, just enough to display our prince close to the walls.'

'Not too close, I hope.'

He grinned. 'Close enough. Close enough to see how a Roman soldier salutes his Prince.'

'And how is that?' asked Martin.

'I shall demonstrate.'

The bodyguard stood up, turned his back, dropped his pants and bowed very low, baring his hairy arse in our faces. Martin choked with laughter.

'Aye, they laughed too, and shouted abuse, hooting and crowing. If my understanding is correct, they were suggesting various animals for the prince to mate with, and others for his mother.'

Martin shrugged. 'So, they do not care for a foreign pawn.'

We looked at each other, covering our frowns with a smile. Later, in our tent, we silently sharpened our swords and checked our bows. Our leaders wisely decided not to attack the city itself but to capture the suburb and tower of Galata, on the other side of the harbour, opposite the city. After months of waiting, preparation, argument and division, no one objected, despite more broken promises. We had come too far and lost all sense of turning back. Now, we just wanted to get this journey finished. Relief and determination flowed through our veins as we took confession and absolution on the night before. In minor skirmishes so far, these Greek-speaking Romans had always run away. We prayed that the Lord would continue to put fear into their hearts.

The next morning, at dawn, we crossed. We pulled and pulled our bows upon the deck of our ship, adding our arrows to the lethal rain that washed the shoreline clean, while our horse transports approached and lowered their ramps. We watched and cheered as waves of our armoured knights thundered ashore, routing the hapless foot soldiers defending Galata. This so-called Roman army fled for the bridge at the far end of the harbour, then back into the city walls, while their rear guard demolished the bridge behind them.

The next day, we archers stood on the hill above the tower of Galata, using the heights, while our army surrounded the tower. We watched brave defenders make sorties, trying to disrupt our preparations. Too brave, as on their fourth sortie our soldiers chased after them so hard, they had no time to bar the gate, and our weight of men pushed it open again. Once our men had pushed inside, the garrison surrendered. At the same moment, we heard a mighty cheer from the Venetian ships.

'Look,' Jacques pointed, 'they've broken the great chain across the harbour.'

That afternoon, our ships slowly filled the harbour on the Galata side, while the population of the city watched silently from the city walls across the water. On the hill, we danced with elation – they did not seem able to stomach a fight. Now it was our turn to wave a Roman salute, and their turn to watch bare arse.

I would demonstrate, Basil, but my old rump is not a pretty sight. In the taverns, I would ask the girls to demonstrate, telling them the moon must be lonely, and begging them to show us more pretty moons from their glorious heavens. Many would do so. And sometimes, when my story was done, I was lucky. A girl would come to rest their moon upon my lap, and I would know that I would not be cold that night. But I digress...

After this initial success we sat down and rested our arses for four days. What would the mighty Roman army do next? By day, silence continued to greet us. No succour here, it seemed, for our Prince. By night, they crept out to constantly harry and raid our camp, so we slept little. Their patient sniping forced us to test ourselves upon their mighty city walls. The Venetian sailors wanted to attack from their ships, sailing straight across, arguing that the harbour walls were smaller. Our pilgrim army preferred to attack by land. We spent eight long days and restless nights repairing the bridge and preparing towers, rams, ladders and screens. Even when I tried to sleep, my mind would not let me, spinning visions of a growing child and its mother...

After much prayer we marched across the bridge, while the Venetians sailed into a storm of missiles. We approached a section of wall and I remember loosing arrow after arrow, my arm aching. Ready the bow, pull, move out from the screen, loose the arrow, duck back behind the screen; again, and again. Meanwhile, other men brought up siege machines and ladders. These men were mostly flung from their ladders. Those who reached the top, died there, or when they hit the ground below. At mid-day we fell back from the walls to rest.

A cry went up to the heavens, 'Hold fast'. I turned to see an army emerging from one of the city gates to confront us. Confusion reigned, before we retreated a mile and formed up on a rise, to use the slope. We archers stood at the front, on each side. I watched their army emerging, and tried to count. They marched out ten abreast, ten rows and then a gap, ten more groups, a hundred men in each formation, and the formations kept pouring out, like water from a stream. There must have been fifty thousand men against our ten. I could see damp legs around me and smell the piss on the breeze, as we watched their army grow. I touched my fingers over my embroidered cross, whispering, 'Now, you have work to do.'

Jacques nudged my arm, pointing. A rider galloped off toward the harbour. 'We're not the only ones shitting our pants.' Our throats grew dry, while we sweated under the hot sun for over an hour, watching the gleaming spears and shields of the Roman formations forming up. Then we heard shouts on the left flank. Straggling across the bridge, a thousand Venetians in a ragged black line staggered in our direction, weighed down by weapons and armour.

I smiled at Martin as we cheered. 'I never thought I would be so happy to see Venetians...'

Our allies, though, were cursing as they joined us. Three crossbowmen flopped down on the ground in front of us. One glared, pointing at his chest: 'We fight them on the walls. Part of harbour wall, we take.' Then one of his friends touched his shoulder, and pointed out the army facing us. He turned white and crossed himself.

We waited, sweating in the afternoon sun. Who would make the first move? Not us: we had the slope, and had to make use of it. Gradually, we became aware of movement in the rear of the Roman army and I realised their ranks looked strangely thin. Slowly, it dawned upon us. Like a sleepy giant, this Roman army had simply marched out through the city gates, waited, and marched back in, shutting the door again in our faces. They had tricked us and regained their harbour walls without a fight. Our first attack had cost much, but gained nothing. Their Emperor had out-manoeuvred our leaders.

* * *

Wolf At The Door

Bernard vanishes again, taking the days of my youth with him. Darkness is king now within this wretched prison: light only visits my life when someone brings me food. My eyes glimpse figures moving around me in the darkness, sometimes silently; sometimes I hear voices calling out. I can no longer distinguish between wakefulness and dreaming, past and present. I am surrounded by an army of ghosts; they lay a siege around my bed. And the walls of my sanity are crumbling a little faster than I had hoped.

How to break a siege? Well, as Justin once said to me, courage is often born from the womb of desperation, fathered by fear...

* * *

When the shadow of the Latin fleet first fell across the centre of the world, like one giant raindrop on a hot day, it caused a ripple of curiosity, nothing more. During the previous century several ill-disciplined hordes of these curious, troublesome northerners had streamed past the city, headed for Jerusalem. By comparison to past expeditions, this army was tiny. Some of these hordes had meandered on into the hot, dusty mountains at the entrance to Asia, ill prepared for thirst, poisoned wells, and ambushes; simply vanishing, never to return. Many in the city assumed that these men would disembark and follow a similar path.

Thanks to my brother, I had a unique appreciation of the dangers which, once again, I tried to explain to Luke of Antioch.

Though Luke remained sceptical about my deeper fears, he agreed when I insisted that we should take our ships out of the harbour. His eyes narrowed while he considered the implications. 'If a siege does happen, the price of food will double.'

'We have one boat just arrived, still loaded with unsold grain. I could send that back west, to intercept our other boats heading this way.'

'Good idea, Basil. Instruct their captains to wait with their cargoes at Heraclea until they hear from us.'

'We have two others already unloaded, waiting for cargo.'

Luke scratches his head. 'I will try to arrange a cargo for you to take east, to Nicomedia.'

'What manner of cargo?'

Luke tapped his nose. 'A cargo in a hurry. Then, at Nicomedia, you can buy more grain before the price rises. And it will, when word of this gets out.'

After informing the crews of our plans, I went to find my brother. I told him, 'I need to find a way to bring food into the city, if a siege occurs.'

Justin raised his eyebrows for a second, then smiled wryly and nodded. He put his hand on his chin and rubbed it. 'Come on, then. It sounds like good sense to me, though I'm not in charge. But all we can do is to ask...'

Justin took me to the commander of the walls overlooking the Sea of Marmara; but the man laughed, dismissing the idea out of hand and sending us away. Like most of the population, he could not believe the crusaders would be so foolish as to attack the city. And I had thought I was a stupid peasant. What else were they going to do?

On my return to the harbour, I found Luke waiting there with a group of men, women and children. Luke drew me to one side and told me, 'You are not entirely alone in your fears, Basil.' He gestured at the people waiting. 'Many wealthy families came here as refugees from the Holy Land. They all have a horror of crusader armies, having seen what they can do. Most of them do not wish to stay anywhere near this fleet'. He paused for effect. 'They are paying us top prices for an immediate passage to Nicomedia. And I mean top prices...' He opened his hand; I glimpsed a fistful of gold coins.

I blinked, and whispered, 'I can buy a granary with that.'

I reached Nicomedia with my human cargo four days later, and spent another two refilling the boats with grain. I also bought a small dinghy which I planned to use for carrying messages back and forward. With three of my best men, I set off back towards Constantinople in the dinghy, dressed like local fishermen. Soon after we set off, we hailed a cargo boat passing in the other direction and asked for news.

'Be careful if you're headed that way, lads,' the captain told us. 'That foreign fleet appeared again, and those galleys didn't seem very friendly; God knows why, but they blocked all the other boats behind us. We'd just left the harbour in time. If I were you, I'd turn around.'

After that, we moved slowly and carefully, stopping at each headland to scan the horizon ahead. A trickle of people from Chalcedon and other settlements around the city became a flood, first passing in boats and then by foot along the coast. Sobbing and wailing people complained loudly that the Latins had robbed them, taken their homes, and worse. My men watched them streaming in the opposite direction and looked at me, pointedly. What should I do? I felt my lion's heart shrinking...

On the fourth day, we spotted Venetian war galleys in the distance. My men looked at each other, muttering mutinously. 'Don't worry,' I told them, 'They'll ignore us. They're only interested in boats full of soldiers.' I touched wood behind my back, though.

My men shook their heads, and began to argue with me.

Eventually, I capitulated. 'Yes, yes, all right. We'll wait here and hide ourselves during the day. If we move at all, we move at night.'

Two days later, another group of fleeing refugees gave us the latest news. 'It's terrible. Everything goes from bad to worse. First, the Latin fleet and army landed at Chalcedon, across the mouth of the Bosphorus. Rather than pay for supplies there, like civilised men, they just stole anything they wanted and beat anyone who resisted. No-one was safe. Then, once they'd rested, they crossed the Bosphorus and attacked the city. They landed their army at Galata, on the north shore just outside the Golden Horn. After a short battle, they captured the Galata tower, broke the chain at the mouth of the harbour, entered the Golden Horn and made camp opposite the city walls. Now, the city itself is under siege.'

The trap was sprung. Yet now that the crusaders had crossed the Bosphorus and made camp, I was able to persuade my men that we could advance safely to Chalcedon. From there, we could see both the city and the crusader camp a mile away, across the channel mouth. But I wanted to put the city between the Latin army and ourselves. I reasoned that the crusader army was too small to surround the city completely, that there must be a way to sneak through on the western side. So in the darkest part of the night, we sailed out into the Sea of Marmara in a wide arc and back to shore a mile west of the city. There we waited, hidden in a small bay. On the second day about thirty monks appeared, walking along the shore away from the city. I stepped out and hailed them. 'How goes it?'

The bearded man at the front shrugged. 'We heard there are lots of small skirmishes outside the walls. And that the Latin army prepares siege machines to attack the city; they seem to mean business. But inside the walls, life goes on.' His face gave nothing away.

'So, have you all come out from inside?'

Finally, a hint of a smile; 'Yes, but we are pilgrims. We only came to the city to worship at the great churches and see the relics. We had intended to return earlier, but it was difficult to leave. Eventually the church elders persuaded the guards to let us leave last night.'

'How difficult was it?'

He shrugged. 'It took some coin, if that's what you mean. We left through a small postern gate furthest from the Latin camp, near the Golden Gate fortress.'

So ways did exist to sneak in and out of the city. And I had now heard enough stories of crusading armies, of rape and murder, to think that I needed to discover this way myself. The next evening I left two men with the boat and persuaded the third, the one with the sharpest eyes, to accompany me. We walked silently along the shore towards the city in the deepening gloom, hoping to find the same postern gate.

Would the Latins send out foot patrols at night?

Our muscles were tense, ready to run or hide, but while the light lasted, we saw no one. We heard movement occasionally as the darkness gathered around us, which made us drop and hug the earth. I smelt the sharp scent of animals. Was that what moved? We crept slowly on, and on. I became aware of a deeper darkness, and my companion tapped my shoulder, pointing upward. The walls. Yes, we had come very close. We backed away, fearful of an archer with the eyes of an owl. Now what? I whispered, 'Let's wait a little and listen.'

After an hour, the moon rose and the dark shapes around us took some form. Soon after, we heard movement and soft voices.

'It must be people coming out,' I whispered. 'Which direction; can you see?'

'Over there...'

We hurried towards the noise, and arrived at a small door in the wall just as it shut in our faces.

'Wait,' I pleaded, knocking upon the door, 'wait...'

'Push off.'

'Listen, I know your commander. Tell him Basil of Makri is here.'

'Why should I bother?'

'Because I have a gold piece for you here, that's why.'

After a pause, a chink of light appeared through a peephole. 'Let's see it, then.'

I held it up to catch the moonlight. I heard the noise of something heavy being lifted, and the gate opened a little. The coin got us both through the gate. I had hoped Justin might be in charge, but my heart sank when we were brought before the same commander who had chased us away before we left. His expression was grim.

'Christ, it's you again. You don't bloody give up, do you?'

'There's a lot at stake here, commander, for everyone.'

'And have you brought food, already?'

I saw my chance. 'Not yet, but I will; and when I do

you will get a good share of the profit.'

He looked me up and down, and his face softened. 'In that case I won't have you both flogged as spies, just yet. Come back tomorrow and we can discuss the details.'

After all my efforts, I discovered Luke and Sophia in the same complacent state as when I had left. They looked concerned when I told them of the chaos in the area surrounding the city and the difficulty I had gone through, but Luke shrugged off any personal sense of danger. 'Within these walls, we occupy the safest refuge on earth. Granted, it may be a long siege, but what can be done?'

Their smug confidence in their city walls seemed maddeningly unshaken. I had an urge to bang my head, or better still Luke's, upon the floor.

Luke rubbed his hands and added, 'But think of the profit we'll make on the food, Basil. You've done well there.' He hesitated for a moment, as if trying to choose his words carefully. 'Though maybe you didn't need to take such a risk and rush back to us – it might have been better if you'd remained with the boats.'

Luke had never criticised me in front of Sophia before, even as mildly as this. I snapped back, 'Look, my men do not need me to watch over them all day. I trust them. I needed to find a way to send messages to and fro. And most of all, I came out of concern for your safety: yours and Sophia's.'

Father and daughter smiled knowingly as they looked at each other, and I could see Luke holding back laughter.

My face, already hot, now burned. I turned away from their grins, feeling like a little child caught stealing honey. I knew I had revealed the depth of my feelings for Sophia, and that seemed to amuse them. That hurt. I wanted to bang their heads together, to make them listen. I managed to control myself, somehow, and told them, 'You can laugh if you like, and I hope that I am wrong. But you have not seen what I have seen.'

Luke sighed, and nodded. 'Of course. You must forgive us, Basil, if we seem light-hearted. But here within these walls seems to me far safer than outside them.'

I bit my tongue. It struck me suddenly that, in this matter, Luke was treating me like a child. Thus even Luke, who had the wisdom of Athene, could be stupid. This realisation helped to lessen the insult. Sophia also had the grace to recognise my embarrassment. She kissed me on the cheek and thanked me for my concern, and everything I had done. Her actions balanced the persistent feelings of ridicule that I continued to suffer for the next few days.

* * *

My skin itches terribly. The last time light entered this place I saw a trail of ants upon the floor. Perhaps having finished my spilled food, now they feed on me. This thought makes me remember what Luke of Antioch said to Sophia after the first fire... 'I thought Basil was looking at ants and seeing scorpions, but I was wrong; they were snakes.'

* * *

That day we awoke, hearing noises in the distance: the sounds of a crowd calling out continuously, like spectators at the Hippodrome, mingled with a hammering of distant smithies. Rumours spread through the city, about fighting on the harbour walls.

Just before noon Luke said to me, 'Let's go to see for ourselves. I know a good vantage point on the roof of a building near the monastery of Chora, on the highest hill. We can look down on the walls near the harbour from there.'

An hour later, we balanced precariously on a roof, watching ferocious fighting, witnessing how cleverly the Venetians used their ships.

'You might be right,' Luke finally admitted, 'about the danger. Look at the size of those Venetian ships, and the height of their masts.'

Around the tops of these masts, wooden castles perched, covered with hides to repel missiles and fire.

'Oh, Good Lord, Basil, look.' While we watched, bridges swung out from these castles, filled with crouching men, towards the walls. Ropes with grappling hooks flew from the bridges to the walls, like claws. Arrows and missiles flew in both directions. Attackers pulled, while frantic defenders tried to cut, the ropes. One claw after another was cut; but meanwhile more grew, so that the bridges inched inexorably towards the walls, until men began to cross the gap. Some leaped and fell; some stepped over, only to be thrown off, but others managed to hold on, and fight upon the wall.

I could not take my eyes off the scene. 'It reminds me of a battle between red and black ants,' I told him.

Luke pulled a face. 'They are men like us. But the wrong side seems to be winning.'

My stomach slowly tightened while we watched the Venetians capture one of the towers along the wall. Soon after, another. After an hour, they had captured a length of wall. Smoke began to rise into the air from adjacent buildings.

'I've seen enough, Basil.' Luke turned and slapped my shoulder. 'Come, we must go back: Sophia may be in danger.'

Oh God, yes, I thought. They could enter the city at any moment and Luke's house is not so far distant from those walls... 'We should run.'

'Yes. First, we find Sophia. Then we take her to the west of the city, near the gate you used. And we take the valuables.'

The nearer we go to Luke's house, the more chaos we found in the streets. Smoke blew into our faces from burning buildings next to the city walls; householders ran about searching for buckets and water to protect their homes. Others, having lost their houses already, staggered tearfully away from the fire. Groups of soldiers tried to push their way through the streets towards the walls.

Along our most direct route, the smoke began to choke us. A burning fragment landed on my hair, singeing it badly. A large district next to the wall seemed to be burning now. Our lungs and eyes burned so much we had to stop and shelter in alleys and doorways. Even the soldiers were turning back. I heard a crash; a building had collapsed somewhere near. People were running in all directions, shouting and crying.

'Look out!' Luke grabbed my arms and pulled me into a doorway as a shower of roof tiles and other debris landed nearby.

I realised that, as with water, so with fire; wind direction was the key. I pulled Luke to me and spoke into his ear, my voice hoarse with smoke. 'Let's try to approach your house from upwind of the fire, if we can. We're downwind of it, here. We need to go back and use the smaller streets and alleys, there's more shelter from the wind and smoke.'

We worked our way backwards and sideways out of the smoke, then forward and sideways again, around the fire, back to Luke's house. This worked. We found Sophia working with the servants, covering all the shutters with wet cloths. She had already gathered together the valuables. A practical woman, I noted. And this time, she looked expectantly at me, not at her father. Now, they both listened to me...

'It's too risky here if the wind changes; we could get trapped and burned alive. Gather the servants and take whatever we can carry, and leave the rest.'

We made up small bundles, containing Luke's money, his gold and silver utensils, and his most precious books and belongings. Luke led us to the house of another merchant, near the western walls. We waited out the day, and that night the wind dropped and the fires died down. We returned to find the house had escaped serious damage, though Luke had lost the contents of his kitchen and storerooms to looters. He fell on his knees and thanked God that his library had escaped. Then he stood up and ordered his servants to prepare all his books for transportation.

Turning to me, he added, 'Maybe we should all go to Makri, while we can. Let's rest tonight, and leave the city tomorrow.'

My heart danced at his words. And it leapt in the air later, when Sophia took my hands and whispered how grateful she was that I had come back into the city to help them. I felt real hope now; she might really be mine, if we all went together to Makri. I slept very deeply that night, despite the constant noise and movements in the streets outside.

*   *   *

A hand grasps my body and shakes it, and then a spoon laden with swill is thrust into my mouth... a rude interruption to my reverie. The food is plain, but I am hungry.

Soon I am left alone in the dark again, thinking about my younger self. My dream of becoming Sophia's hero would also suffer a rude interruption, I remembered. I allow the tide of my past to rise around me again, and float gently away on a raft of memories, once again dozing in a haze of happy anticipation, just as I did then. I knew that they would come with me; we could escape the city together before the next attack. I slip back in time, into a body young and strong again, leaving my weary old carcass to rest...

*   *   *

We awoke to hear groups of excited people hurrying past in the street outside. What was happening now? Rubbing my eyes, I dressed and went down.

At the front door, I found Luke listening intently to a well-dressed man. 'That miserable coward fled in the night. He must have been scared the mob would lynch him. And they would have too, after he failed to use his army. So now the Patriarch has restored the last Emperor, old blind Isaac, to the throne. Perfect solution, don't you see? This stupid war will end. It's Isaac's son Alexios, who fights with the Latins. Everyone is celebrating that...'

Luke asked, 'Surely the Prince wants to be Emperor himself?'

'Yes, but the Latins are fighting for Isaac's line, not for the Prince himself. Anyway, Alexios will become ruler soon enough, since Isaac is blind. I tell you, this war is over.'

Luke and Sophia, like the rest, began to jump for joy. While everyone else rejoiced, I reluctantly swallowed a lump of disappointment. With the fighting finished, danger had vanished. Sophia had no need of rescue. One more day of war and she would have been on my boat, heading for my home. Under my breath, I cursed the peace. What an idiot. But passion and wisdom always make quarrelsome bedfellows...

Luke began to busy himself unpacking his library again, and I had business to organise. I could not hide my disappointment from Sophia; she read me like a book. She came to me as I prepared to leave the house and kissed me on each cheek. 'Thank you, Basil.' Then she smiled and lowered her voice, and whispered for my ears only. 'Be patient.' Hearing this, my spirits lifted, and my battered hopes revived.

The shortages produced by the fighting, plus the demands of a foreign army, raised the price of food. When our boats returned we sold at more than double our usual price. We bought incense, silk, and other luxury goods cheaply from merchants who needed cash. People made homeless in the fire also pleaded for passage to cities where they had relatives. Since few ships from the main harbour remained intact, these refugees then outbid each other, increasing our fares threefold and more. I was also learning how war and profit delight in sharing the same bed.

I itched with curiosity to see the Latin soldiers. Their cavalry, with enormous armoured horses, terrified everyone – even the imperial Varangian guard. But the reality disappointed me. I did see some of their nobles on horses, but even they seemed unkempt and badly dressed, without armour. The common soldiers who walked into the city looked and smelled worse than provincial slaves: unwashed, dressed in plain woollen garments. I soon learned to cross the streets to avoid the smell. I thought I had been naïve when I arrived, but these Latins had obviously never seen anything civilised before. They wandered around gawping at everything, like idiots.

And most did not behave like pilgrims. Those that did visit the churches stared for hours at the pictures on the walls, arguing among themselves in their own language, as if they had never read the Bible. When I mentioned this to Luke, he said, 'Don't be so surprised. I have a friend who is a Latin, a merchant. He says that that most of the soldiers cannot read, so they do not know the Bible stories.'

My mouth dropped open. 'How can they call themselves pilgrims?'

'I know. But their church services are spoken in Latin, which the common people don't speak; only the nobles understand it. So the only way these soldiers know anything from the Bible is through pictures, or fragments a priest might choose to translate for them.'

I shook my head. 'No wonder they are such poor Christians, with such strange ideas of fighting a holy war. That always puzzled me. Anyone who knows the scriptures knows what Jesus thought of war and fighting.'

Luke laughed at this, and nodded, 'Holy war. Holy fools! He would have got down from his cross and hit them with it, would he not?'

But the Latin army made me uneasy, and I tried again to persuade Luke to winter with me in Makri. But rather than deaf, Luke now seemed blind to the menace in the streets. 'The city walls remain unbroken, and after all, the war has finished, hasn't it? But you can find me land or a house, in Makri, for the future. You have milder winters there, I know.'

The old habits of our lives took up the reins again, as that first crisis receded in our minds. We parted that September, and I took my little fleet back down the coast, dropping off refugees as I journeyed. Back in Makri, the usual trade and exchange with the capital had been prevented by the war. I arrived to find the town short of luxury goods, with a surplus of food; perfect for me. I made a great profit, and filled my storehouses with grain and oil. I had ridden the storm. Indeed, it had brought me a basket of wealth.

I had no plans for more voyages that year – sudden storms in late autumn had ruined many a merchant, and spoiled the ambitions of kings unwise enough to take their armies in boats. So I prepared the boats for winter and kept an eye out for land where Luke could build a villa. As it happened, a farmer wanted to sell some land in a quiet part of the town, next to the monastery. The abbot, unwilling to pay a fair price, had pressured the man to sell cheaply. I stepped in and bought the land for a fair price. The position was ideal for what I had in mind; slightly elevated to give views out to sea, but hidden from the land below. Antoninus puffed out his cheeks when he next saw me, but he dared not make trouble.

On the twentieth day of October, a boat owned by a trader from Cyprus came to Makri bringing more refugees from the capital. The boat also delivered a letter to me, from Luke. The refugees looked troubled; as I read Luke's letter, I understood why:

My dear friend Basil, greetings from Luke of Antioch...

It seems a short time since you left, but events have tumbled over each other since then. Two weeks after you left us, citizens who had lost their homes (in the fire that nearly took my own house) stirred up, and led, a mob. This mob looted and destroyed the homes of all the Latin merchants who lived within the city walls.

Vengeance has a double edge, never clearer than for our own citizens. The following day a group of Latin survivors returned for revenge. They set a fire within our city walls, in a warehouse of oil. A blustery wind caught this fire in the dry conditions here – we had not had rain for months. This terrible fire, like the hatred that set it, could not be controlled. It destroyed fully a fifth of our city. The stink of burnt timber, goods, and flesh hangs in the air. Because of the fire, another hundred thousand people have no home. Some have left the city, some are with friends (I have two here) and many now beg in the streets.

To make matters worse confusion reigns; not Emperor Isaac, nor his son. One of my well-connected friends told me the last Emperor took the treasury when he fled, yet Isaac and his son have promised to pay the

Franks an enormous sum. These rumours seem to have substance, for imperial officials are stripping all the minor churches of their wealth, as I write. My friend also suspects there may be more trouble ahead when the full payment cannot be made. I realise I should have asked you to stay a little longer, or listened better to you and your brother about the dangers of this barbarian army.

In truth, my friend, a vat of trouble brews already. Dissatisfaction grows rapidly with Isaac and his son – everyone sees this shameless robbery of the churches as an insult to God. The priests say this action will lose our city the protection of the Holy Mother, which has kept these walls intact all these centuries. The smell of fear and foreboding pervades the atmosphere, plus seething anger towards the Latin army that has so humiliated us.

Despite the time of year, I must ask you if you can return immediately with one or two ships to transport us and our possessions. If you cannot do this, let me know what you advise. If need be, we could make our own way to Makri, but my daughter would feel much safer if you and your men were our escort in these troubled times.

With my gratitude and our hope to see you again,
Luke of Antioch

These words sent me into a fever of anxiety and activity, rushing about to get my little fleet prepared for one more journey. How many ships? I decided to take five – leaving two in Makri – all to follow each other two days apart, to avoid the risk of losing the whole fleet together. The cargo? That must be food, to keep hunger at bay in a partly devastated city. I also knew many other refugees would pay for passage on our return. How could I have been so stupid, so blind to my own instincts? Never again, I told myself.

At the beginning of November, I knocked upon Luke's door again. He beamed with surprise, gripping my arms and calling my name. Then Sophia flung herself into my arms and hugged me so long and so hard that it took my breath away. At that moment I felt, for the first time, that she might be mine already, in spirit. Then she looked into my eyes and told me, 'I knew you would come.' With those words, I felt that she had quietly pledged herself to me. This time, I noticed Luke smiling secretly to himself. They did not think me such a fool anymore; especially after all our profits. Then, I asked him, 'What news here, Luke?'

He pulled a face and looked skyward. 'No more fires or riots, though God knows how. Just endless minor brawls, but no big eruption as yet. Everyone expects it will happen, though, with such a large army of barbarians just outside the city gate.'

The last of my ships arrived just in time, with the weather suddenly turning, to unload our cargo before the first of many winter storms struck. We used a quay in the small harbour of Julian, facing the Sea of Marmara; the Venetians had sealed off the Golden Horn. But this drastic change of weather made it impossible for us to return. I sent my ships and men to winter in the harbour at Nicomedia, at the eastern end of the Sea of Marmara, more sheltered from the winter weather than Heraclea.

We planned to leave together in the spring, as soon as the weather improved. Until then, I organised a chain of communication with my men in Nicomedia, using fast horses. We seemed well prepared. Meanwhile, Prince Alexios and the Frankish leader Boniface returned from some adventure, apparently allies. Everything seemed calm.

But war broke out again between them, with no warning. Instantly, the city gates slammed shut, the siege began again. We wished to leave, yet only a fool rushes out into the dark. I had to test the dangers first; meanwhile, Justin assured me the Latin army would not attack until the spring. It seemed we had time and initially, we felt safe within the city walls. But once again we had become the bait, caught in a trap, with a wolf at the door.

* * *

My life has been stripped of all its silk and finery, and what does it reveal? A dark and empty room; visited occasionally by the ghost of a ragged, pungent old fable maker. Bernard has become a constant companion. Now, I miss him when he has gone. Each time he comes, he looks a little older and poorer than before. He and the girl are the only company I look forward to. The other slaves tell me I babble to myself all day, but that must be when they are not here. Well, why not? Who else will listen to my story?

Today Bernard of Chevreuse shuffles painfully towards me, as if he has no shoes and walks on blisters. He looks like an old man, and sighs with relief as he sits down, and then resumes his tale...

*   *   *

The Devil Plays His Hand

How was it during that first siege, inside the walls, Basil? You may not believe this, but we were probably far more scared than you were. Your army was enormous, and we had no walls to defend us. When your army emerged to face us, we thought we were doomed. We faced it down, your mighty Roman army, and thanked God that you did not use it. Still, we had gained nothing, and lost some of our bravest men. Short of food that night, our nobles and cavalry ate their wounded horses. Back in the tent, our stomachs grumbled while we cursed our leaders long and hard. I asked Martin, 'What will happen now?'

He grunted. 'If they keep their patience, the Greeks can slowly wear us down and crush us under their feet. We have no food left. We should leave while we can.' Jacques began to curse, repeatedly.

We called your people Greeks, because this was the language you speak and use in your churches. But we called your army Roman; because your city ruled that part of the mighty Roman Empire that had never fallen in over a thousand years, and we all knew that far too well. I could feel our spirits sinking, to a new low. I prayed aloud, 'Just grant us some sleep tonight, please...'

Robert whispered, 'Amen'.

Jacques chuckled, murmuring, 'Aye, some sleep tonight, but bring me a juicy little whore in the morning...'

We expected more attacks to harry us, to keep our sleep at bay, that night. But silence slowly filled our camp, and one by one we fell into a lifeless stupor.

Our Lord had clearly not forgotten us, for mine was not the only pilgrim's prayer answered that night. The bright sun of a new day brought amazing news. Your Emperor had fled. He had lost the support of his people overnight. Because he had failed to attack us with his huge army, he had been branded a coward despite his cunning victory. Roman impatience had turned our certain defeat into victory. Our Prince's father had been given his throne back by his people; and we had won it for him. Now we would be welcome guests, not enemies, in your great city of Constantine, the jewel of the ancient world.

* * *

We penetrated those enormous walls as guests, not warriors, and wandered open-mouthed for days. The great cathedral of Saint Sophia stretched up to the very sky. Everywhere we looked, gold and silver gleamed, framing icons of the saints, and decorating jewel-encrusted altars. The main altar, a treasury in itself, left our nobles gaping like beggars at a feast. Yet no treasure, not even a mountain of it, could fill this vast space, for it seemed so high you could see the clouds under its heavenly dome. I swear it. Even the ceiling was fashioned to look like heaven, with the face of Christ our Saviour gazing down from the enormous dome above. On seeing this likeness, Robert fell upon his knees and began to babble, begging forgiveness for his many sins. He truly believed that God Himself looked down upon him, and not even Jacques could dissuade him.

Inside that place called the Hippodrome, your great long enclosure of stone had seats enough for ten times our army. And along the central spine of that long oval chariot track, the host of statues was an army of stone staring back at us with curiosity equal to our own. Men, women, lions, bulls, every creature imaginable; I felt their eyes upon my back whenever I turned away.

When we looked at your citizens, with skins of every hue, in their silk clothes, brightly coloured and embroidered with gold, we wondered, how many nobles did you have in this city? You looked back upon us poor soldiers just as intently, but more in fear and horror than in awe. Ah, the silk. How many of us had seen silk with our own eyes? A few. How many of us had touched silk with our own hands? Almost none. When I told my tale in the taverns, I would describe silk as like cobwebs, so fine a cloth that you could not see the threads, and as soft as a virgin's kiss. So it is, and it was just as arousing to us to see it, and feel it, upon the female form.

What astonished us most? One simple fact: that in this city, some of the slaves were dressed in silk. Not one, but many. I began to understand what had drawn the barons there.

Our bodyguard friend later swore to us that he and his Lord saw a tree made of gold, with mechanical singing birds, in one of the great palaces. For me, with my faith, the shrine with the Holy relics of our Lord and the one true cross gave me the greatest blessing. For the first time that year I felt at peace, as a pilgrim should. I felt able to watch mothers with their babes in the streets, laughing as the child sucked on their fingers, proudly pointing out a tiny sprouting tooth. Though I wished to be home, I still felt privileged to be in such a sacred and wondrous place.

This reverie did not last long. Rot had crept into this earthly paradise along with us. We knew the contract with the Venetians expired within the month; they would demand more payment. Would we ever reach the Holy Land? We grew bored, waiting for news. Jacques and Robert sought out the brothels, while Martin and I looked for information. Our bodyguard friend provided it. 'That foolish Greek prince agreed to pay the Venetians for a second year, in addition to the fortune promised to the Barons.'

Martin nodded. 'Imperial thrones do not come cheap.'

'If he can pay...' He looked around and then tapped his nose, lowering his voice to a whisper. 'The last Emperor took the gold with him when he fled. The Prince and Boniface left yesterday with most of our armoured horse, to chase the former Emperor and his gold.'

We looked at each other and I laughed. 'Now we have something in common at last. Like us poor pilgrims, this Prince and his father cannot pay what they do not have, eh?'

As the weeks became months, tension and ill feeling against our army grew in the city. Occasional brawls and altercations with the locals became more frequent; soon most of us dared not venture into the city after dark, for fear of attack by your mob. Then one night, we woke up to hear a succession of cries and wails approaching our camp. We staggered outside and rubbed our eyes. A pitiful column of distressed and injured men, women and children clung to each other as they limped into our camp. They seemed to be asking for help, or comfort.

'Which hell have these people sprung from?'

I was talking to myself, but an older man, bleeding from a head wound, answered me in my own language. 'These peoples, we are foreign merchants here; most of us Venetians, Pisans, or Genoese. Tonight – big, terrible riot in the city. The mob attack our quarter. They drive us out, steal everything, burn our homes. We are lucky: many men killed, women raped.' His wife, her faced streaked with tears, clung onto his arm.

Robert looked at me, then gently took the woman's hand and gestured for them to go into our tent. We cleaned the man's wound, and Robert and I let them use our bedding that night.

The following day, while they were leaving us, the devil played his hand: he blew up a gusting, southerly wind. We watched a small plume of smoke by the city walls rapidly grow in size until flames appeared, visible above the city walls across the harbour. These flames spread slowly up and across one of the hills that dominated the city skyline, out of control. I looked at Martin. 'How did that start, I wonder?'

He shrugged. 'Maybe still burning from last night, or maybe someone's idea of revenge.' Pilgrims and Venetians alike, we watched in horror as the fire spread, consuming a large part of the city. Now, they probably hated all of us.

Boniface and our cavalry returned, with the Prince, in late November. Judging by their sour faces, they had not been successful. On the afternoon of the first day of December we heard the call, 'Arm yourselves; arm yourselves.'

'Mother of Christ...' Jacques grabbed his bow and sword and stepped outside. We followed, in less of a hurry. Men milled around, looking puzzled. Otherwise, nothing seemed to be happening.

After another hour, another knight rode into the camp, 'Stand down, stand down.'

In the tavern that night, we heard the news. 'Another brawl broke out between Greeks and some of our pilgrim army. A crowd gathered to chase the pilgrims away. Each side took up arms, and blood was spilled. The mob grew as word spread through the city. They murdered any Latins and pilgrims they could find within the city walls. We thought the mob would attack our camp; to keep the peace, the Greek Prince has shut the city gates.'

The next day the four of us watched warily from the hill above our camp. Hundreds of the Greek mob scrambled down the harbour walls on rope ladders and tried to cross the harbour in small boats, until the Venetian war galleys appeared and sent them packing. Martin sighed. 'Look at this madness. The Prince and his father couldn't pay the Venetians now even if they had the gold. That mob has murdered emperors before and would cut their throats if they paid us a penny.'

Sure enough, our alliance with the Prince and his father ended the next day; war broke out again. Our bodyguard friend described the scene to us: 'My Lord attended as an envoy, with me by his side. First, we had lots of bowing and scraping, and licking of arses. Then the discussion, led by that fool Conon of Bethune. A great diplomat he is: in short, he said, it's your fault. The Greeks said no, no, it's yours. Tempers, already so hot, just ignited. Great Lords are no different to the fishwives of Paris, arguing over the price of eels, where money is concerned. More wine, lads?'

Now, we owned this war; we did not borrow it from another. It was a golden war, spawned by money and necessity; not a just one, or even a Holy one. Money had been promised in a solemn treaty. To take this money, and feed ourselves through the winter, we raided settlements around the city, stripping all the houses and churches of all their valuables and food. When I asked a monk what he thought of this, he replied, 'Necessity knows no laws.' Think on that, my friends; think on that. Meanwhile the Prince and his father avoided battle, waiting for us to run out of food and patience, hoping we would hear the call of the Holy Land.

This might indeed have happened, but again your people ran out of patience. At the end of January, the mob deposed the Prince and his father, and later killed them. In the common soldier's tents, the refrain was 'Who cares?'

But our nobles looked on aghast, their treaties and debts now void; the new Roman Emperor had not signed them. We had stripped the country of food, and the noise of an army grumbling with both mouth and stomach filled the air. Without a purpose, our army would surely rent apart again. We had lost all faith in our leaders. They had brought us into one mess after another. As usual, they turned to the priests to hold the pilgrimage together.

The Bishops called us together to hear their decisions. 'We asked the Lord for guidance, and this is His answer. God declares the new Emperor a murderer and usurper. Our conflict is a just war against a tyrant; and this new tyrant has openly declared a schism with Rome and the Holy Father. The Greeks are no better than Jews and infidels. So this conflict is a Holy war: if we reclaim Constantinople for the Holy Father, this will be the equal of reclaiming Jerusalem. The Lord will grant you all your privileges as pilgrims – absolution for all sins, cancellation of debts, and entry to heaven.' I struggled to comprehend this message as I watched relief dawn on many of the faces around me. Then I realised what they meant; conquer the city again, and we could go home, having fulfilled our vows. No need to go on to the Holy Land. How strange this seemed, after all that had gone before, but it lifted a great burden from our minds.

Back in the camp, no dissent was voiced. We all felt imprisoned by our long journey, our divisions and diversions; exhausted, sick to our teeth. Suddenly, the door had unlocked and swung open. We quietly remembered friends and comrades who had already spilt their blood. This fight had become personal, and the devil has no higher wage. We would attack in the spring.

By now, my child would be trying to stand on its feet, to reach out and upward. If I could walk away from one more battle, I might yet hold those tiny hands in mine.

Now we have reached the meat of my story, and in the taverns I would say that I must have meat, and more wine, before I would tell how we conquered those mighty walls, which had never before fallen in a thousand years.

* * *

Spring blossomed while we made our final preparations, sharpening our weapons and building the machines of war. The legions of the Roman army harried our foragers, but did not attempt to drive us away. Our leaders, meanwhile, had learned some lessons. We would concentrate our forces on the smallest city walls, across the harbour, fighting alongside the Venetians in their ships. Guessing our intent, we watched the Roman army raise the harbour walls higher, building extra wooden ramparts along the top. We built the castles around our masts still higher, to match their work.

On two dark, moonless nights, cries of alarm from the harbour woke us. We stumbled outside, peering into the gloom below the camp. I glimpsed flickers of flame out in the middle of the harbour and the cry went up, 'Fire ships!' Floating slowly towards our precious fleet, the fire reached out slowly, seeming to lick its lips and then to roar with anticipation as tar and pitch caught hold. We could only watch, helpless; but each time the Venetian sailors use their galleys to intercept the blazing ships and tow them out into the Bosphorus.

The day before the attack, in early April, we readied our souls for battle. That evening after dark, lines of heavily laden men stumbled up ramps and across decks, cursing quietly as we moved into our positions. We archers had to climb into small wooden castles, halfway up the masts, along with crossbowmen. We tried to doze, sitting back to back, but the whispering of anxious men makes a poor lullaby. Soldiers hate the long hours of waiting before a battle. You sit, struggling to blot out visions of your own death, willing Father Time to move, but he stands still and whispers horrors in your ear. I tried to distract myself, feeling the surface of my keepsake, but Catherine's face would not appear in my mind, and I could not picture a healthy child... I found my fingers tracing the shapes of her embroidery repeatedly, my lips silently muttering prayer after prayer.

At last, the signs of first light appeared; the creaking of wood broke the silence as movement began. Peering down from our perch, we made out the dark shape of catapults, sitting like huge scorpions on the decks below. We felt exposed and unbalanced as we swayed from side to side, the black water below.

'God help us.' For the first time, Jacques too sounded afraid.

'We all pray for that,' I whispered.

We attacked as the dawn broke. A hail of arrows, bolts and boulders replied from the walls. I saw most of one sailor vanish through our deck when a massive stone dropped upon him, leaving an arm behind. Time and again the Venetians aimed the ships toward the walls, but a gusting wind blew up and kept pushing us back, so that our bridges would not anchor on the walls. My arms ached, from pulling my bow.

Other men landed on the shore, but oil and fire drove them back. Robert and I leaned out to watch. Then I heard a noise like an angry bee, and the sound of a slap. A hand clutched my shoulder as liquid spurted into my eyes, running down into my lips; I tasted the salt of blood. I blinked my vision clear. Robert's face contorted, his eyes bulging. His lips moved but no sound emerged; one hand grasped a feathered stick jutting out of his neck. Around the shaft of the arrow, blood and bubbles of air spurted from his neck. Strong hands grasped us both and pulled us back behind the screen. I heard a long wail from Jacques, while a wide-eyed Martin gently slapped my face. 'Are you hit?'

I shook my head. 'No, not me; it's Robert's blood.' Martin carefully ran his hand over the top of my head, to be sure. We turned to see Jacques on his knees, cradling Robert tenderly in his arms. We could do nothing to help him. He kicked and gasped for air, the blood spraying from his neck and spluttering out of his mouth as he tried to speak. All the time, he grasped the arrow shaft, as if trying to hang onto his life. Jacques began to cry, repeatedly begging God to save Robert, and stroking his face. He bled his life away, held tenderly in Jacques' arms. At the end, Jacques cried like a baby. Meanwhile, our first attack had died along with Robert.

We buried our dead and then our frustrations burst like a boil. A crowd gathered outside the grand marquee where the leaders held their council, shouting advice and abuse:

'This siege is impossible. Armies ten times our size did not succeed. For eight hundred years those walls have not been broken.'

'They have a vast army within the walls, plus the mob. We should leave before they use their strength on us.'

'Why did we come here? This is madness.'

'God has showed His judgment upon us, for all our diversions.'

'Aye – this is His displeasure. Open your eyes, barons!'

The faith that makes a pilgrim army such a force was draining away. Once again, the nobles turned to the priests. That evening, the bishops called us together. 'Your righteousness is not in doubt. Today was not a judgement, but a test of your faith. God is displeased, but only with your lack of faith in His purpose. You must have faith, and try once more. This attack is not a sin, but a righteous effort to defeat a tyrant and restore the true faith. They have called us dogs; and they treat us, their friends, like dogs, promise after promise. They murder their emperors for no reason, attack their allies, dishonour their solemn oaths, and do not behave like men. These Greeks are heretics and traitors and cowards, who are worse than Jews or infidels.' So the priests gave us communion and absolution, with these words of hatred for the Greeks echoing in our ears, stirring our anger and contempt to the surface. We expelled the prostitutes from the camp to purify our purpose, and made ready for one last effort.

Three days later, we attacked again. We pulled and pulled our bows and watched the battle rage until noon; Martin's face grew darker by the minute. 'Even with two ships upon each tower, we can't get near the walls.'

But then, a reluctant sigh escaped from heaven. Martin noticed it first. 'It's changed.'

Jacques paused as he picked up an arrow. 'What?'

'The wind. Feel the air. The direction has changed. Look how it drives the ships on towards the walls.'

Brave men leapt from our bridges onto walls and towers, human anchors, tied with ropes to pull the bridges in and secure them. Most were cut to pieces with axes, or stuck like pigs on spears. But one fell inside the city wall, his rope intact, and the weight of his body dragged his bridge across a tower, where the defenders were soon swept away. On the next tower, an armoured knight landed, ignoring the blows bouncing off him, standing long enough to pull his comrades in. Now, by God, we had a foothold. Our ship was next in line. We fired arrows furiously to keep Greek heads down while we delivered our bridge of men to reinforce one of these towers, and then moved away to the side.

Have you seen a man fry and burn? Do you know that smell of hot and burning oil? I remember it well. I have heard men shrieking until they breathed the fire into their lungs. I watched them writhe, pulling off their own skin in desperation, and then collapse. It can pour all over a man's body in the blink of an eye. If he is lucky the oil is aflame, so the end is quicker.

We archers fired and fired. When we had used all our arrows, the captain of our boat looked up and shouted, 'Take your swords onto the shore.' He pointed. A dozen men were clustered at the base of the wall, calling for help. We clambered down and splashed ashore, glancing upwards, muttering prayers and curses. They had found a walled up postern gate. So we dug or hacked at the ground below and the bricks above with axes, swords, and pikes – while others held shields above us against a growing rain of rocks and arrows. In our heads we all screamed, silently, 'Please God, no oil; please, no oil.'

A small gap appeared under the bricks; above it, bricks began to fall out. We worked in a frenzy to widen and deepen this hole before we all fried, or burned. Soon, a single man might crawl through. A knight knelt, peered through the gap, and cursed. 'There are hundreds of Romans running about on the other side. It's suicide.' He moved back, reaching under his chain mail to scratch his neck.

A monk stepped forward, a quiet and pious man whom I respected. He had never lied about our destination, remaining silent while others misled. Without a word, he dropped to his knees and crawled into the hole. The knight cursed and told him not to throw his life away, but his feet disappeared. We listened for the sound of butchered flesh. Then I understood the monk's madness – if this business is not God's will, let me die now. And if I am honest, I felt more terrified of the oil than of their soldiers. So I could not stop myself, and crawled into that hole.

On the other side of the wall, my head emerged to see the monk on his feet and alive. He stood holding his sword with both hands, blade downwards, raising it in front of him like a cross, glancing impassively about him. From behind his feet, I looked around and hesitated. A small circle of Roman soldiers gaped at him, astonished, while others ran here and there through the noisy chaos around us. One man with a spear could defend this hole easily; yet no one moved.

It dawned upon me that this monk had them under a spell. Perhaps they had never seen a warrior monk; perhaps his own stillness made them fix like statues in the ground. Slowly, I rose to my feet and joined him, shoulder to shoulder. Still they gaped. Others followed behind me, more rapidly. By the time one of the Romans awoke and shouted the alarm, the call came too late. Half of those facing us broke and ran. The rest, poor soldiers, followed after a token fight. Soon seventy men had crawled through that narrow hole; it seemed to me with God's own help.

Our hesitant knight then took command. We ran along the base of the wall towards the nearest gate. Once there, we fell on the astonished defenders from behind. These men fought like soldiers – but we had cut half of them down before they could fight, and the rest, outnumbered, did not last long. This sword here killed two Romans that day: one with a slash across his neck, and the other with a thrust upwards under the chin, into the skull. Two of our men slipped out from this gate and ran to signal our fleet. Somehow we remained invisible for an eternity, while the Venetians slowly brought our lumbering horse transports nearer to the gate.

We heard trumpets, and the growing tramp of marching men along the street leading to our gate. Turning the corner, a legion of giants strode steadily towards us, double-bladed axes at their shoulders, blonde hair spilling out around their helmets.

Martin turned pale. 'The Emperor's guard,' he whispered, 'the grim reapers, in person.'

As they formed a line and began to swing their axes, I dimly heard the sound of ramps dropping. Without my bow, the sight of these men froze me to the ground with fear. I pissed myself when they started to run towards us, roaring a battle cry, their double bladed axes singing through the air. I could not take my eyes away from them, though the creaking of hinges distracted me. The city gate opened behind me while the gate to another world ran towards me, sucking my last breath of air away. I blinked. Suddenly, those grim reapers in front of me had gone, replaced by a thunderous noise – the roar of armoured horses storming through the gate, brushing them aside like corn.

We watched the Emperor's fearsome axe men retreat towards his fortified palace, while the rest of his army broke and ran. Our foot soldiers flowed through the gate, moving into the side streets, killing off any resistance and taking what they could find in the houses nearby. By nightfall, our army had occupied this small corner of the city.

The three of us Chevrotins had long since sunk to

the floor, our backs to the wall, too exhausted to move. The ghost of Robert sat next to me, and tapped my leg gently with his sword; 'Fucking good fight, Bernard.'

I swallowed, confused, looked again. It was Jacques.

'Is it over?' I asked, hopefully, after a long pause.

Martin shook his head. 'Their army still outnumbers us three or four to one, if they reorganise.' He spat. 'I need a drink.' He patted his sword. 'Then there's the population of the city – their mob alone could sweep us away. If only a fifth of them arm themselves, they would still outnumber us ten to one. Better we sleep outside the walls, tonight. We don't want to risk being trapped by the mob.'

We got to our feet wearily and slept little that night, jumping up at every sound. Fires had started around the fighting, and we could hear them spreading. In the morning, a great swathe of the city burned, blocking our path to the rest. So we let our exhaustion grip us hard, and dozed for another day and night while the fire took its course. The battle was only half won.

This tale of fire is hot and thirsty work, Basil. You too should rest a little, before I return with the bloody finale of my pilgrim's tale.

*   *   *

A Hero's Costume

In the darkness of the night around my bed, I glimpse shadows shuffling forward and hear them whispering, a line of refugees waiting to board my ship. The aroma of spring, of new growth, fills the night air, mixed with the stink of fear, piss and sweat.

I fall back into sleep until a female voice calls to me repeatedly. At first I hear Sophia's voice, telling me to get up, to get ready to leave the city together. I hear a note of such tenderness in her voice that I want to hang on to this moment, and keep my eyes closed. But then a hand touches my shoulder and shakes me. Oh no, I think; this is no dream. The little slave has come to feed me. I am an old man again, with no hope of ever holding my Sophia again...

The little slave giggles as she lifts me up and sees how I stand to attention again for the memory of Sophia. She smiles and puts her fingers to her lips, and wets them. I shut my eyes and try to remember and relive our last night, alone together in the city of Constantine... I slip through the curtain, as I did that night, feeling my throat swell with wonder as my eyes meet hers. I pinch myself three times, unable to believe my luck. We touch, Sophia's skin caressing mine and mine caressing hers, our bodies moving closer together, unfolding so carefully into each other, here, into this heaven; moving slowly at first, our eyes together, our bodies and feelings growing into one another, hearts beating faster and faster, our bodies entangled in motion, so deep, so deep, until we both cry out together...

* * *

When I looked back on those events years later, I saw that my confidence grew too fat on my own success that winter. A young man, unused to such profits, I was drunk with the heady taste of my good fortune, and with my unspoken betrothal to Sophia. I wanted to gorge myself on those feelings, to make them last. Perhaps that is how I lost her... I had been given a warning; how much time did I need to act upon it?

By now, I had an arrangement with the commander

of the wall for our mutual benefit. Whenever we left by his postern gate, two of his best men would scout ahead and guide us from the gate to the nearest point on the shoreline. When we returned, one of us first went alone to the gate, so that his scouts could come out to meet and inspect our cargo. We paid him and his men a generous tax for the cargoes going in and out.

The winter that year began badly, but the worst storms did not persist beyond January. As soon as we had periods of calmer weather, we slipped out to use the dinghy and began to test the route we had used before, moving along the coast by night and hiding in small bays by day. A week later, on a moonless night, we brought one of our cargo boats with food from Nicomedia, staying well out at sea until the last moment. We come inshore at a bay three miles west of the city. There we loaded the food onto waiting mules and brought it along the shoreline to meet the scouts. We guided our mules to the wall, and then escorted a party of refugees to the shore. It seemed safe enough: at this time the crusader army foraged only in daylight, and the galleys rarely ventured out of harbour, and then not far. By the time daylight returned, our ship was a dot vanishing over the horizon.

The weather continued to interrupt our trips during February. But each time we risked a voyage, the refugees who wished to leave filled our pockets with more and more gold.

Back on land, things had gone from bad to worse politically. At the end of January the mob rose up and demanded a new emperor. The resulting palace coup deposed Alexios and his father and imprisoned them. The mob had chosen a man they thought could fight the Latins, Alexios Dukas. Hearing of this, the crusaders arranged a parley; approaching under a flag of truce, they treacherously tried to kill him. But Dukas escaped, and in revenge he had the Prince and his father quietly killed. Now, the Latins could never put them back upon the throne. Murder had crept out from his lair.

In March I made enormous profits: however much I increased the fare, men would queue to pay it, and more. It seems like madness now, to take such risks, but I felt charmed, that nothing could harm me. And I got such adoration from Sophia, who thought me a hero. Did she realise the profits, or did she think that was immaterial to the task? Eventually, fear got its grip upon my men, and they made me see reason. They demanded to go home to Makri. So I agreed that at the beginning of April all our ships would make one last trip from Nicomedia on successive days, exchange cargoes overnight, and then head out of the Sea of Marmara and down the coast for home. For speed, we would take mostly refugees out, with a minimum of other goods.

I returned to the city to help organise our own exodus. Luke met the first ship himself. He loaded his library and valuables plus some refugees he had organised, and this boat left. So far, so good; but then events began to move too fast for me. The next day, the crusaders attacked the walls again using the Venetian ships. Worse than that, some galleys were spotted patrolling the shoreline from the city walls later that day. I worried that the second boat might be intercepted, so we did not use it ourselves. I ventured out to watch it leave with more refugees that night (at an unbelievable price) and it seemed to get away safely.

Now, fear had a grip on us all, in different ways. Sophia flung herself upon me when I returned to the house from the postern gate. 'Thank God, you're safe.'

I could not help myself. In a teasing manner I told her, 'I will have to marry you now – people will think this behaviour unseemly.'

I meant it as a joke, but she didn't laugh. Colour flushed through her cheeks and she looked down at the floor with her dark eyes. I could see her thinking, deciding whether to take it as a joke or not. Luke looked on, suddenly alert and standing tall, searching her face to see what might be revealed. Eventually she looked up and smiled, though the set of her brow revealed her determination. 'Yes, I think you should, Basil of Makri. Today would be a good day.'

We Romans have a saying – marry in haste, and

fornicate at your leisure. Why did this pop into my head that day? Something in my gut told me to wait, to leave the city before we married, but how could I refuse? Sophia had offered herself to me. Would this moment come again? I had learned to grasp unexpected good fortune firmly with both hands. We had all breathed an atmosphere of fear in the city for many months; maybe Sophia wanted to marry me at that moment because she did not want to risk dying a maid. I could not blame her, and it matched my own desires.

Suddenly conscious of her eyes upon me, I nodded. 'Today would be perfect.'

She clung to me, and then to Luke, making little jumps and cries, and then watered both of us with her tears.

I remember Luke said to us, 'I would rather have chosen a happier time, but you have my blessings. I understand more than you think, both of you. This...' Frowning, he waved his hand, trying to pluck the right words out of the air, '...this strange and terrible background uncannily matches the circumstances of my own marriage. I hope you will have the same happiness, but for much, much longer; for a lifetime.' He started to cry too. 'It is a wonder and a joy, to see my daughter so happy.'

Yes, she certainly seemed as eager as I. My heart burst with pride that day. But the result was that this happy event once again delayed our departure, while we organised a priest and a church. This took a whole day, and meanwhile...what was happening outside the walls? The third boat took more refugees away while we celebrated our wedding. I could not even find my brother to tell him my news; that also troubled me.

But Sophia and I had one wonderful night together in the city of Constantine as man and wife. That night, we were fireflies, burning up all our passion in that one night together. I remember thinking please, please, let this be the longest night of my life. And now, as I relive it again, I try to stop time, to stay in that memory forever, just as I wanted to stay in that bed forever...

* * *

I awake again to find myself crying aloud in ecstasy. The slave girl laughs, but then looks worried when we hear footsteps approaching. Quickly, she wipes me and covers me up. Someone flings the door open. I see Timon's face; he raises his lamp high while he examines us coldly. He steps forward, throws back the bed cloth, and he too laughs. His amusement does not bother me; laughter is cheap. But then his eyes fix upon a book and candle, also hidden in my bed. They narrow, cold and staring, as the girl shrinks away from him. 'Where did you get this book?' he hisses at her. She silently shakes her head. He leads her away by her hair while I watch, impotent once again.

In the middle of my most precious memory, the poor little slave girl and I are both exposed. Humiliation, anger, sorrow, and wonder all run together in my veins. Is there no pity in this world? And how could I have forgotten that night for so long? By hardening my heart, all those years ago, I had put aside the most wonderful night of my life from my memory. What curious creatures we can be, to throw away such a jewel. I remember now, though. These dreams of Sophia have brought it all back.

* * *

When the light crept through the curtains I stroked her hair one last time and reluctantly rose to dress as she watched me, smiling. Even my young lust had exhausted itself, leaving a residue of caution deep within me. I wanted us to have a second route to safety, to have one boat in reserve; just in case. I knew that we must leave that night, on the fourth boat.

During the day, I asked one soldier after another about my brother, only to see them shrug; it seemed I could not say farewell to him, or offer him the chance to come with us, though I knew he would refuse. But that night, as Luke and I stepped through the postern gate with the other refugees, the commander called after me, 'One moment, Basil. Aren't you the brother of Justin, also of Makri?'

I turned and nodded; at last. 'Yes, of course? Is he

here?'

'No, I've just found out myself. He was wounded in the fighting on the walls two days ago. It's not a lethal wound; but in the shoulder, so he can't fight. He's been trying to get word to you, to tell you where he is. He's with the monks in the hospital of St John.'

There it sat, grinning at me, the devil's choice. I could either go with Sophia and Luke to safety together, or try to rescue my wounded brother. I could either risk separation from my new wife, or abandon my brother, the hero who had kept me safe as a child and warned me about the current dangers. I could not do both. Of course, my instinct roared at me to leave. But how could I? With hindsight, I should have sent one of my men to find Justin. But at that moment my pride took over; I wanted to impress Sophia. Already intoxicated with my own success, I swallowed my doubts, thought rapidly, and turned to Luke.

'Go with my men to the boat tonight. Wait one hour for me, no more, before you depart, in case I find him quickly. If we cannot catch up tonight, I will bring Justin in the other boat tomorrow night. But you must get away before dawn. The boat will head for Heraclea initially; I will catch the last boat tomorrow and meet you there. Whatever happens, get away from here. My men will take care of you. If the sea route out through the straits of St George is blocked, go back to Nicomedia or any other safe port, and from there go to Nicaea overland. It has the best fortress in the Empire. The local ports may not be safe for long, if this war continues.'

I hurried back into the city. I left a man to wait by the gate, in case Luke and Sophia had to turn back and return that way. But other events were hidden from my eyes that night. Justin had already sent a messenger to Luke's house and discovered our plans from the servant left in charge there. While I instructed Luke at the gate, a monk was helping my brother to dress. While I hurried to the hospital, this monk brought Justin to the postern gate. We may even have passed in the street; both in such a rush, we missed the other. Balancing on such small events, our lives toppled one way, and another. At the gate, my brother found the man I had left there; he took my brother to the boat. And by the time I had reached and searched the hospital, and then returned, I had missed that fourth boat. So it was me that was left behind, raging at my own stupidity. I cursed the vanity that made me don the hero's costume, only to find that it made me look like a perfect fool...

* * *

My memories are like a spider's web, spun out of painful connections to the mistakes I made as a young man. Only now can I bear to remember them. Such anguish I suffered, after I found myself separated from Sophia and the others; my only comfort was to tell myself that my brother, wounded or not, would keep her safe... in my mind I want to go back, back to our night together, but my memories march on and carry me with them, struggling and protesting...

My last day, alone in that great city, felt like an eternity. Rumour and panic swept through the streets all day. I awoke to hear soldiers running through the streets, and in the distance, the sounds of battle. The snap of catapults, the crash of stones upon walls and roofs, and distant shouts and screams, continued all morning. Shortly after midday, I watched a rush of people pass by. Others followed carrying valuables, crying out that the Latins had a foothold somewhere near the harbour walls. Before nightfall, a soldier limped past from the same direction. I exchanged water for news: 'The Latins have taken part of the city; they robbed and murdered all those they found.' On the gusting wind, the smell of smoke and fire brought panic, invading every corner. Frightened and angry crowds became mobs, and then dispersed again. Desperate talk filled the air, prayers and appeals for a new Emperor, to save us. But who could that be?

At last, my hour of departure arrived. My pockets had been filled to overflowing with gold by my passengers, on that night. With these companions I crept out through the little gate that night. We were not alone; hundreds of other wise souls were also paying to flee into the darkness, all hoping the Latin army slept, exhausted, on the other side of the city. And mostly, they did. We reached our boat safely, and as first light approached my crew prepared to get under way, a fresh offshore breeze on our faces. All seemed to be going to plan...

Among the crew, the relief was palpable as we cast off. We used the oars to move out from the shore and then unfurled the sails as the breeze picked up. But suddenly, in the dim half-light, something approached, out of the gates of hell. Low in the water, far too close, two dark shapes passed from east to west like giant serpents. In the terrified silence, everyone heard the steady, rhythmic splashing of oars. The Venetians had sent their war galleys out to patrol again, to prevent reinforcements supporting the city's defenders. With the misshapen land behind us, I realised our own boat must have been invisible. But these galleys now blocked the route along the coast to Heraclea. And how many more galleys would be out there?

I waited until the silence returned, and then we moved our boat quietly and carefully away from them, forced to head east, past the city towards Nicomedia. Risky, but in the growing light I had no choice. As the wind began to pick up, I smelt smoke; then, as we rounded a small point we all saw a terrible red glow in the sky. The whole city seemed to be burning. Gradually, the light of dawn slowly revealed the horizon, revealing patches of thick mist or fog upon the sea. I scanned the horizon, hardly daring to breathe, as we picked up speed in the morning breeze. No galleys, yet. A patch of what I had assumed was fog brought an acrid smell of burning timber. Of course, I realised; it wasn't fog, but smoke from the fires. We made our way east for almost a mile, almost at right angles to the wind. Astern, we could see fairly well. Ahead, the smoke patches gradually thickened, forming a wall of cloud in the distance. The silence began to be broken by muffled coughs. Then the steersman called out, in a hoarse whisper, 'They're coming back. Mother of God, help us.'

I ran to the stern. The wind was moving the boat,

but how quickly? On the horizon, two small shapes were gradually growing larger. 'Steer south-east, we need more wind behind us,' I shouted. 'And get the women and children on deck, the men below.'

We picked up speed, but still had a distance to travel before we could disappear into that cloak of choking safety. Time dragged, while I desperately tried to judge the speed and distance. 'Have they turned, too?' I asked.

We peered behind. Nobody spoke. The outlines grew larger, but had not changed shape. They were following us. Everyone was paralysed, mesmerised by the sound of their own beating hearts. After a while, I could see their oars, rising and falling.

A child wailed, speaking for everyone. I glanced ahead and my heart skipped a beat. Now, I could see no more than a few hundred paces. By Tyche, I thought, it must be spreading as it drifts, though by now the galleys were far too close, and gaining rapidly. How far, how fast? A minute seemed like an eternity. Astern, I could now make out the ram of the leading galley, with the white bow-wave around it. But even as I watched, the shape of it began to disappear as smoke drifted around us and slowly swallowed us up. Once the galleys had vanished completely, I counted a hundred beats of my heart, then another fifty, and shouted, 'Turn about.'

The steersman looked at me in horror, unable to move. I grabbed the tiller from him and pulled it until I felt the wind on my right arm. The steersman's voice choked as he whispered, 'What are you doing? God help us.'

Ten, twenty seconds; I started to pray to Neptune but at that moment, sounds interrupted me. A drumbeat, a splash, a drumbeat, a splash – and out of the smoke, the first galley appeared, the bow wave hissing as it passed us, moving very fast in the opposite direction to our own movement. The galley had no time even to turn towards our boat, causing a wry smile to appear on the face of the Venetian captain as he turned to inspect us. One of the little children on my boat waved at him; the captain's hand twitched a little, before he restrained himself and his galley disappeared back into the smoke. We heard the second galley pass, but did not see it.

I took the steersman's hand and placed it on the tiller. 'Turn south,' I ordered, 'out across the sea of Marmara, away from the coast. They'll never find us in this, even if they wanted to. Those galleys will go back to the shoreline now. They're here to protect their army, not to pursue women and children. Once we're well out to sea, we'll turn west again.' Heraclea awaited; the straits of St George beckoned us on. Gradually, everyone relaxed. A small ship, obviously filled with fleeing refugees, would not be worth pursuing.

Two days later, we made port at Heraclea. My first three ships all awaited me there, but my most precious cargo, the fourth boat, had vanished. I went through agonies during the next few days, when survivors from the city begin to arrive, telling dreadful stories. Without a leader, the city surrendered, expecting a Christian army to show restraint. Instead, the Latins engulfed it in an orgy of unspeakable cruelties. Each story I heard gave me awful visions of Sophia and Luke suffering at their bestial hands. I began to believe they must have been captured or sunk by the galleys. We waited five long days, listening to tales of broken lives.

Two of my passengers traded their places on my boat with other refugees while we waited. They were fools: I knew that once they had rested, the Latins would start to loot the surrounding area. We could not risk waiting here much longer. What had happened to them? There would have been no great cloud of smoke to hide in, that night, I realised.

I waited, and prayed.

*   *   *

My little treasure – the one who comforts me – will be punished. Not for pleasuring me, but for bringing me the books and candles from my great-grand-daughter. First, Timon and another man bring her into my dark little room. They tie her wrists, then her ankles, and suspend from the ceiling, all of her limbs tied together. Is this her punishment?

The ropes creak while she turns slowly and twists her head around. She looks at me, her lips trembling. Then Timon brings the child Sophia in to watch, so that she will know what her kindness has brought upon the girl. Leo does not involve himself; he has probably taken his wife away, so that she cannot interfere. The girl whimpers when she sees the whip in Timon's hand.

He does not hold back; on the first blow she screams so loudly that I think she might die of shock. She does not, though her cries lose none of their anguish. Young Sophia tries hard to pretend that nothing happens, but she bites her lip, clenches her fists, and tears run down her face. Timon silently carries on, hitting every part of the girl while she shrieks and tries to twist away, until the sweat stands out upon his neck. He stops. The girl passes out, at last.

Once I might have enjoyed this spectacle, but age has changed me, perhaps because I too have suffered this. I find myself flinching when Timon hits the girl. The scene returns to me in my dreams, when it may be my little donkey who cries out, but it is my body that feels her pain. It puzzles me, that her plight affects me so much. But then, only this slave girl deigned to touch me when no one else would, and she did it out of human kindness. Perhaps she touches me now, but with her pain. I confess, I have never before felt this thing called sympathy so vividly. I thought that I had hardened my heart, my ways set in stone.

* * *

Penance For A Knave

Wake up, Basil; it is I, Bernard. Are you thirsty, old man? Now you will hear how men thirst for blood at the end of a battle. Be warned; this is not a foolish ballad. I will tell you what really happens after the heat of battle, what men will do in war. If you are squeamish, cover your ears.

While my body rested as we slept for two nights and a day, my mind ran back and forward between events and places. I dreamed I was tunnelling, trying to crawl and dig my way back to my Catherine, to my child, away from the battle. But wherever I surfaced, I saw soldiers and burning houses. I was searching for my hopes and dreams. But my search for hope ended, for someone was shaking me, shaking my dreams of Catherine out of me. Martin's excited face stared down. 'Get up,' he said. 'Get up, something is happening.'

I rubbed my eyes and stumbled after him, Jacques following behind. Inside the city gate, a crowd of pilgrims gathered in a circle around seven Greek nobles on horseback. Martin pushed his way to the front, with me in his wake. On one side, Boniface waited impatiently, surrounded by his bodyguards.

'What's happening?' whispered Martin.

A man turned and whispered back, 'He's waiting for the other barons to arrive.'

I noticed the brave monk standing nearby. I pointed him out to Martin and Jacques and moved closer to him, tapping his shoulder. 'What do they want?'

He narrowed his eyes for a moment as he bit his lip. He glanced around to see who was nearby and whispered, 'The Greeks have sent a delegation to Boniface, saying he can enter the city as Emperor. The usurper has flown the nest. His army must have deserted him.'

Martin asked, 'What about the mob?'

The monk shrugged. 'I assume this delegation represents the city.'

'That makes no sense. Why would such a mighty city surrender without a fight?'

He placed his hands together, as if in prayer, and looked down at the ground. After a heavy sigh, he added,

'I assume they think that Boniface wants to take the throne, and that his success will end the destruction. It seems logical. We came here to put that Prince upon the throne, remember? Why not another palace coup, now? After all, Boniface shares a bloodline with that Prince and his father. So they think we can be at peace again, once he is offered the Imperial throne.' He glanced over at Boniface, who paced back and forward anxiously. 'I'm sure Boniface would love to accept, but he knows none of the other barons will agree.'

Martin whispered, 'Why not?'

Another deep sigh escaped, while the monk studied a beetle crawling past his foot. 'Our leaders have already agreed to divide the booty from the city equally. One of them might be Emperor later, but only after the division of the wealth. The Greeks make a terrible mistake, assuming that Boniface can hold back the rest. There can be no Emperor elect here, to keep the city alive like a tethered bull. We are more akin to a ravenous horde, each and all wanting a pound of flesh from an animal that must be slaughtered and divided. Look at Boniface – he does not know what to say.'

We looked at each other, open-mouthed. An army that conquered a city by force of arms had the right to put it to the sack. Did the Greeks not know this? We had fought them for months now... were they blind, or stupid?

Jacques spat in contempt; 'Cowards.'

At the time, I felt the same. Now, I realise this monk understood that Boniface lacked either the wisdom or the strength, or both, to hold back the rest and gather a council. The Greek envoys began to look puzzled as they watched Boniface's silent pacing, while our host gradually roused itself and gathered round, scratching and yawning. Those who understood this little charade told others as they arrived. As the sun began to warm us, a realisation began to dawn upon the crowd – the road into the city lay open, undefended. Men began to edge forward, to check. A small step sideways here, and another there, became a gradual shuffle. This became a walk, and then with a collective roar we all surged forward into the city, each man wanting to grab his own riches before the others found them first...

In the city streets, many citizens had already turned out in their best clothes and finery to welcome the new Emperor. According to their custom, brightly coloured decorations fluttered across the streets in the morning breeze. Men waited to hold their gold and silver crucifixes aloft, with their wives alongside them, wearing their finest jewels. Excited children tugged at their sleeves.

The crowd sensed that the drama was about to begin. They heard noises in the distance, and necks craned to look along the street. Some with sharp ears began to feel uneasy as they picked out sounds in the distance. Was that a scream, a cry? A few sharp-witted ones began to move. *Come quickly now, children; we must hurry.* Others shrugged, sighed, and waited. The cacophony approached, growing all the while; men looked puzzled, trying to fit their expectations to the sounds they heard. And then, too late. A tidal wave of human greed and lust and hate swept over them all. A wave of our soldiers and Venetians, and even local Latins bent on revenge; they all began to loot and rape and kill.

Many citizens did not understand until the last moment; they held out their crosses of silver to greet soldiers with the customary words; 'Our Holy Emperor, hail the new Emperor Boniface.'

Grateful soldiers made to seize these offerings.

Some citizens saw the blades and let go quickly, escaping with a bruise at worst. Others who did not understand were cut down or beaten. Meanwhile, a second soldier had grabbed the citizen's wife, while a third stripped her of her jewellery. She has barely had time to gasp, let alone scream. An older wife might then be tossed aside; a younger one was stripped of her clothes, too, and dragged aside to be used as a plaything. Older children scattered into the crowd, while younger ones stood like skittles, frozen in silent panic. And this, my friend, was only the beginning...

As for my part, I will not feign innocence to excuse my actions. Those priests had made us believe that we had reached the Holy Land, that we fought infidels, not Christian men. Our army had learned to live by taking loot. We had sacked Zadar and watched our leaders take the profit; for the last few months we had made a daily chore of robbery. And we all had a score to settle with their army or their mob, and thus the people of the city. We followed the rest, blind and deaf to all pity, grabbing what we could, until this cruel wave ran its course, scattering our host through the city to pick the houses clean.

As the soldiers of the nobles took over the grand houses and palaces, we found our way to a district of small but still prosperous dwellings.

We burst into one to find two men inside, standing with weapons waiting. At the sight of us, one dropped the long knife from his hand and bolted away through the back of the house. The other, the owner of the house, backed up warily, calling on us to go.

Jacques began to move forward but Martin touched his arm, whispering, 'Wait, he is more useful alive.' Martin gestured for him to put down his sword.

He looked at the three of us, grim-faced and decorated with gore, as we slowly encircled him. He soon obeyed. While Martin and Jacques tied him to a chair, I went to look around the house.

Mosaics and paintings decorated most of the floors and walls; the tables and cabinets were finely carved of aromatic cedar wood. I moved upstairs, entering first a small chapel and then a bedchamber, with fine drapes of patterned silk. I noticed a slight movement behind the drapes and I gently pulled them to one side, revealing a young woman who gasped and then shook with fear. Like her husband, once caught she did not resist or run. One of my hands reached out to cover her mouth, the other clutched at her dress; her eyes widened with silent pleading, while her whole body trembled. But like all of us after a battle, my lust overwhelmed me; having caught her there, her helpless trembling body simply hardened my own desire. Holding her dress within my hand, I could feel her warmth underneath. I pulled her closer and smelt her skin and hair, while my hands explored the softness and warmth beneath her flimsy coverings. I carefully cut off her dress with my knife. She whimpered. Scrambling out of my cuirass and tunic, I held her warm body to mine, trying to quell her shaking for a moment. I felt something cold against my skin, and wrenched my undershirt and keepsake over my neck before Catherine's memory could interrupt me. I pulled that trembling body back, skin onto my skin, and stroked her body with my own. She sobbed, and whimpered, and pleaded, but my ears only heard desire within these sounds. I pushed her down onto the bed, and allowed my arid, thirsty lust to drink its fill from her quiet terror. I cannot deny that I took great pleasure upon her. Only after Martin had also taken her, did I begin to hear her cries as those of grief and fear, and feel shame clutching my throat.

When Jacques tied her to the bed, she wept quietly. Martin and I escaped to the kitchen to eat and drink. There, we found the husband still tied in his chair, looking much the worse for wear. Jacques had beaten him thoroughly to make him reveal his gold and valuables, which now sat upon the table. He looked broken in mind and in body. Martin took him outside and loosely tied him up, but he soon escaped and vanished.

That afternoon, Martin agreed to stay and guard what we had already collected. Jacques wanted to see what else he could find. I was drawn to see the sights of the city again and by my soul's desire to find a church and pray. But as I wandered closer to the centre of the city, I came closer to the horror that now infested it. Spread-eagled corpses decorated the streets; all ages and both sexes, mouldings of flesh painting the cobbles red. Predatory groups roamed: Latins bent for revenge, soldiers looking for female victims and Venetians pushing carts laden with goods for their ships. The cries of women echoed in all the streets, the squares, and even within the churches. Drunken men laughed in the midst of stripping these churches of their altars, their gems and precious metals. No one could pray here.

As I passed the back of one large house, a pilgrim

led an old man out of a door, holding his hand. Seeing me, he waited until I had walked on. I glanced back to see the pilgrim grasping the old man from behind; a blade flashed, cutting the old man's throat. He wiped the blade on his tunic, watched him die, and dragged the body away into a side alley. I heard raised voices from within that house; another soldier came out and walked in my direction, crossing himself and shaking his head.

As he passed me I asked, 'What's going on back there?'

'That family tried to save their gold and jewels by swallowing them. We caught them in the act. My friends are too impatient...' He shook his head and walked away.

I looked back to see a pregnant woman being led out into the street. Yes my friend, it is true. I could not watch and walked on, my head spinning with thoughts of my Catherine and her child. And yes, my stomach still heaves at this memory.

I tried to escape this nightmare in the great cathedral of St Sophia, hoping that at least here there would be sanctuary. But in that church of Holy wisdom, men were cutting and smashing the altars to divide the precious stones and metal. Others took turns to force a woman, right upon the Bishop's throne. I even saw the Abbot of Paris stuffing holy relics into a sack.

I shrunk into a dark corner, where I discovered a monk silently praying. He, too, wanted to blot out what he could see and hear. I knew him; this same monk told me about Boniface, and yes, I remember now. This brave monk crawled alone through that hole under the postern gate, into the unknown. I knelt beside him and tried to pray too.

He turned and recognised me, said he would pray for me.

'You'd better pray for us all,' I replied.

'I am,' he said.

'If the Holy Father were here to see this, he would regret sending us here.'

He looked away and replied, 'Those who sin in ignorance will surely be forgiven.'

'What do you mean?' I asked.

He looked at his feet.

'Who is in ignorance?'

He sighed, and looked me up and down. 'You saved my life, so I cannot lie to you. You have all been kept in ignorance. The Pope did not consent to this diversion from the Holy Land; He forbade it. That is why I am praying for all our souls.'

His words shook me to the very core, but now I understood his act of bravery. He had wanted to die. That is why he went through the hole. Because the Pope had forbidden all of this... it turned my world upside down. While we crossed the world to do the Lord's work, the Devil had whispered in too many ears. First in the ears of Boniface, then the Venetians, and as we went around in circles he kept on whispering, whispering; keep the army together, do whatever is necessary, until even the bishops had started to listen.

Who directed this army now? No soldiers of Christ here, only a host of demons, stealing, hacking, smashing, and ruining lives. Not pilgrims, but a pestilence, eating away at one of the holiest cities in the world. And as for me, what had I become? Damned for all eternity, for sure. How could I now return home, knowing that no Bishop's letter could ever save me from my debt? I would lose everything in this world, as well as the next. For Catherine's sake and my child's sake, it would be better not to return. I looked up to see the eyes of the saints looking down at me from the walls, and I could not bear their gaze.

Wandering back to Martin in a daze, it came to me that *I must make some act of penitence.* And God did grant me a chance to do this. I had already decided to free the woman at the house and take her to safety, when I saw a soldier dragging a young girl by a rope along the street ahead. The girl was crying and wailing in misery and fear; he ignored her, pulling her steadily along. An old Greek man following them also seemed to be calling and pleading to the soldier, telling him she was but a child. At first I did not recognise him, for he had discarded his tunic and leather cuirass for a silk shirt; then I realised this soldier was Jacques. More shocking still, I see something hanging from a cord around his neck, glinting in the sun... had he stolen my keepsake?

The old Greek man fell on his knees as I passed him, imploring me to help. I pretended to ignore him and hurried on. As I approached Jacques he recognised me and called out, 'Look, I have found a fresh one for us. They say the younger the juicier, don't they?'

I took a long look at her: small, a pretty face, but not yet a woman. Not even a youth. She covered her face in her hands and wailed again. As I walked around her, I gestured for Jacques to pull the rope upward, to lift her arms. 'Let me see her face,' I said, and stood to one side of him.

He grinned. 'For sure. She's worth a good look.' He lifted his own arms up above his head, pulling on the rope to make her do the same, and my silver keepsake glinted again in the sun. I stifled my rage for a moment, waiting until he stared at the girl in satisfaction. Then, I disabled him with one quick slash of my sword across his stomach. I had become a good soldier; the best fight should be both quick, and easy. He doubled up and sank to his knees, holding his wound, trying to stop his guts spilling out, calling out for Jesus to help him...

My anger was cold. I wanted him to know some truth before he died. I said to him, 'Jesus is not here; and you will have no absolution, for we are all in sin. The Pope forbade our leaders to come here. All our souls are damned. Welcome to hell, fellow pilgrim.'

I watched him understand this, and then gave him the blow of grace to send him on his way. Tell me, Basil, was I right to offer such a bloody penance? What would you have done?

The girl and her father followed me back toward the house, grateful and terrified in equal measure. I made them pretend to be my prisoners so that no-one else could claim them. When I entered the house, Martin and I both looked at each other curiously. He was sat at the table feeding two small children, while I untied an old man and a girl.

'Where's the woman?' I asked.

He looked glum, scratched his head, and spat on the floor. 'That scum Jacques must have strangled her.' Then he gestured at the children, 'I found these two after you had both gone.'

'Jacques will not be returning.'

Martin shrugged. 'He was useful in a fight; good riddance, otherwise.'

That night, after dark, we tied the Greeks together, and walked with them to one of the city gates. I had half of our coin, leaving the rest for Martin. There, we parted. A few miles further on, I discarded my pilgrim garb (except for my sword, my keepsake, and the linen shirt) and donned Greek clothes. I untied my companions.

You see, Basil, that journey became my true penance, to take those four souls to safety. I had crossed the world for the sake of a long walk to Nicaea, escorting an old shopkeeper, his granddaughter, and two small children. And two years later by some strange miracle, I found the children's father and reunited them with him. That became the true goal of my pilgrimage, and the end of my tale. Pray for my soul, I beg you.

*　　*　　*

Flesh And Spirit

An angel comes this morning... is it morning? No matter; I am having a most peculiar dream. I dream once again of Sophia, but not of our wedding night. Instead she appears here in this dark prison, looking much older and going grey, though still beautiful. She calls me over to the other side of the room and shows me a door.

'This door, Basil, is for entry by the others. You can lock it if you wish to be alone, but if you leave it open someone will come.'

Somehow, even in the darkness, I can see the outline of the door and feel the latch. She waits for me to speak but I cannot say a word, because I do not wish to have this conversation. My wish is to remember our youth, our past. Her future strikes me dumb.

'Has Athena taken your tongue? Most unusual, Basil...' She pauses, and waits again. Eventually she sighs, exasperated. 'After all this time, Basil, are you not pleased to see me?'

The child in me feels chastised, so I whisper, 'Yes'.

She sits by the bed, watching my face. I feel a curious mixture of relief and anxiety; just as I did back then...

* * *

At last, after five days of agonised waiting, a small boat came into the harbour and then approached us, its two occupants shouting and waving. I recognised them immediately; the captain and mate of the fourth boat. Relief flooded through me. 'Thank God. Where are the others?'

'They're safe. We had to turn east to avoid the Venetian patrols. We managed to get clear, but they forced us to head for Nicomedia.'

Yes, I remembered, there was no smoke that night.

'Luke and the others decided to head overland to the fortress of Nicaea from there. The two of us preferred to take our chances and come back this way. We both have wives and children in Makri, and we hoped you'd wait here.'

So at least Luke, Sophia and Justin had survived,

for the moment. I had to accept my separation from them; we needed to leave Heraclea, immediately.

As we tied the small boat to our stern with a rope, to tow it, a badly bruised man with bloodstained clothes limped along the jetty. He shouted, 'Is this your boat?'

I nodded. 'As you can see, we are full.'

'Do you have a house?'

I thought he must be a little crazy, but harmless. So I humoured him. 'No, but if I did, you would be welcome to it. A house here is not much use, now. But I am having one built, back in Makri.'

'Would you like it beautifully decorated, like a royal palace, with the very finest mosaics that you have ever seen?'

Perhaps he was crazy, but now he had my full attention. 'Are you joking?'

The man shook his head, looking back through blackened and bloodshot eyes, and held up his hands. 'These hands have decorated royal chambers in the palace of Blachernae. I come from a line of great artists. My father who taught me was one of those who decorated the walls of the great cathedral of Monreale in Sicily for the Normans, which many say is unsurpassed. Take me away from this awful place, and I will work for you until your house has the finest rooms you have ever seen.'

I nearly refused, but an image sprung into my mind. What a wonderful expression of surprise would appear on Sophia's face, when she saw a home like that. I would not seem such a country bumpkin, then, would I? I murmured to myself; 'By Tyche, I swear ...we'll be the envy of Makri...'

But how could I fit him in? My overloaded boat already wallowed low in the water. Then, I remembered the small boat. I pointed at it and told him, 'It won't be comfortable; you'll be like a cork in a storm, but you can sit in that. That's all the space there is.'

'Thank the Lord.' The man came aboard to shake my hand, and then kissed it. 'My name is Menas. I escaped the killing in the city. My family are either killed, or slaves.'

I had no answer to that. But having come so close to this fate myself, I felt convinced that Tyche had sent Menas in my direction.

Our Roman Empire descended into chaos after the Latin rabble ruined the city of Constantine. The Venetians stole most of the art; they and the Latin barons took the large gold or silver objects, or at least any that had not been hacked into pieces by the common soldiers. These barons then divided our empire up among themselves, though most of them did not have the wit or the strength to take or defend what they claimed. Small kingdoms sprang up everywhere. Latin barons fought against our own nobles, especially our three would-be Emperors. These were the Emperor who had fled after the first battle, the next one who had tried to fight, and the yet-to-be Emperor Theodore Lascaris. The last named had based himself in Nicaea; his family would succeed and return to rule the city of Constantine many years later, after my hair turned white.

But that spring I returned to Makri, hoping that I'd be able to set out for Nicaea, to find Sophia and the others, later that year. The first thing I did was to store my goods and gold carefully in various hiding places, well inland, since I guessed that soon we would have new rulers who would rob us of all our wealth. Never was I wiser; the Latin army arrived quickly, thanks to their Venetian allies. Such was their arrogance that I wondered how exactly they could fit their ugly heads into those armoured caps. Landing in all the major ports along the coast, they took our castles and best homes, and anything else they wanted, including all my trading boats.

I could not travel anywhere that year. The Latins killed anyone on the road who might be a soldier. Menas and I took the small boat that they had deigned to leave us, and went fishing for the rest of that summer, to keep busy and feed ourselves. Our new rulers had their heavy feet planted firmly on our necks the following winter; many struggled to pay their taxes and to eat. My secret stores kept my parents and my friends alive.

Things changed abruptly the following spring. We

Romans received secret letters from Lascaris in Nicaea; the majority of the Latin army had been destroyed by the Bulgarian Tsar, and their so-called Emperor Baldwin captured and killed. We could therefore rise up and get rid of them. We gathered our fighting men together, to act before they heard this news. That night, the castle guards received a surprise gift: a cask of fine wine from my stores. This was a good investment; after the guards had drunk themselves stupid, our secret army crept through the gates. Next morning, the Latin Baron of Makri awoke to discover a very unusual tableau in his bedchamber. The captain of his guard, or rather his head, gazed back at him from the end of a pole, held proudly aloft for his attention by a grinning Roman soldier. The Baron then followed his wife, flying from his own battlements onto the rocks far below, joining the other bodies scattered there.

All along our coast, the Latins either fled or suffered a similar fate. The core of their stolen Empire survived a few years, under Baldwin's brother, but they never ruled our coastline again. The survivors of their garrisons fled to the islands to become pirates. We reverted back to our Roman ways, though for years no Emperor ruled us; we became one long frontier, ideal for trade, with Turks inland and various small kingdoms around us. We Romans have a saying from this time: 'Better the turban of the sultan, than the cardinal's hat'. Infidels the Turks may be, but at least they behaved like civilised men.

My time of fretting and restless waiting neared its end, that summer of 1205. At last I could begin my journey to Nicaea. Having regained my boats, I left my father and best captain in charge of my business, and Menas in charge of building my new home. 'Spare no expense,' I told him. 'Build me a fine villa, which you can decorate as if it were your own. We have good local stone, plus marble brought from the ancient cities inland, and fine Lycian cedar.'

His eyes lit up. Menas began to live again, poring over the plans. The day before I left, he asked me, 'Would you like some golden mosaics? If so, I will need some gold.'

I must have looked shocked, for he added hastily, 'It's just the finest layer of thin gold leaf upon a stone. For a small room, a few gold coins will suffice.'

I suppressed a smile. My last batch of passengers had given me a fine wedding present in exchange for their lives. 'Go ahead, I have enough. I will give my parents plenty, to give to you as you need it.'

I do not care to remember that journey, but I suppose I must. I could only take a boat part of the way, for the safest route lay inland that year...

* * *

I had crossed one hot dry mountain after another; my bum ached constantly from sitting on the mule, day after day. As I climbed the path up to each pass, I could almost feel the watching eyes upon my back. I was dressed in old, torn clothes, and carried my money hidden inside a stinking cheese. I found myself wishing, give me a ship anytime; at least a breeze will cool you, and blow away the flies.

I bounced up and down on the mule for forty-three days before I saw the walled fortress of Nicaea, sitting on its high promontory with the lake on three sides. Once inside the city, I wandered through dense crowds of locals and refugees, questioning anyone who would answer. On the second day, a woman sitting outside a shop recognised Luke's name. 'Is he with a young woman, his daughter?' I nodded. 'You'll find them at my cousin's farm, outside the city walls. They have children with them; food and rooms cost less, outside the walls. It's safe enough now, since the defeat of the Latin army.'

I followed her directions; back along the road south, then up a small path to the east, my heart running ahead of me, beating like a drum. Eventually, the path topped a hill and began to descend again. My heart felt like a bird at that moment, and I wished I had wings to fly. A house lay far below in a sheltered and fertile valley, with steep slopes on three sides. My path meandered down one of these slopes through scrub, then terraced olive trees, with fine views over the valley. I hurried the mule, while birds fluttered from branch to branch in restless sympathy. My mouth dry, I dismounted to walk down the steepest slope, pulling the mule impatiently and stopping here and there to look through gaps in the trees.

I spotted some figures in the distance. I felt sure it was my brother and Sophia, playing with two children, swinging them around and around in a meadow by a small orchard of apricots. I recognised the way they both moved, and paused to watch. I could hear the children screaming with delight. An idyllic scene seemed to welcome me far below, after all the chaos I had witnessed. I watched them play for a while before I started to descend again. They disappeared from view until I turned a corner and there they were again, within shouting distance. I resisted the temptation to call out as I wanted to surprise them. As I watched, the two children ran off toward the farm, leaving Sophia and my brother standing side by side with their backs to me, watching the children disappear. Together, they reached out to join hands. It seemed so natural, but it took my breath away. Sophia leaned her head upon Justin's shoulder. He turned and reached around her with his free arm, stroking her shoulder, and turning her body into his. I blinked, took a step forward, and then stopped. I could not believe what I was seeing. I felt the cold pain of that moment being thrust through my chest, like a long steel blade. They kissed, and I felt the blade twist, and twist again. I did not witness a relative's kiss. I watched two lovers kiss, as they gently wrapped around each other.

I sank to the floor in shock, putting them out of my sight, wanting the earth to swallow me up as I gasped for breath. It felt as if I had been struck with a club, and hard. I have no idea how long I sat there; but the sun had slipped low in the sky when the mule came to nuzzle my back, and brought me back to myself again. First I felt the wetness on my own face, and then the numbness in my heart. I turned the mule around and started the long journey back to Makri. I pushed that mule so hard that it died; I had to walk the last two hundred miles. As I walked, I fought my feelings of misery, and began to feel a cold rage growing in my chest...

* * *

Now I repeat that long walk, back and across this little room, endlessly. Walking now, on my old and crippled legs, brings a different kind of pain. I must still be dreaming, for in truth my legs are useless now. In this dream, I pace and pace this room like a crippled snail, trying to keep myself awake; I don't wish to remember that time, to dream of it any more. But I can't help it; even in my dreams I am repeating that endless walk. Worse still, now I am caught between two nightmare worlds, between my prison and my memories of that time.

My soul felt so empty on that walk; I had become nothing, a husk of a man. Even now, I am merely an empty room filled by mysterious ghosts; though I can guess who will visit me next. I lie awake in my dreams, waiting for him. I wait for Luke of Antioch: I know he will come. My first father-in-law, the man who took me from a small world into a big one, who gave me my chance of great fortune; he helped me become what I am, or was. He was my mentor, my friend; so now I wait for Luke, just as I did then.

* * *

By the end of that year, my villa had been completed. There was nothing like it in the area, perhaps even in the whole of Lycia. Menas had worked like a man possessed upon all the decorations; the love and grief for his lost wife and children had inspired him.

He created a gallery of mosaics throughout my new home. Look within the library, and see portraits of wisdom in various guises: a wild-eyed Moses looks with astonishment upon the tablets of stone, Solomon the judge beckons a hesitant woman to speak, and white-haired Aristotle tutors a young Alexander. In a small chapel, a ragged Jesus preaches on the mount while two weeping women clutch at the tatters of His robe and a man falls onto his knees, struck by the sheer force of His words.

Upstairs, frescoes of hunting scenes dominate the hallway that leads to the bedrooms. Menas called it the hallway of leaping deer, because these animals immediately catch the eye, most of them in mid-air. They leap over bushes with wide eyes, as if to escape from whatever is pursuing them. Wild boars also hide among the bushes, sniffing the ground, and two goats also turn warily to look behind them; an elephant peers down imperiously from the far end of the corridor. Just when you think you have seen everything, you spot the crouching lions, each hiding in a shallow recess built into the wall, about to spring out into the corridor. At first sight, they take your breath away; children often scream when they turn and see them.

Inside the bedrooms, mosaics create an atmosphere of peace and rest. Animals and cupids listen to musicians and lie down to sleep, and women gather flowers against backgrounds of orchards and sunsets. On the ceilings, Menas painted patterns in pastel tones, Moorish designs from Sicily. He assured me these would help bring sleep. His work made me weep, when I saw it the first time. But would the glory of all this, and all the furnishings he chose, be wasted? My heart was an empty, silent house, even when I finally received this letter from Luke, the following spring:

My dear Basil,

I fervently hope you are alive and well; we have all been much concerned about you. This is the fourth letter I have written to you without reply, though I know how dangerous and difficult the roads have been these last years, so you may not have received any of them. We are all alive and well; our ship found its way blocked, so the crew took us to Nicomedia. There we sold the ship, and travelled on to Nicaea as you suggested. We gave the crew money to travel home. We hope they did so safely.

We waited here, hoping you were alive. We expected you would come to find us in Nicaea, but perhaps you cannot travel. We hope you and your parents are still well. Whatever has happened to delay you, we have waited here long enough. We hear the roads are safer, now, and your brother and another soldier will accompany us. We will set off in one month's time, by which time this letter should have arrived, to ensure that our paths do not cross in opposite directions. We all hope to see you and your parents soon.

Luke of Antioch

My parents could not contain their excitement at the thought of Justin's return, demanding that I hold a feast at my new villa. I found myself in a trap. I had told no one what happened at the end of my journey. What could I say? Shame and the fear of humiliation had gagged me. I had simply told my parents that I had been forced to turn back; what was the point of telling them the truth? My elder brother would remain the apple of my parents' eye, whatever happened.

Looking back, I should have told them what I knew. Better still, I should have run to confront Justin and Sophia that day in Nicaea – even if I had attacked them both with my bare hands, it would have been better than poisonous secrets and cold, cold silence. But at that time, I did not have the confidence in dealing with people that I developed later. So I began to rage at the unfairness of my situation; at the misfortune of our separation, at their ingratitude, their lack of faith in me, their betrayal.

I realise now that I still loved them both, but I also hated them. What could I do? Luke would always forgive Sophia... but could I? I told myself that she might have behaved like the whore of Babylon, but I would try to forgive her if she was honest and confessed...

*   *   *

I busied myself in mindless activity at my warehouse, distracting myself as I had for weeks. I heard someone call out. I turned around and saw Luke watching me from the door, while Sophia ran toward me. She flung herself into my arms, as if she were a true and faithful wife. I had steeled myself not to respond to her, but how could I stop the wind blowing? I held her tightly and choked up for a moment. She whispered, 'I thought I had lost you...'

I could not speak. I thought, at that moment, if only

I could wipe my mind clean and forget it all. I heard Luke's voice, telling me, 'We did begin to think the worst, Basil...'

I considered this for a long moment, as an excuse for what I had seen, but then rejected it. I spoke slowly and carefully. 'I was also frantic at first. But the captain of your boat caught up with me, so I knew you had got away. I was sure you would be safe once you got to Nicaea. I tried to make the journey there last year, but I had to turn back...'

'Then thank the Lord we are all alive,' added Luke. 'That is all that matters...'

I thought, *If only that were true,* but I nodded, as if in agreement.

I understood immediately that Sophia was going to behave as if nothing significant had happened in Nicaea. She and Luke barraged me with questions about my own escape, about events in Makri since I returned. If Luke knew anything of the betrayal, he gave no outward sign. Sophia continued to cling to me, and I had to resist an urge to push her away. My senses began to fill with panic. I could not feel her usual warmth at all, in that way I did before. Why not? Did she only pretend to care? Or were my own senses now hidden away, frozen with my rage? To my relief, she released her hold on me, allowing me to turn to Luke.

With Luke, by contrast, my senses could feel and receive his warmth and affection; I moved to embrace him with no reserve. This helped to beat down the panic and anger rising within me. I discovered that by focussing upon Luke's presence and company, I could play my own part better, as an innocent ignoramus, and wait to see what transpired...

I answered their questions, emphasising how fortunate I had been; both to escape the galley in the smoke, and to regain most of our boats after the Latins were overthrown in Makri. As time passed, I saw that Sophia gradually became puzzled and hurt by my apparent indifference to her; but then this was exactly what I wanted her to feel. Indeed, I started to take a perverse pleasure in limiting the attention I gave to Sophia. Meanwhile I lavished it upon her father, explaining the local geography and situation in terms of trade and territory. I did not ignore Sophia completely; that would have been impossible. But sometimes as I turned away from her I glimpsed tears beginning to brim in her eyes, and that pleased me, while I became louder and more jovial with Luke.

One unspoken question dominated my thoughts. Eventually, I voiced it. 'Where is my brother?'

Luke glanced at Sophia, who blushed slightly and replied, 'He's helping our fellow travellers find a place to stay. He knows the town and wanted to get them settled in.'

I nodded. I felt relief, primarily; even more so, when another thought occurred to me. 'In that case, let me take you to meet my mother and father now. Best to do that before Justin arrives there. When he does, they will have no attention for anyone else.'

I fell in with the pretence of normality, and the meeting of my wife and parents provided another useful distraction; both for me and, I realised, Sophia. My parents made a great fuss of her, compensating for my own inability to do so. Meanwhile I was able to stand back, feeling less pressure to act the joyful spouse.

Perhaps Luke sensed my strange mood. He took me to one side, and began, 'Basil, I had better warn you now...'

Hearing this, I expected the worse; finally, something about his brother and Sophia...

But Luke surprised me. 'We did not come alone from Nicaea. On the road there, we met a foreign soldier with two small children in his care, orphans that this man had rescued from the sack of Constantinople. He had also brought out a shopkeeper and his granddaughter to take to their relatives in Nicaea. When we got there, that family helped us, finding us places to stay.'

'That was useful.'

'It was. But this foreigner, Bernard, and those two children remained with us. Since they have no mother, my daughter has been looking after them. She has grown so attached to them, Basil. I know it is a lot to ask, but she is desperate to keep them. It would be a great kindness to her, and to the children, if you would allow this.' Luke paused and looked at me, half-smiling.

I really did not know what to say. Two children? Whatever next?

I struggled to fit this idea into my crowded mind, while Luke continued. 'If not, then perhaps I will adopt them so that she can see them often. Or perhaps we can find a wife for Bernard who might mother them?'

Luke smiled, while I bit my lip, lost for words. I stared blankly back at my father-in-law.

He seemed to sense my uncertainty; he coughed, and added, 'You should not decide now, Basil. Let's wait until you have got to know these children.'

I felt another flood of relief, and nodded. 'Of course.' My confusion made me feel like a child again, making me feel as if I had to explain myself once again to Luke. 'When I tried to make the journey to Nicaea last summer, the roads were too dangerous... I should have hired an escort, like you.'

Luke nodded, looking down at the floor, as if a little disappointed.

'But I knew from my crew that you had got away to Nicomedia and would go on to Nicaea. I knew you were safer there than anywhere else.' I felt as if my voice did not sound quite right. I looked at Luke's face to check his expression, and continued. 'I knew you would come eventually. So I decided I should get our business running once again, and prepare houses for us both.'

'Logical,' Luke agreed, 'though for a young man, Basil, not very romantic, don't you think?' He said it very lightly, a little teasing aside to remind me of my role as a son-in-law, but it hit me like a brick.

I felt cast as a failure, or a coward, whatever I did. Then, I felt a rush of anger at the unfairness of it all. 'I had to survive first. Besides, I knew you would be well protected by my brother.' After I told him this, quite sharply, I regretted it. The mention of my brother gave my voice a tone that I wished to avoid in front of Luke. He could be far too perceptive.

Luke raised his eyebrows, but then nodded and raised his hands in a gesture of appeasement. 'I'm sorry, Basil. Of all people, I should not criticise your judgement after all that has happened. But, you see, we did not know if you were safe. We heard only terrible stories, from everywhere. We feared the worst for you when you did not come and then we did not hear from you.'

I nodded, thinking, *Yes, I should have tried to send letters.*

Luke turned away as if finished, and then turned back. 'Is there anything else?' It sounded like a casual enquiry, but I could sense that Luke was offering an opportunity to spell out what was bothering me. Should I do so? No, I decided, I had to give Sophia a chance to confess, first.

I also saw a chance to change the subject. 'Well, there is something. We should also go to see the land that I have bought for you, a place for you to build your own house here.' Luke smiled at this; he too seemed relieved to have a practical distraction.

The following day, I met Bernard and the two children when Sophia brought them to my new villa. I watched Sophia and Bernard play with the children in the garden. Bernard swung each of them round and round, first by their arms and then by their legs. While he did this, Sophia put the other child on her shoulders. When that game had finished, she produced sweet dates from her robe and dangled them from her outstretched arms, on either side. The two children, Mark and Anna, both had Sophia's dark hair and looks. I watched them run around and around Sophia, giggling as they leapt up for the dates. She kept giving instructions, but dangling the dates just out of reach. 'Higher, now, jump up, little ponies...' After a while, she gradually lowered her arms until they both claimed their prizes. I had to admit, a stranger would assume she was their mother. I felt a lump growing in my throat, watching the way she shone her full attention upon them, without reserve. I remembered what that felt like. Now, it seems, I had a lot of competition, some from unexpected quarters.

For all his rough ways (he behaved like a peasant) Bernard acted like a father to the children too. So, observing this little scene, I could not help wondering, what am I to be? Am I to be a cuckold, twice over – first in flesh, and then in spirit?

Having studied him closely, I felt suspicious of Bernard's claim to be one of the Varangian guards. Most of the Emperor's guards were Norsemen, giants with long blonde hair and blue eyes. Bernard stood tall, but he was slim and dark, and not really broad enough to swing the double-bladed axe. He did not have an axe, either; though I suppose he might have lost it in the chaos. I did not confront him, but by his manner and speech I felt sure he must be one of our enemies, a Latin foot soldier. What on earth was he doing here, with us? Was he simply a mercenary, perhaps?

* * *

The Last Supper

Sometimes I seem to float above my broken body in the darkness, listening to myself gasping for breath. I look down on myself as others do, feeling a mixture of pity and revulsion...

At other times, I dream of food and feasts. Usually, it is my hunger that wakes me from these dreams... but this time, I feel a tug on my sleeve and there he is, sitting by my bed. Luke of Antioch. He has not changed, a little more grey hair perhaps, but the same proud but patient expression as he waits for me to speak. I owe him so much, so much; and most of all, an apology... but I do not know how to begin. How can I explain my actions to him?

Eventually, his presence combines with my hunger to prompt my memory of that feast in Makri, my last supper with my brother, wife and Luke of Antioch. My parents had asked me to organise a celebration to mark my brother's return to Makri, one year after I turned my back on him at Nicaea and walked away. I had begun to hope that in time, within my beautiful new house, Sophia and I would grow close again; but all my hopes washed away that night in a flood of unspoken feelings, within a river of hidden secrets. At this last supper, the devil first broke the bread, then stole it, and spilled the wine for good measure...

*   *   *

I held the feast two nights after their return at my new house. Despite everything, I still itched to show off the magnificent mosaics that Menas had been working on over the last year. I hoped their magic might somehow put everything right... I still expected that Luke would remain in Makri, and that Luke would also use Menas to build his villa. You can understand, from this hope, that I was still uncertain what to do...

I had met my brother the day before, outside my parent's house. He had also behaved as if nothing had happened, greeting me warmly. But I felt rigid, as stiff as a board, and as cold as a winter wind. He knew that something was wrong. He pulled back and looked at me, puzzled. 'What is it, Basil?'

I looked him in the eye. 'Don't you know, brother?'

He looked confused, as if he had forgotten his own name. I sensed the panic behind his face, while he fought to stay in control of his expression. He tried to work it out. I could sense him thinking, hard. What else could explain my coldness to him? 'I... I suppose you must be angry with me for not bringing them sooner.'

He looked for reassurance, but I remained passive, made of stone. After a second, he took my silence for assent and looked down, avoiding my eye. 'I am sorry, Basil, truly I am. But travelling was unsafe until this year. We wrote letter after letter, and Luke felt sure you would come to us, if you were alive. The letters must not have reached you.'

'True enough,' I replied, and instantly regretted saying this, because he took my agreement as confirmation that his delay in travel had caused my anger. He looked relieved, and muttered more apologies. But he could not look me in the eye for more than a moment. His face remained pink, and his forehead damp.

I simply did not wish to see him, so I quickly made excuses about my work and left him; I could not stand being in his presence. He scratched his head and blew air out in a loud sigh, as I left. The feast – well, how strangely that began...

* * *

I had asked Menas to arrive early, so that we could decide how to show the visitors his work. We were still discussing how to do this when Luke and Bernard arrived. I introduced Menas to them. Menas shook hands with Luke, and then turned to Bernard. They both stared at each other, transfixed first with curiosity and then, it seemed to me, with horror. A look passed between them as if they had both been shot with red-hot arrows. As Luke and I glanced at each other in bemusement, Sophia entered the room with a child on each hand.

Menas gasped, and fell to his knees. His eyes brimmed with tears, and he gasped for breath, choking back emotion. We all watched, astounded; meanwhile Bernard's face turned a deeper red than I had ever seen upon a human skin. Menas attempted to speak, but mostly succeeded only in choking himself. After a few long moments, I realised what he was trying to say – the names of the children. 'Anna...Mark...'

The children, meanwhile, stared at him in shock. Then the girl cried out, and her cry explained it all... 'Daddy... is that you, Daddy?'

Tears streaming down his face, Menas nodded and held out his arms to his children. They did not run to him, though; they seemed wary, unsure whether to trust their eyes or perhaps their memories. Instead, they started to cry too. The rest of us stood aghast, until Sophia dropped to her knees and put her arms around the children. 'It's all right, hush now,' she told them, 'come and see your father with me.' Then, taking each by the hand, she led them over to him. Menas clutched them to his chest and they cried together, while Sophia comforted them all.

Watching her closely, I saw sadness glistening in her eyes too. She must have realised that now, she would have to give these children back to their father. I felt a savage flush of satisfaction at this turn of events. I wanted her to be punished. If anything, my anger with Sophia and my brother had multiplied because of their silence. I had begun to imagine that perhaps they want to carry on behind my back, hoping that I would not notice.

I offered Luke and Bernard wine and then showed them around the new house, leaving Menas and Sophia alone with the children. Bernard seemed glad of the distraction, and did not comment on what had happened. I gave Luke a quizzical glance, but he shrugged his shoulders to indicate his puzzlement. When we returned everyone seemed calmer; Sophia even took the children outside to play. I expected Menas to make some announcement, perhaps to explain, or to thank Luke and the others publicly for the return of his children, but he remained silent, looking very troubled. I broke the silence by asking Luke what he knew of the Lascaris family, the rulers in Nicaea. While Luke and I discussed this, at some length, I noticed Menas shuffle closer to Bernard and whisper to him. I was conscious that Luke and I were not really listening to each other, and I had very sharp hearing...

Menas whispered, 'What happened to their mother?'

Bernard looked down at the floor, 'I wanted to save her too, but she died.'

Menas blinked, his face hard and grim, 'How?'

Bernard shut his eyes for a second, and sighed. 'The short crusader killed her.' He glanced across at Menas, as if struggling to find his words. 'The one who beat you... he enjoyed hurting people. Jacques, was his name...I was not there when he did it. I would have stopped him, I swear.' He looked down at his hands. 'Later, I killed him, to stop him doing more. Then I brought your children out of the city, with a young girl and her grandfather, and brought them to Nicaea. We met Basil's family on the road. Ask them, if you don't believe me.'

Menas nodded, 'I will.' Then he shuddered and closed his eyes for a moment, as if trying to let go of the past. 'Thank you for bringing my children out of that hell.' There, the conversation ended. How did they recognise each other? What on earth had happened when they first met?

When my parents and my brother arrived, Menas conducted another tour of the house, explaining his work and the myths and ideas that inspired it. Everyone admired the mosaics; but the unspoken tension in the air smothered all sense of celebration, except perhaps for my parents. The food was eaten with many murmurs of appreciation, and much wine was drunk, but the mood was subdued, cautiously polite rather than raucously joyful. I felt a sense of impending disaster; a voice in my head kept whispering about falseness, telling me to speak out, to rage against the wind, one way or another.

The guests finally left; Luke retired to his room and Sophia and I were left alone together. The first two nights, I had feigned sickness as my excuse not to share her bed. Part of me wanted her, needed her, but the coldness of my anger still dampened the fires of my lust. Not until she had confessed, I told myself. This night, I had other excuses; I told her she must be upset about the children, that she must be exhausted. Now was not the time to talk. 'Go on, go to our room and sleep,' I said. 'I am not tired yet.'

Sophia's eyes glistened, and she bit her lip. She looked up, 'When will you come?'

'When I am tired.' I reached for my cup of wine.

She hesitated. 'Have I displeased you, husband?' Her dark eyes tried to hold onto mine, a look of mute appeal. Or was it guilt?

'You tell me, wife.'

A look of horror crossed her face. She seemed to struggle for words, and held her forehead as if in pain. But then she shook herself, dropping her hand and holding her head high. She looked me in the eye. 'It would seem so.' She stared, daring me to confront her.

But I had already steeled myself; this is up to her, I had decided, she must tell me herself. So I glared back at her, until the long silence finally snapped.

'I am bored with you pestering me. Go to bed.' My voice sounded far too loud.

Her mouth opened in shock; I had never struck her before with such barbed words. Then, she turned and ran. After a minute, I went up to listen at the door. I could hear her sobbing quietly, inside the room.

* * *

If I could change only one moment in my life, I would return to that moment, listening at that door. I would open the door to go in and talk to Sophia, to confront her with the truth. You see, in that room magic does surround you...

Upon the walls around the bed, Menas brought the myth of Paris to life. To the left, Aphrodite, with poppies and golden roses to each side of her, smiles confidently as she extends her hand for the golden apple. Swallows fly above her head and swans float upon the stream that flows around her feet and away, behind her. Her thin, loose robe slips open above her breasts, while a breeze moulds that robe around her lower body, hinting at the gap between her legs, the promise of what is to come for

Paris – but for how long, and at what cost?

On the opposite wall an athletic Athena leans back against a tree in an olive grove, her arms partly folded, a coolly appraising look upon her face. She dresses minimally, as if for the gymnasium. Snakes curl suggestively around her feet and lower legs, while a hint of a smile shapes her lips. This is a clever and dangerous woman. One of her little fingers just happens to point suggestively behind her, where the olive grove ends by a waterfall. Look closely, though – the last tree, no olive tree this, has fruit on the branches, and they look like golden apples. Athena is suggesting, 'If you want to have all three of us, look over there, and you will discover the means...'

On the wall between them a larger than life Hera, the queen of heaven, reclines, floating in the air. Naked except for a golden crown, her beautiful body stretches out in profile, one leg extended, the other half bent, with pointed toes. All the fruits of the earth lie scattered below her feet and legs, as if she has given birth to worldly pleasure. Her body and head float above a pile of gold and silver and gems, the riches of Asia, which she will exchange for the golden apple. While her body stretches languidly across the wall, her head turns to look outwards. That look dares you to touch her, dares you to reach out to her. She has a confidence that whatever the others do, she will have her way eventually. On the ceiling of this room, one simple pattern repeats; two hearts, intertwined together.

In a curious way my own life has aped this myth; three females claimed me, though only one divinity. First I had Sophia, for whom I felt overwhelming desire; and whom I loved with all my heart. She even looked like Menas's Aphrodite; though he told me he had modelled the goddess upon his own wife. Then I had Eirene, who embodied wisdom and fun. She may not have resembled Athena in her looks, but her attitude was identical. Finally, I married Hera's treasure, the riches of Asia. But who gifted this to me? Not Hera, but an older goddess; Tyche, protector of sailors and traders, and the bringer of unexpected good fortune. She was always my mistress, and I became her slave. She gave me many blessings, but Tyche's particular pleasure consists of raising hopes, only to dash them into pieces. I became her plaything, while she became a constant visitor to my life. So perhaps I belong to her more than the others. And Tyche has another persona: when men do not use her gifts wisely, for the benefit of others, she adopts another name, another face. Nemesis.

I knew them all. And I am certain that if I had gone into that room to be with Sophia all those years ago, the magic in those mosaics would somehow have healed our wounds. Somehow, I know it.

Now, I slip back into that moment in my dream, hoping to change history. But I am still paralysed; trapped within this memory. I must watch as I clench my fists like a fool and go downstairs for more wine. What am I doing? I watch myself in horror. After an hour or so, I fall asleep on one of the couches, surrounded by cushions and bitter thoughts.

* * *

My memories become more and more discomforting, with more of these damned ghosts who arrive to torment me with their stories. My brother comes next. He has acquired the grey pallor, muscular arms, and whip marks of a galley slave. He does not speak to me at first, but simply sits for hours, staring at me angrily. Eventually he speaks. 'Eleven years. I lasted eleven years on the galleys, Basil, before it killed me. I will tell you all about it, the next time I come. Then you will know exactly what I went through'. Then he wheels away, as if he finds my very presence offensive, and strides away into the darkness.

* * *

I awoke when someone tugged at my sleeve and poked my chest. I had slept a little, tossing and turning upon the couch, after the feast. I opened my eyes to discover a very agitated Menas, hovering over me. I sat up, blinking in the dawn light. 'Dear God, what is it?'

'I can't stay in the same town as Bernard.'

'Why ever not, Menas?'

'That man may have saved my children, but he is a Frank, a crusader. I recognised him; he is one of the men who robbed my house in Constantinople, and they all raped my wife, even if he was not the one who killed her. I cannot stay here. I will have to kill him if I do. I need to take my children away from here. Help me, please, Basil.'

One mess followed another... how appalling. But at least I could easily deal with this situation. 'Alright, calm down. I have a ship leaving for the town of Antiphellus and some other settlements near the old city of Patara, this morning. It's a short local trip with a light cargo going out – some incense and silk in exchange for honey, cheese, and olive oil. There will be plenty of room for you and the children. It's far enough away, and I can bring you back when Bernard has gone, so that you can work for Luke.'

I still had no idea what I would do to solve my own problem. Part of me still thought that maybe we could carry on as if nothing had happened. While the others slept off the food and wine I took Menas and his two children, both half asleep and half complaining, down to the boat with a bundle of clothes. I gave him money, though not all the wages due to him – I wanted him to return, after all. As I waved him off, I thought suddenly that maybe I could also ask my brother to take Bernard away somewhere. That would get them both out of my hair, so that I could think more clearly. I noticed one other trading boat in the harbour that morning, not a local boat. I didn't pay it much attention.

After that, I went to my warehouse to start marking up the goods for the next two trips I had planned. I had nearly finished when Luke appeared. He looked anxious, not his usual self. I wondered if Sophia had been talking to him about my behaviour. I felt grey and wretched for lack of sleep and too much wine; in no mood to play polite games. I watched him silently as he approached.

'Greetings, Basil.'

I nodded.

He rubbed his head with both his hands. 'The children are missing. Do you know where they are?'

I turned my back upon him, in irritation, and chalked a mark upon the sack of grain in front of me. Then I turned back to face him, with my hands on my hips. 'They are not missing. Menas has taken them. He is their father.'

'Ah...Sophia is terribly upset, Basil. I know he's their father, but they hardly recognised him last night.' He sighed, and scratched his head. 'And Sophia promised them that she would look after them. They will be terribly upset if they do not see her at all. Where has he taken them?'

A long silence followed, while I filled up with a cold rage. How could my faithless wife presume to make such a promise? As for Luke, what business was this of his? If Menas wished to take his children to the end of the world, that was still none of their business. I knew that I harboured jealousy for these children; I certainly wanted them out of the way. But I had not engineered this. And Sophia was my wife, not their mother. I would have to teach her that too, as well as faithfulness. But how should I reply? Menas had made me promise that Bernard and his friends should not know where they were. So, I decided a little lie would suffice, for now.

'He's taken them north, to Halicarnassus.' Then, I thought, maybe I should explain about Bernard to prepare the ground for when I told the full story, later. So I added, 'Menas has met Bernard before. Something very bad went on between them. He took the children away from Bernard, not from Sophia.'

Luke nodded, as if he suspected as much. 'Ah. Maybe we should have sent Bernard away, and not Menas, eh, Basil?' I had to admit, he had a point; but that was hindsight, after all.

Then, the last words he ever spoke to me as a living man left me completely speechless. 'We must talk later, Basil. I need to talk to you about my daughter. But that can wait.'

He turned his back and walked away, in the same way that I had turned my back on him. After he had left the building, my anger and frustration burst out of me. I took out my knife and I repeatedly cut and stabbed a sack of grain while I wept, until I had released some of my helpless rage. Then, exhausted, I took a nap.

I woke in the afternoon. I went for a swim in the sea to refresh myself and then walked back up to my villa, only to find it empty. The servants told me Luke and Sophia had gone out together late that morning. That must have been after Luke had returned from seeing me. I walked to my parents' house. My father looked worried. Normally he was placid, unflappable in his deeds and words; that day, for once, his mood surprised me.

'It's too late. They've gone,' he said.

'Gone? What do you mean? Who? Gone where?'

He sighed, 'Luke and Sophia; to Halicarnassus, to go after the man with the children. By chance, another boat in the harbour happened to be going there. It left at noon. They said you looked busy, and they didn't want to disturb you again. So Justin has gone with them to protect them. They would like you to send one of your boats after them in a day or two, to bring them back. But Basil, you really should look after your wife, and not spend so much time looking after goods in your warehouse. She looked dreadfully upset, did you not realise?'

I laughed at first, when I realised they had gone on a fruitless and well-deserved waste of time, exactly what those busybodies deserved. But then as I considered it, my suspicions of Sophia and Justin increased. Nevertheless, I did as they asked, and sent a boat after them three days later, with a load of grain and oil. But by now, I felt a little uneasy. Halicarnassus was not a simple journey, for the Franks still infested the islands of Samos and Chios. These Frankish pirates occasionally raided the coastal strip to the north. My ships always travelled that way very carefully, with a small boat going on ahead to look around each point, to signal the main boat whether to proceed. (If the smaller boat ran into trouble, the crew would beach it and escape inland.)

When my boat returned, having turned back with news of a raid further up the coast, my heart sank. What a mess, what a dreadful set of coincidences. What had I done to offend Tyche, to gain me such bad fortune? We could only await news and hope.

As time went on, they still did not return. And what news we got was bad; a big raid. It seemed likely that their boat had been swallowed up, along with Luke, my brother and Sophia. I cursed them for their careless impulsivity. I prayed that the boat was captured and not sunk, that Luke and Sophia had survived. (Though not my brother, I hoped that he had died fighting.)

It took me days to find the courage to tell my parents what had probably happened. Horror and shock filled their faces. My mother wailed, distraught while my father held her; but neither attempted to comfort me. They did not say it, but I knew what they thought... they thought it should have been me, not Justin, on that boat.

In an effort to defend myself, I told my father, 'If they had been on one of my boats, they would never have been taken.'

My father looked at me coldly. 'Don't you think we don't know that, Basil? I told you, if you had not been so busy with your work ...'

They blamed me for it all. I couldn't bring myself to tell them the truth. Inside, I seethed with anger that all this blame heaped up on me, when this was a mess of their own making. Shame camped outside my front door, while deception waited patiently at the rear.

* * *

I feel another tug on my sleeve, and there he is again, sitting by my bed; Luke of Antioch. I swallow, trying to find some words. My eloquence deserts me. Eventually I blurt out, 'What happened to you?'

He looks down at his hands, then into my eyes. 'I see you are straight to the point, Basil, at last.' He looks down again, and scratches his head. 'Let me see. Two months after they captured us, they took me to Egypt and sold me as a scribe. They knew I could read and write in several languages. At first, my new master did not seem so bad. I had good food and sometimes, wine. I worked hard and he let me read some of his books, as my reward.

He promised me my freedom after ten years, if I did well. But gradually I learned that he gave empty promises, never honoured, and he could also be exceptionally cruel when someone displeased him. I tried to escape, you see, to find my daughter. The first time they caught me, he had me beaten severely. The second time, I acted very foolishly. I forgot my new position in life, and I insulted him. I also told him I would keep trying to escape...'

He raises his wrist and hands, and lifts an ankle, to show me the marks. 'Upside down, Basil...he had me crucified upside down, like St Peter. I will tell you all about it later. But for now...' He purses his lips, frowns, and sighs. 'How do we begin?' He studies me intently, as if he can see my thoughts. Then he nods to himself, stands up straight, narrows his eyes, and looks down upon me. 'For now, just remember what you did. Can you do that, Basil?'

I shake my head from side to side. My head hurts. My heart pounds in my ears, trying to block out what he has said to me. 'Go away. Go away.'

'I am a very patient man, as you well know. I will come back when you remember.' With that, he goes back through the door in the wall, which I lock after him, to stop any of them coming back. But as I lie there listening, I can hear them through the wall, whispering about me. Meanwhile the slaves busy themselves around me, taking out a bundle of stinking rags from my bed and replacing them. But Luke of Antioch knows how to plant a seed in a person's mind... despite my reluctance, I find myself slipping back into that time, slipping back into the body of a young man, once again...

*   *   *

Feet Of Clay

During my last days with Sophia, I felt hemmed in, trapped, longing for space in my overcrowded mind. After her departure, I lived in a void. My beautiful new villa suddenly echoed like a ransacked tomb and to counter this I invited Bernard of Chevreuse to come for supper again. I still had to solve the problem of his presence, and I wanted to know what sort of man I had to deal with. Strangely enough, I found that I liked him.

I decided to be direct. 'You didn't really swing an axe, did you, Bernard of Chevreuse? And where exactly is Chevreuse?'

He grinned and shrugged; I liked his disarming honesty. 'No, I pulled a bow. Perhaps you have noticed, this arm is much stronger than the other.' He mimed the action. 'Chevreuse lies on the river Yvette, near Paris.'

'So whose army did you escape from?'

He laughed aloud. 'My God, Basil of Makri, you read my mind. We called ourselves pilgrims. But you call us Latins, Franks, or crusaders. And escape is exactly what I did. How did you guess?' He looked relieved, pleased even. He didn't have to lie to me anymore.

I learned a good deal about his country, and the customs of the Latins, during our conversation that evening. He answered all my questions in a matter of fact way. I began to I wish I could keep him, to work for me. But I had made a promise to Menas.

After our food and much wine I said, 'I'm sorry, Bernard, but I must warn you. Menas has told your history to others in the town. That means a death sentence, if you remain here. Plenty of refugees in the town will not hesitate to take their revenge. But because you have helped my family I do not wish to find you with your throat cut, or swinging from a tree. You will have to leave here, soon.'

'Ah. So that is why you asked me here.' He frowned, and then met my eye. 'Thank you for warning me.'

'What will you do?'

He drew a circle with his cup upon the table while he considered this. 'I could always look after goats somewhere... but perhaps I will try to go home now. I have made my penance by these children. Your land has its own beauty, but it's nothing like my land. I did not think that I could go back at first, but there has been so much chaos... perhaps, now, who cares what a poor soldier has done? Maybe God will allow me to return now. And even if I do not see my Catherine again, at least I want to die knowing that I tried.'

I remembered something. My brother had asked me to pay him as an escort should be paid, for helping them on their journey. At least I could send him on his way with hope. 'Wait here,' I told him.

When I returned I held up a little purse. 'My brother asked me to give you this.' I threw the purse at him and watched his face. He had not expected this, and almost fell backwards in surprise. As he opened it, his eyes lit up as he counted the coins. He came toward me, fell on his knees, and grasped and kissed my hand. 'God bless you, Basil. This will pay my debt, if I can work my way back home.' Then, suddenly as embarrassed as I was, he stood, embraced me tearfully once more, and left.

* * *

Sophia sits me down upon my bed, and takes hold of my hands. Seeing them, I realise my body is very old, much older than hers. She waits until I look again at her face and then smiles, a little wistfully. 'You know, Basil, they sold me to a rich Egyptian. I suppose I should think myself fortunate not to end up in a soldier's brothel. And Ahmad did not treat me badly. I never left his house again, but he never hurt me, and eventually I became his favourite concubine. My education gave me a great advantage. Once I had learned the language and customs, I kept his interest.' She pauses and smiles. 'Tell me, what else do you want to know?'

Alas, the shock of seeing her again empties my mind. I do not know what to ask. My head starts to spin a web of thoughts but soon they lead nowhere; this happens again and again. I end up feeling puzzled, lost for words. So after a while she smiles, shakes her head sadly, and disappears through the door. Who else will come? Now, in this dark and empty room, I wait.

Take my brother, for instance... he came again last night, with his tale about the galleys. As I listened, it was me that relived it, me that was chained to an oar, pulling with all my weight to the beat of the drum, at times sitting in my own filth, with nothing but stale bread and almonds to eat, and watered vinegar to drink. Dreaming of escape for the first seven years, but then gradually began to dream more and more of death ...

Justin described a feast they had once, after winning a great battle. 'Our reward came from a mound of enemy stores, bread and meat and fish and fruit, brought to us by captured camp followers. What a feast – a mountain of food. I felt foolish, at first, because my stomach threw most of it back up. Others who ate their fill and kept it down, they laughed at me. But later I felt lucky, because they began to moan in pain, and later to scream. They had burst their own stomachs with their greed.'

*   *   *

After I dealt with Bernard, I felt great satisfaction that I could so easily direct the lives of others. I never saw him again, except in my dreams, and I often wondered whether he made it back to his home; and what awaited him there.

I settled back down to my work and waited for news while I slept alone each night in my empty villa. I began to think that I might never hear, though my anger plumbed so deep that sometimes I thought this might be for the best. For weeks we had no news until a man finally brought a ransom message in the middle of the night. He looked unhealthy, half-starved, with a white pallor like a ghost. He told me he had been ill with a fever. But only desperate men take such work.

The Franks demanded a high price, worse than I had expected. They obviously knew their prisoners had wealthy relatives. I would have to sell Luke's land, to raise more cash. Then, I begin to have tempting thoughts. If only I could ransom Luke and Sophia, without my brother. But Luke and Sophia would know what I had done, and my parents would be sure to find out. Perhaps I should punish them all by letting them wait a while. Perhaps I could even let them be sold as slaves, and then find them later and buy them back. It seemed an appropriate punishment. I tried to put these thoughts out of my mind, but they kept coming back. Anger whispered in one ear, temptation in the other, giving me feet of clay.

Sometimes, if a ransom demand was too high, then waiting for, or offering, a lower price became the only option. It sometimes worked. But I also knew that even the wealthiest traders familiar with all the routes and ports could never be sure of finding people, once captives had been sold as slaves.

I needed gold for the ransom. Who was the obvious buyer for Luke's land? Antoninus, the Abbott of the monastery, would now have his own unexpected good fortune. In my troubled state of mind, I went to see him. I did not mean to tell him about my troubles, but I suppose he had not become an Abbott for nothing. I told him why I had decided to sell, about the ransom; he asked me how their journey had come about. In my anger, I told him, and one thing led to another. I had not been in church for some time, though I still had a little faith at that point in my life. Somehow my need to confess led to all my anger spilling out; I told him about my brother and Sophia, my belief that they meant to continue behind my back, and even about my suspicions that Luke did not come from Antioch and had not been born a Christian.

He listened to all of this carefully. I could see him thinking, and I imagined he would bargain with me about the price for the land. Well, he certainly made me an offer. He began by saying; 'I do not think it reasonable that you should have to bankrupt yourself in such circumstances...'

I started to say, 'It will not really bankrupt me...' but he quickly put his hand across my lips to keep me quiet, while he continued.

'God knows that you entered your marriage in good faith. But He also knows that you have good and just reasons for annulment. God is wise and just and all seeing. He knows that, by their betrayal of the most sacred vows, Sophia and your brother have both lost their right to God's protection – and to yours. As for this foreigner Luke, it is unfortunate that he too is mixed up in this. But as an educated man, he will certainly not be mistreated, even as a slave: the infidels, too, respect knowledge. He will be well treated, I can assure you. It may even be better for him, if he returns to his own land. Whether he's a Christian or not, you have my sacred promise that I, with all my monks, will pray every day for his soul. We will intercede for his soul with God, so that he will one day surely enter paradise. I understand your other difficulties. Your parents shouldn't have to bear any further suffering by knowing of the disgrace of your brother's act. As far as the world's concerned, I will make it well known that you tried diligently to ransom them all, using the church as an intermediary; but we failed, having been tricked by the Franks. I will also help you by buying the land, at a reasonable price.'

So his offer boiled down to this; sell me the land cheaply, and the church will help you get rid of your embarrassing problems, forgive you all your sins, and help you start your life again. He even made me think for a while that this might be the right thing to do. In the end, of course, this episode ensured that what little faith I had left in the church disappeared. If God's blessing could be bought so readily, what need did I have of it?

At that time, though, my thoughts began to race in different directions. I could not take it all in, and so initially I nodded, thanked him, and said that I would consider this carefully. I went home and repeated to myself what he had said, again and again and again. Sometimes in my deepest anger it seemed to make sense, though I had to harden my heart and stop myself from thinking about my future in this empty villa. I went back and took the money that the Abbott had offered. With what I had already, it was enough.

I told myself that I needed his money for part of the ransom; but in truth, I had not yet decided what to do. Perhaps I could track them down and buy them back later, with my connections... so I waited. I waited a long time: to punish them, I told myself, to put Justin and Sophia through the same agony I had suffered since my journey to Nicaea. I knew this was unfair to Luke, but I was sure they would not be harmed. *Thinking about it now, I no longer needed Luke for my business.* That thought hurts my conscience, and fills me with shame.

I told myself I would rescue them, after just a little longer. Perhaps this poisonous temptation itself made me ill; maybe my mind sought refuge from my dilemma through the very same malady my ghostly messenger had brought with him. Either way, I tumbled into that terrible fever. During moments of lucidity, I felt glad that only a servant attended me, and not my mother, to hear my feverish, rambling confessions.

Afterwards, for many years, I made excuses to myself. I told myself that none of it was my fault: that I would have rescued them if I had not collapsed with the fever; that nervous exhaustion had made me delay; that all the terrible events of that time had weakened my body, otherwise I would have acted much sooner. I truly believed that I had not acted badly, only slowly, and thus was not responsible. Their fate was not my fault... now, though, I see through this self-deception. Judge a man by his actions, not his words, even to himself. My waiting spoke volumes: a form of action, in truth, by non-action. The truth was that I could not put aside my rage. It consumed me. And thus it consumed Sophia, Justin and Luke.

I woke after my fever, alone in my room, surrounded by the goddesses on the walls. I called out, and a servant appeared.

'How long have I been ill?'

'Two weeks.'

'Bring one of my captains,' I demanded. But I somehow knew, already, I was too late. And so it was, and is. They had gone to the slave markets of Egypt, and there they had all vanished, without a trace. How empty that felt, and feels. Time has not healed that self-inflicted wound.

* * *

I am feverish now, and sleep. I wake, to feel someone wiping my face with a cool cloth and talking to me. It is Sophia; I knew she would come back.

She talks to me now. 'Oh, Basil, look what a bitter old man you have become. Was it worth it... all that hatred, just because I fell in love with Justin? Of course not... I guessed you knew, though I did not know how. I still believed you would rescue me again... but you should know the truth.' She picks up my hand. 'I was unfaithful to you, but not so often, and probably less than you would have been to me if we had lived all our lives together. I was so young, remember that, and your brother...well, he had been wounded and we needed his strength, so I nursed him as he recovered. He could be so boyish and playful. He made me forget all the danger around us, and I felt like a girl again in his presence. So we grew close. Later, we both began to think... that you might not have escaped the city. We turned to each other. Foolish, I know, but we both needed comfort. So yes, yes, you were right to be jealous. But we stopped, and if you had treated me well I would have been a good wife to you. I do not doubt that.' She puts my hand down again. 'Would you have been a good husband to me, Basil? Would you? I wonder... in the end, you let me go too easily, and then you pretended it was not your fault. Is that what a good husband does? Did you really love me, or was it just the idea of a beautiful wife? You chose to let me go, didn't you? Think about that, Basil, and don't be so bitter...'

She has gone, but now I see Luke's face, looking down at me with a curious mixture of pity and determination. I shrink away in horror, for I know he has come to tell me about his fate.

'You should understand this, Basil,' he tells me. 'I did not know exactly what happened between Sophia and Justin. I knew something had happened, but I thought it fairly innocent, best ignored. They had both been through so much fear, when death surrounded us on all sides. This sense of constant danger dissolves our usual loyalties. We cling on to others for comfort, when we might die tomorrow. And if you do not die, the relief makes you giddy. Most important, they did not know that you still lived. Whatever went on, they fought against it, when it would have been easier to give in. She felt so lonely, Basil – and your brother too. He had also lost much. You judge them too harshly.' I feel ashamed listening to him, because he has, as usual, more concern about others than himself. He does not complain about what I did to him.

But then, he does not need to. He simply says, 'Now, I will tell you my tale.' This takes him a day and a half, and throughout that time his story comes to life within me, so that I feel that I am inside Luke, shrieking as they drive in the nails and hoist him up, and then gasping for every breath. As I hang there upside down, the pain makes my body want to move, to get away from the agony, but whatever I do, it worsens. The ropes stop my hands and ankles tearing apart – but they do not stop my weight shifting the torn flesh and broken bones upon the nails. I beg for water; then for my life to be finished, pleading to be killed as I stare at my master's feet. He looks down upon me, and laughs. With his foot he pushes a sponge filled with vinegar and water towards my head. I know that he uses it to wipe his arse, but I cannot help myself, and twist my neck to try to drink, whimpering with the pain.

At the end, I beg repeatedly, 'Kill me, please. Kill me, please. Please, kill me...' This becomes a mantra, screaming in my head even when I have no breath left, and no voice to say it.

* * *

I had one more choice. I could spend the rest of my life in a fruitless search, torturing myself for the rest of my life, or I could harden my heart and forget, blot out my feelings, and move on. I took the second road. I closed up my beautiful villa, and did not live in it again for another twenty years.

I am Basil, and I am Roman; and once I traded with lives and souls. That is my boast and my confession. By not acting, I traded the lives of those I loved for money.

The wealth I gained by doing this became the seeds for the riches of Asia that later grew around me. I realise now that the soul I traded was, in fact, my own. I had hardened my heart, on the outside. And inside, the emptiness within filled with cruelty and bitterness, especially after the death of my son. The ghosts of that era are yet to come, but come they will. Now, I lie alone in this dark and empty room remembering the art of Menas. The mosaics in the villa above me are glorious, the best things that remain of my wretched life...you should seek them out. The artist, Menas of Constantinople, he should be remembered...

*　　*　　*

Basil's Children

My dreams now swell to bursting point, pregnant with visitations from the past. Recently it is my second wife Eirene who emerges out of the night, looking young, sometimes carrying one of our babies in her arms, or another in her belly. She must ferry herself here from the era of our young family, for she holds none of the bitterness that filled the void between us in our later years. She cannot stop talking; and despite myself, I cannot help listening. She sits by my bed, and I swear I can smell the fragrant oils that she rubbed into her skin, and feel her soft hand patting mine, to keep me awake.

'I know you thought of me as a frivolous girl when you met me, Basil. You were ten years older; self-educated, but successful. I also knew why you wanted to marry me – you needed my father's help. Once the Empire had struggled back onto its feet again, in Nicaea, the imperial taxmen returned to bleed you dry. My father's position as the local magistrate for our small peninsula appears of minor importance, but you understood its potential. Climb the mountain pass above the sheltered bay and the main harbour at Makri, follow the path through the forest, and you drop down into our fertile bowl of land, encircled by steep hills. Our peninsula juts out into the sea; with a wide arc of small bays and natural harbours, hidden around its edge. Cut a few trees, and you have a jetty here, a jetty there. After you have unloaded your most valuable cargo, well away from the prying eyes of the taxman, local crops can be loaded onto your boats. A web of paths and roads criss-cross the peninsula leading to the bay opposite the ancient ruined city, Karmylessos; and other ruined and abandoned buildings and settlements provide plenty of hidden storage. Best of all, our outer ring of hills allows you to see for miles from the old watchtowers. No one can approach unseen. So why should you pay taxes in the harbour at Makri? You can pretend to be a poor merchant and bring in a cargo of cheap goods to the harbour, now and then. But quietly, a small load of incense comes over the mountain and goes to the monastery in exchange for the best of this crop of honey, or that crop of oil. A boat comes and goes; but not in the harbour, where the tax-collectors take ten per cent. And what better man to hire all your sailors and mule drivers from our local villages, than my father? What better way to seal all of these lips than for the whole community to realise that they will share in this prosperity only by keeping it quiet?'

I nod and laugh. Had I been that transparent?

'You knew my father was no fool, Basil. Neither was I. He told me all this before we married. But I felt pleased, Basil, fortunate to be marrying a clever man, someone who took charge of life and made his own decisions. I knew you had come from a family of fishermen, but you had already become much more than that. So many men are slaves to convention, and I did not want to marry a slave. Do you remember how I showed you all the best places to hide your goods and ships, where to place your lookouts, and told you who you could trust? I surprised you, then. A slip of a girl, you thought me, and not beautiful, either. Yet I knew exactly what you wanted. You paid me little enough attention on our wedding night, but after I had shown you the secret harbours of our coastline, then you also discovered mine.'

I blush at the memory of that. Eirene did indeed have sweet and hidden depths, in more ways than one. The disastrous end to my first marriage had left me with an empty space inside my soul and I entered my second marriage thinking of it as a business arrangement. I felt I could never trust another woman, never rid myself of bitterness and suspicion. It suited me to have few expectations, to keep my distance, at first.

'When I discovered you had no strong religious customs, that pleased me too, Basil. Some of the boys from well-off families became so boring, afraid of their own shadows. The priests who taught them hate Lycia, our land of light, because we have so many old tombs, and ancient sacred places. Evil spirits, they say, inhabit all these places. They cross themselves until their wrists grow sore. My mother knew better than they. She took me as a small and innocent child to those old shrines and taught me that no devils live there, only the ghosts of our ancestors. She taught me that the priests invented the idea of devils when they arrived here to discourage people from worshiping at the old shrines. Then the old fools forgot the reason for their own invention and became afraid of their own shadows. My mother had wisdom, and knowledge. She taught me how to use plants and herbs for medicines, and which could not, except as poison. Do you remember how it saved our lives? Do you?'

I nod again.

'I saved your life as well as mine. You never thanked me, but I saved us both.'

I do not argue, though what she says astounds me. Did I really not thank her? Her voice lifts and lilts, my Eirene, as if she is about to burst into song (and she could sing well). I thought my heart had been hardened as a young man, but Eirene befriended me and slowly softened it, as I gradually let my barriers down. Even then, I hesitated to have children, believing I would be too jealous of them. But Eirene was a fertile garden, and her mother insisted that I watch the births, telling me that if you witness a miracle, some of the magic enters your eyes.

Something did change within me, making me feel whole again. I struggled uncertainly as a father, but Eirene's voice when she soothed our children grew to sound like music to me. She looked plain and sturdy, but she transformed into a nymph, soft and delicate, in my arms. For the first part of our time together, I put away the nightmares of my past and not only lived again, but cherished our young family.

While Eirene talks, sitting by my bed, the song of her siren voice transports me back, to relive the time she describes. I married her and left my beautiful villa in Makri to stay with her parents in their farmhouse in the old citadel on the peninsula. We spent our happiest times there. Ten years or more, it must have been. This citadel, a small castle dating from the early days of the empire, guarded the northern corner of her family's peninsula. From the battlements, you could see the entrance to the long bay that leads to Makri harbour. I kept my profits there under her father's authority and protection, knowing he could be trusted. The castle sat on a steep hill; only a small army could storm it. We felt safe. But when that army appeared, like locusts from hell, it shattered our lives into pieces that would never fit back together, however we tried.

* * *

In the middle of the night a distant clamour of anxious people, knocking upon gates and doors, shouting, disturbs their rest. Basil strokes Eirene's hair, slips out of the bed, wraps himself in a goatskin, and pads along the corridor. The night is warm, but what he discovers when he opens the outer door sends shivers of alarm and fear tumbling through his body. Frankish pirates have come to raid Makri, in force. Their fleet has crept in at night and already landed; they surround the town itself, cutting off the escape route that leads inland to Kadianda and the mountains. The people outside clamouring for shelter have somehow stumbled up and over the dark mountain pass into this peninsula. Everyone knows that soon, perhaps even now, ships will be landing other men around the peninsula to cut off any further escape. After stripping Makri, their main prize, they will come to take everything else they can find. The trap has already closed around them.

Basil returns to wake Eirene and inform her. For once, she sits silently, looking first at each of the sleeping children, and then to him for counsel. Basil's brow furrows; he bites his lip as he tries to concentrate, tearing his eyes away from the children. He swallows, forces himself to use his reason. If they remain together here with their money in the citadel, and it falls, they will all die, probably as slaves, once the raiders have their money. They should hide their fortune. His wife knows the terrain as well as he... but greater safety also lies in separation, since one survivor can then ransom any others who might be captured. Eirene knows all the hiding places in these parts, after all. Her hand creeps into his, as he swallows his doubts and speaks.

'Leave the children with your father in the citadel. Your father will make a stand there with the fighting men. Dress the children in their finest clothes so the Franks won't kill them even if the citadel does fall. We'll split our money in two, so you and I will each hide half, and then hide out in the woods. That way, even if one of us is captured, the other will be able to ransom the children and each other, if we need to. Take a slave to help if you wish, one you can trust, but go quickly, while it's still dark. And stay hidden during the day.'

She nods. 'Where shall we meet?'

'Go to the woods next to the large rock tombs. One thing about the Franks, they have superstitious ideas about evil spirits, so they won't hang around there.'

While Eirene attends to the children and speaks to her father, he fetches their hoard of coins and splits it, also dividing her jewels. Not a great fortune, but enough, even split into two parts, to start again. He leaves one half within its small wooden chest, and puts Eirene's part into a large leather bag. They both embrace the sleepy children. Will this be the last time? The daughter, the youngest, whimpers at her mother for a moment, and closes her eyes. The oldest, Adrian, sits up looking dumbstruck, as he usually does at this hour. The second son, Basil, sleepily asks if he can go with his father, and then puts his thumb back in his mouth.

The older Basil shakes his head hurriedly – although as soon as he has stepped outside he wishes he had agreed. It would have made sense to separate the children, too, and he would have chosen little Basil. But there is no time: his mind brims over with the need for speed, already fighting against his desire to keep his wife with him, and his fear that this farewell might be the last. He tries to ignore those nagging doubts, that sensation of his small family tearing itself apart.

He slips out of a door at the rear of the building into the shadows, careful that no one follows. As he walks, his mind fills and refills with questions. Should we have told each other where we plan to hide each half? What if the Franks capture one of us, or both? And what if they torture their captives? Things will be safer this way, he tells himself. Fears and doubts keep assailing him, while he stumbles over rocks in the darkness, avoiding the well-used paths and houses, trusting no one. He travels on foot, slowly and carefully, carrying a small supply of food and water. He has decided to hide his box near an abandoned farm. He remembers the delicious figs he sampled there last year, in the overgrown garden of the ruined house, while riding with Eirene's father to one of the quiet bays. No one lives nearby. The ground around the fig trees was surrounded by grass and thorn bushes, perfect to hide the signs of digging. Spring has also just arrived, so no one will pick the fruit for months.

Light is cautiously creeping over the distant mountains by the time he arrives. From a nearby hill, he checks that he has not been followed. Then he chooses a spot between two of the fig trees in the undergrowth, and lifts a square of vegetation and topsoil carefully with his long knife, laying it on one side. He lays his cloak on the ground and uses it to catch the soil while he digs a hole, not too deep. Disguise is his purpose, not depth. He wants to find his hoard again easily – not to spend the rest of his life digging. He places the box in the hole, replaces some of the soil, packing it down, and then replaces the square of vegetation. Even standing nearby, he can't detect anything unusual.

Satisfied with his work, he checks his surroundings again from the hill and creeps away, retreating into the refuge of the pine forest, scattering the surplus soil under vegetation a good distance away. Then he lies down to rest. The trees give plenty of shade, and he needs his water to last.

Over the next few days, he inches cautiously towards the meeting place. He travels only at dusk, in gloomy light – enough to run away and hide, if need be, without falling and breaking an ankle. He avoids paths and trails, except when he has to cross them. One evening as he nears a trail, he hears raucous laughter and foreign voices. He drops to the ground and crawls behind the nearest bush. Peeking from behind it, he glimpses a party of Franks, driving a herd of goats, no doubt on the way to feed their army.

These Franks carry the swords and shields of a crusader army, but now they wear a hotchpotch of clothes, as pirates do. Basil knows that most of them came here as pilgrim soldiers, expecting to fight infidels in the Holy Land. Somehow they are stuck here, fighting a war against fellow Christians to keep the islands that have become their home. This war has become a series of raids and counter raids, each seizing the valuables of the enemy, kidnapping and extortion, selling their captives into slavery if no ransom is paid. That said, for a Frankish soldier it's not a bad life. Their pay is good. There are no major battles now. This is a rich land, with a warm climate, plentiful food and wine, and they can take their pick of the peasant women they capture.

Basil listens to their laughter fading into the half-light. Each night, he wraps myself in his thick, dark cloak and dozes. Several times he hears animals, or people, moving nearby in the darkness. How many others have scattered into these woods?

By the time he reaches the place of the tombs, he has finished his food and water. Eirene has told him a hermit lives in a cave somewhere near; there must be water nearby, but where exactly? He searches, but sees no signs. His heart sinks. Where is Eirene? Surely she has been careful? That night, he tosses and turns, unable to rest, his mind plagued with terrible imaginings. Eventually, as first light begins to creep through the trees, he dozes off in exhaustion. When Eirene wakes him, for a moment Basil thinks he is dreaming.

*　*　*

In my nightmare, a dog held me by the throat; then shook me, shaking me into the world. I blinked, sensing Eirene's silhouette looming over me, whispering, hands reaching out of the semi-darkness. We have found each other again. That night, so long ago, we clung to each other for a long moment, trying to hang on to that moment of relief, that brief interruption to the madness that threatened to swamp us. Then she pulled away from me. I

151

felt puzzled, somehow knowing that something was wrong. My relief slowly dissipated, but I didn't see the bruises on her face until later. They slowly dawned upon me, as it grew light. But even then, she insisted they were nothing, the result of a fall. The slave she had brought with her, Peter, confirmed this.

Now, she sits by my bed and looks at me with that same bruised face, and I still do not know what to say. I knew then something bad had happened, but she would not tell me of it, ever. How could she? We had to save our strength, to remain alive, to hang on to our capacity to reason. We could not give the reins to our feelings. Only now, in my doting dreams, does she tell me. She holds my hand, but cannot meet my eye.

'I must share my shame and pain, Basil, or it will always fester between us.' She sighs, and shivers. 'They were Franks – about six or seven, I lost count. They blundered across our hiding place, foraging for food. They used me as their toy. They assumed that useless slave Peter was my husband and forced him to watch, at first. They laughed at him when he made no attempt to help me, and later they made him join in. He resisted none of it, you understand?'

I nodded. Now, I understood why she had turned on him.

'They did not cut me, though they threatened it, often. They seemed to enjoy hurting me, making me cry out. That seemed to satisfy them, I realised, the louder I cried. I thought I would tear apart. You can't imagine what it feels like, Basil. It takes away all pleasure from the act of love. Afterwards, every time I wanted to love you, I never could. That night was the reason. You thought it was grief, at first, I know.' She pauses, and I watch a tear trickle slowly down. 'That didn't help, either. Your grief made you irritable, and impatient. I needed you to be patient.'

I did not want to know all this, but it explains much. I can't hate the slave, Peter, for not resisting. He would have been killed instantly, had he tried to interfere or refused; but Eirene would not forgive his acquiescence.

'I told myself not to struggle, but to cry out louder, and stay alive. I told myself, I can bear this, as long as I find my family again. That was the bargain I made with the old goddess of Karmylessos. If I found you and the children again, she could keep the treasure. She kept most of us alive, Basil, so I kept my bargain. That's why I made you promise to leave it hidden, for the sake of my soul. Do you understand now?'

I did, at last – my stubborn, superstitious, pagan Eirene.

She sighs, and shakes her head again. 'Whenever I tried, Basil, that night would always force itself upon me. You could tell that something had gone wrong. And you grew more and more suspicious of me. You believed I had another lover, didn't you? I know you had me followed; but there was never anyone else...'

She kisses me, and tastes like sweet olive oil. She talks again, and suddenly I find myself catapulted back in time again, reliving the past...

* * *

By now, a plate of stale bread and a cup of sour milk would have looked like a feast to Basil. At dawn, Eirene fills the water-skins from the spring that keeps the hermit alive. At last, his thirst is quenched. Later, she comes back with edible roots and wild plants. They eat a peculiar, herby salad. Anything feels better than an empty stomach. At least, so he thinks. After their meal she rubs one special herb briefly onto their faces, saying it will comfort them. Then she gives it with the remaining plants for Peter to eat.

An hour later, Peter cries out with pain and doubles over. He looks puzzled for a few moments, and then vomits. He begins clutching at his gut and moaning, gasping for breath. Basil turns to Eirene, and sees her watching Peter carefully, with a satisfied expression on her face. She looks at Basil coolly. 'Don't worry. You didn't eat what he has eaten.'

Peter lies there moaning for the next half hour, while death sits down by him, caressing his stomach. Basil watches Peter's throat turn red and swell, so that he can hardly breathe. A bright crimson rash slowly covers his skin and face. He dies slowly, gasping, as his tongue and throat become so swollen he cannot breathe.

When Peter has stopped moving, Eirene tells Basil to help her move the body. He asks her why.

She looks away. 'In case the Franks come back here. You'll see.'

They drag the body to the largest of the tombs, and she props it up against the side. Basil is exhausted. He has no sense of what she intends, and feels too tired to care. They find some shade on the hill above the tombs and rest there. Basil's face itches with the heat, while he tries to doze.

He wakes to the sound of a shout, perhaps several shouts. He reaches out, but Eirene has left his side. He sits up, then stands – and sees her down by the tombs, out in the open. On the opposite slope a group of Franks spread out as they move to surround her. Two leaders, on horseback, watch and laugh to each other. What on earth was she doing? He starts to move down the hill towards her, and then stops. Hopeless – surely it is better for him to stay hidden. But how can he stand back and watch such diabolical theatre?

He hears her call out to them. The soldiers nearest to her stop and listen as she speaks first in Greek, and then in Latin.

'Help me, my children are all sick, they are dying, help me, and pray to the Gods who live in these tombs.'

One of the Franks shouts to the others, in their own guttural tongue, translating her speech. Basil begins to move down the hill again, knowing this makes no sense, but he feels drawn toward her. Now, he can see that the other Franks have stopped, and stand pointing at Peter's red-faced corpse, swelling in the heat, and muttering. Then one of them spots Basil and shouts, pointing at him. Two others shout something else, gesturing at all the tombs among the rocks around them. These men start to cross themselves, backing off, and they turn to look for guidance from the two leaders on horseback. One of these men, with hard, glittering eyes, reaches for a bow. At least we die together, Basil thinks. Then, the other horseman puts his hand out as if to say, no, don't waste your arrows. He snaps a command. Abruptly, they all began to back off and move away. Basil watches, spellbound, as they all leave, talking heatedly in their jabbering way. When Eirene turns to face him he sees the bright red rash on her face, and realises why his own face is itching so badly.

'How do you like my plague?' she asks, smiling in triumph. And clearly, she has made them believe exactly that. Over the next two days, all the Franks leave the area. Basil and Eirene watch their ships depart from the cliffs above the hermit's cave.

They return to the citadel, only to find it sacked. They find the bodies of her parents, among others, but their children have vanished. They can only hope that the Franks have taken them for ransom. Eirene lapses so deeply into despair, Basil fears she may take her own life. He keeps himself busy, and tries not to think too much. Each day is a long walk in the desert, without water.

*   *   *

My past invades my present, a ravaging army of memories. Yet I cannot resist, for with this army comes the great mercy of my remembered youth. My body craves to be young again, and so I slip back among them within my dreams.

After the Franks had left, we repaired what we could and buried the dead. They had plundered the whole area, leaving everything in short supply. I had lost most of my goods in storage, but Tyche had smiled on me in one respect – all but one of my ships were away, out at sea, so that when these ships returned over the following months with their holds full, I had a near monopoly of trade and soon made good my losses. Meanwhile, Eirene and I cried with relief when we heard what we hoped for, so desperately. The Franks sent a message saying that their captives could be ransomed for a fixed price within three months, after which they would be sold into slavery.

I immediately sent a fishing boat with a message describing my children and their clothes, agreeing to pay. The reply told me to meet them on a small, uninhabited island to the north. This time, I went with the boat myself.

That moonlit night I met Godfray, the Frankish pirate captain, for the first time. We arrived to find the island deserted, made a campfire for the night and settled down to sleep. A few hours later, something nudged my shoulder. I opened my eyes and saw a large foot, in a leather shoe. I looked up the leg to see a huge man towering over me, grinning like a monkey as he nudged me again with his foot. 'Wake up, Greek, my name is Godfray. I take it you are Basil?'

I nodded and sat up, glancing around. This large, redheaded man had a sword and axe swinging from his belt, like most of the men surrounding our camp. My men lay still and silent, equally helpless, looking sheepish. We could easily have been killed or taken as captives ourselves. I felt very foolish, and swore silently to myself. Never would I let this happen again.

He laughed. 'Don't worry, little Greek. My prisons are already too full. I was just making certain that you were not trying to trick me.'

I stood up and looked him in the eye. 'That would really be foolish.' I meant it too; after all, he had my children.

He still looked down upon me, being a full head taller. His mouth twisted into something resembling a smile, and he nodded. He took a burning torch from one of his men. 'Come then, Basil, come and find your children.' My life's great crisis was just a little game to him, I realised.

His men watched over mine while the two of us walked across the island towards his ship, waiting in a small bay. He had confidence – enough to walk ahead of me without looking back. In a boat beached by the shore, I made out the shapes of three children and, as we drew near, I cried out to them to let them know I had come.

Two of them rushed into my arms – my daughter Theodora and Adrian. I felt a great rush of relief and my throat thickened. But why did little Basil not move? Godfray went over to him, holding the burning torch above his head, and pointed at me. 'Go to your father, boy,' he said, gently.

The boy did not move, and as I looked again I knew why. His face had changed. Another boy, dressed in his clothes.

Godfray looked at me. 'Is he stupid?'

'This is not my son.'

Godfray looked from me to the boy and back again. He grabbed the boy by the hair and held a knife to his throat. 'Then you will not mind if I kill him, will you?'

I shrugged. 'Go ahead'.

Godfray watched the boy; he whimpered, but did not react to either of us. He released his grip, and put the knife back into his belt. 'I can see he's not your son. One moment...' He shouted over to his ship in his own language. A man slipped over the side and swam ashore. Godfray had a long conversation with him in his own language, which I could not follow. Eventually he turned to me and said, 'I am sorry about this, my Greek friend. If you wish, I can return in a week with the other children we have. Then you can see if your boy is among them.'

I swallowed my disappointment and nodded, taking the money for the ransom out and gave it to him. 'Keep it. And if my other son is among them I will give you the same again.' Too generous, perhaps, but I wanted to ensure he returned.

He looked at me with some respect, probably because I had kept myself very calm. I had learned in business that emotions achieved little, especially from such a weak position. 'Very well, Basil of Makri. You can take this boy now, and I will meet you here with the others in seven days. But do not try to trick me.'

I shrugged. 'I want my son back. Why would I be so stupid?'

And I did – so much that I could not rejoice about the others, yet. Eirene had more hope; she convinced herself that little Basil would be found. I also took the boy who had been dressed in his clothes back to the peninsula and watched him smile at last when his mother came to claim him. That night, two of his uncles came to see me and swore they would repay me somehow, though they possessed nothing. I told them they could pay me with loyalty by working for me.

I did not sleep for a week. Then I met Godfray in daylight, the second time. He had clearly decided he could trust me; I felt the same about him. We anchored our ships close together and I swung across to his on a rope. He had kept his word; he had brought twenty-two children, most of them looking either sullen or absolutely terrified. He had also brought girls, which puzzled me initially, but then I realised he probably wanted me to see them all, in case I knew their parents. I looked along their faces carefully, and then once more. But I could not make little Basil's face appear.

Godfray did not look surprised. He nodded and stroked his red beard, put his hand on my shoulder, and said to me, 'I suspected as much. I have been making enquiries of my jailers, Basil. I have learned that there is one who enjoys taking boys and using them for his pleasure. This disgusts me, my friend, and it is bad for my business. The others think this man went too far and killed your son, then dressed the other boy like him to try to hide his crime. So I will sell you all these children and give you this man, for the price you offered. Perhaps in future, we can help each other again, yes?'

He clapped his hands. Three of his men brought out a man, bound hand and foot, with rags stuffed in his mouth to stop him crying out, and laid him at my feet.

Godfray's men, professional soldiers, outnumbered mine; I could not risk refusing his offer. I passed the last of my money to Godfray while I looked down upon the face of the man who had murdered my favourite son. He was trussed like the carcass of a chicken, and his eyes bulged with fear as he saw the look on my face.

Godfray, my enemy, became my most useful ally. He must have felt a debt, because in the years that followed he paid it many times over. He began by selling me his captured goods cheaply, and later we helped each other to survive by warning each other of danger. I took precautions never to be caught by a raid like that again. I built another home in the mountains inland from Makri where, for the next ten years, my family lived. We kept good horses there, with a bodyguard of Cuman archers, to keep them safe. Cumans are small in stature, but they fight like tigers, and they gave me great loyalty. Most of them took wives from those who had been widowed in the raid, and settled down to serve and protect my family. They kept us alive on more than one occasion. But even they could not protect my other son, Adrian, from his own stupidity. He loved to swim, and ten years later he dived off a boat without paying attention and split his head upon a rock; gone, in an instant.

Eirene grew thin with grief after that second lost son. The following winter, her body weakened, she died of a fever. Only then, after her death, did I return to Makri, to live with my daughter in the villa that I had built for my first wife, the house of the mosaics. I threw myself more and more into my work, to numb the pain.

Now, I open my eyes to find Eirene sitting here, looking thin and ill, as she did in her last days. 'You should have let yourself grieve, not shut yourself away. You grew cold with all your suspicion of me. I could not bear that. Did you imagine that I would poison you? Was that it? You became cruel to all of us, all except Theodora. Why did you become so cruel? When Adrian died, there was no warmth, no light, to bring me back from my fever.'

I close my eyes. How can I explain? Anger can be a shield around the heart. Sometimes, we know we do wrong, but we do it anyway. My grotesque gift from Godfray set me on a path towards deliberate cruelty; through him I learned to enjoy inflicting pain. That Frankish jailer suffered terrible agonies at my own hands before I let the widows of men killed in the raid finish him off. To those who find this repulsive, I say this – find me a man who would not enjoy hurting the creature who has spoiled and murdered his most beloved child. If you can find such a man, he will no doubt either be a saint or he will become one. I am not such a man. They say revenge is sweet; but they should also warn you that the taste of it will grow a hunger in you, a need for that sweetness, especially when the rest of your life is bitter.

I open my eyes to explain, but Eirene has gone. That raid had other effects upon my life. Eirene had refused to tell me where she had hidden her part of our hoard, insisting we should leave it where it was, for some future emergency. By the time she told me the location of her treasure, on her deathbed, I had no need of it. But during earlier times of need we argued, while she withdrew further from my affections. She and I drifted apart. Her secret shame and my own guilt at not taking little Basil with me filled the gap between us. Our arguments widened it, and the shadow of my first marriage cast my dark suspicions upon her.

My little Basil's soul was picked far too early; the taste of this bitter fruit filled the empty space within my own soul. Inside, I felt so much bile and anger. I had hardened my heart once before, as a young man, so that I would not feel my own pain. Now, I became blind to the pain of others. I will not dwell on the loss of my son, save to say that I would have traded all my later success for his safe return. But his life had been traded already by Eirene. Years later, I realised that Tyche had taken him, in exchange for all those other children, who became my unexpected good fortune. Tyche, like all river goddesses, loves children. So, Eirene, my sweet pagan, be careful whom you pray to.

Godfray's greatest gift turned out to be those other children, returned to their families. Thereafter, every family on that peninsula bound itself in loyalty to me; and to me alone. On this rock I founded my business empire. Whatever my rivals planned to do, I would discover. Men risked their lives for me, and women exhorted their children to be loyal to me, and to work hard for me. Why? Someone in their family, someone they knew and loved, had been one of 'Basil's children'. In my dotage, grandmothers and grandfathers would suddenly approach, throw themselves on their knees, and kiss my hands and feet. I did not recognise them, but I knew at once who they were.

But where are Basil's children now, when I need

them? In their dotage... and where are my bodyguards?
All dust. By Hades, I would trade a warehouse of silk for
one good Cuman now, if only I could. Ha!

*   *   *

The Smell Of Time

The slight, bare-footed girl struggles with the weight of her burden as she ascends the shallow steps. Behind her, a white-haired Basil reclines on a stretcher among red silk cushions, lost in thought. Behind him, a dark, muscular man gives a grunt of derision and slows his pace, looking up to the heavens. Snail-like, the procession creeps out of the garden and enters a half-enclosed corridor. On one side, mosaics portray trading ships upon a bright blue sea; along the other, shutters have been thrown back, drawing a cool breeze into the house through open arches. Halfway along, the girl hears the old man clearing his throat. She hesitates for a moment, waiting for a command, only to find that her hesitation forces her to take a longer stride. Her foot slips on the marble floor. She stumbles and loses her grip with one hand, then the other. The litter sways sideways for a moment before it clatters to the floor.

'Aphrodite's arse! I am not a sack of olives. Bring me a whip for this donkey, now...'

Basil sends her a withering look; the girl shrinks away and bites her lip, blinking back her tears. Newly arrived, she has nothing familiar to cling to. As the youngest of the slaves, she is the lowest of the low in this house: no one will take her side. Behind them, the muscular man lowers his end down, quietly spits on his hands, grins to himself, and shakes his head.

At that moment, however, a rotund female figure enters the other end of the corridor, waddling towards them with short, staccato steps. She tries to ignore the tableau before her, her eyes seemingly fixed on some distant purpose of her own as she steers around them.

But the old man raises his hand and calls out, 'Theodora, my dear. I wish to visit my old bedroom again, to see the mosaics that Menas created there for me, all those years ago.'

A waft of sweet perfume, roses and jasmine, cascades over the young slave girl while she exhales slowly, relieved to hear that he seems to have forgotten her clumsiness already.

Theodora's silk robes, enfolding her in blues and greens, swirl as she slows and turns. She sighs, tuts, and shakes her head, as if her father is a stupid child. 'It's my room now.' Her eyes narrow, as she sees the expression on his face. She snorts, 'No, you can't go there.'

Basil's jaw drops, 'Why not, in God's name? I built this house.'

Now, she turns away, waving her hand, 'It is my wish.' The girl notices that Theodora has decorated her grey hair with jewelled pins around a purple scarf; purple, the imperial colour. She briefly but pointedly adjusts it while the old man watches, before she starts to move again.

'You cannot refuse me.' He blurts out these words and then frowns, is if in pain, for a moment. He hesitates, then clears his throat as if to rid himself of his discomfort. 'I beg you, daughter. Those mosaics are the only treasure I have left.'

Theodora stiffens. She stops, turns, and looks the old man in the eye. He colours; perhaps it occurs to him, too late, that his last phrase might have been unfortunate. The young girl can sense midwinter in Theodora's quiet voice, which seems to come from far away.

'I seem to remember asking you to let me remarry, five years after Simeon died, when I was still young. You refused me, even when I begged you. You said that was your wish, then, and I had to accept it. Well, things have changed. And now, this is my wish.'

He scowls and looks at the floor. 'Julian was not good enough for you. He would have ruined you.'

She steps closer and raises her voice. 'Julian was an old friend. He may not have been rich, but he cared about me. And people respected him; you used him yourself to build your warehouses.' He starts to open his mouth again, but she speaks too quickly. 'And you can't fool me with your tricks. I know his business failed later, but only because you made it fail.'

For a moment, her words seem to sting him into silence; but the girl sees from his face that he will not give up easily.

'He did not show me the respect our customs demand. He assumed far too much. You know that.'

'He was an old friend.' As she says this, Theodora colours a little.

'Aha... I did not realise...'

Her colour deepens; he presses on, his tone suddenly more confident.

'Granted, I may have been impatient. But I had a lot on my mind. And Julian was far too sure of himself given the nature of his request. He should have asked for my blessing, not demanded it.' He pauses, but she does not respond. 'I know only too well that a hurried and impulsive marriage will bring trouble.'

Theodora almost chokes with fury. 'We were not impulsive. We knew each other for years. You were the impulsive one. You refused outright, waved him away, and then insulted him.'

'He can't have cared for you that much. He married another, soon enough.'

The tears spring into her eyes at this, and for a moment she stares back at him like a wounded animal. Then, she seems to adjust her armour. She moves closer still, and fixes her hands on her hips.

'You were not the only one with too much pride. Julian had pride too. Listen, father of mine – all my life I respected you. I learned my lessons and worked hard. My mother trained me to run a house well. You found that I also had an instinct for business, that I could be trusted to help you. So I trusted the wisdom of your choice for my first husband. But love did not guide your choice. You wanted an alliance of great houses; you said it yourself. I put up with that. I bore Simeon two sons, and we grew to respect each other, but we never felt passion for each other. When Simeon died, I brought our two households together, at a time when that suited us both. You had no wife; my sons had no father. Then, for once in my life, I saw a chance for my happiness. One chance... and what did you do?'

For once, the old man cannot seem to meet his daughter's eye. 'If I had known this was in your mind, perhaps I might...'

'Don't pretend you didn't know. I tried to reason with you the next day, I told you exactly what I felt. And what did you do?'

Her words take him back. While he ponders, the silence gathers. Eventually, he tells her, 'You were insolent. And defiant.'

'And why not? What good had a lifetime of respect done me? You still took away my happiness. Why? Because you wanted me to run your house, you wanted my sons under your control. When I objected, you struck me and locked me in my room. Remember that, father?'

He sighs, and shakes his head in defeat. 'I was wary of my enemies, at that time. I could not allow anyone to manipulate me...even you. At another time...'

'There was no other time, as you well know.'

Finally, he is silent.

Now she hisses at him, wagging her finger. 'So just be glad that I don't beat you, or lock you in your room. From now on, I will make sure that you stay out of all the best rooms, for two reasons, dear father. First, you stink of piss and I do not care for it. Second, it is my wish.' She turns her back on him and walks on, her perfume drifting in her wake.

The old man leans back, sighs, and shuts his eyes. The two slaves exchange a long glance; after a pause, the old man lifts an arm, waving them forward. They both take a deep breath, grasp and lift. As they begin to move, the old man begins to mutter to himself... 'So, now I know why Theodora took to stuffing her mouth. Ha! ...I suppose I must tolerate this irritation... a doting father must indulge his daughter... such gall! I take this from no other, not even her mother, long departed from this life...'

He pauses for thought; his tone changes. 'But at least my daughter did not die young, like my sons... as for Julian, ha! I could have berthed a ship in his mouth that day... he must have thought the way prepared...and now she pays me back, alas, perhaps more than I know...'

* * *

The young slave girl tiptoes quietly along the corridor and

pauses outside his door, listening. She hears nothing. With luck, he'll be asleep. She takes a deep breath and opens the door, moving quickly into the room. From behind her, the sun, low in the sky, shines through a half-shuttered window. It steals into the room so that a shaft of light momentarily illuminates his face.

'Who is it? Shut the door, the light blinds me. Do I know you? Ah, little donkey. Have you brought water?'

She moves quickly to the table, pours water from a jug into the silver cup, and brings it to him. He sips it noisily.

'Thank the Lord for small mercies, and the devil for life's pleasure.'

She shakes her head as if in exasperation, but the trace of a smile appears. Over the last weeks, she has discovered the old man's bark is worse than his bite. He pats the bed, inviting her to sit and rest. She accepts the idea but slides down against the wall, out of his reach.

'Come closer, little donkey, you shall hear my story.'

She nods. She is new to this house and to his storytelling, but she knows enough to humour him, to keep the peace. Besides, he knows how to command attention: how to pause, and raise or lower his voice, and how to reveal his passions by small gestures.

'I, who provided my family with the finest silks and jewels, who built this magnificent house, who paid for all their slaves and indulgences, whose hand they kissed, no longer receive the loyalty and obedience that is due to me. Why? Age has withered me, so that my physical strength has gone. I have no strength left, even to beat the slaves...'

She glances up at this, finding his eyes watching her face. Is he teasing? Some of the others still fear him.

'My limbs pain me until I can hardly walk, and so my daughter persuaded me to take this modest room at the back of my beautiful villa, nearer to the terrace that looks over the garden, and also to the bathing rooms. I have to admit – she is right about one thing. I have less indignity to face when you carry me from one place to another, or throw me onto the floor like a sack of olives...'

She glances up again, and this time she sees

amusement on his face. She bites her lip.

'But I should have realised that my displacement from the finest rooms of my house would be seen as the final sign of shifting power in my family. And so it is, and I find that it cannot be undone. When I demand to return to my own rooms, my daughter refuses, and when I lose my temper, she laughs and walks away. I am left like a child watching his parent disappear with his favourite toy. I can only stamp my gnarled old feet. But this is no toy, for she has taken my power away. Now, the household obeys her will, not mine. Most men pray for a long life, but age will always have the last laugh, and makes clowns of us all. I can do nothing but laugh at that furious child that has somehow survived within me...'

She settles back against the wall, allowing the luxury of inactivity to seep through her bones, and finds herself enjoying his performance.

'When our great ships arrive and unload their goods, my grandsons no longer bother to tell me, let alone report to me as they once did. They tell Theodora, a woman. She runs the business well, I will admit – after all, I taught her. Her sons do the hard work – yet they can drive a harder bargain when the world thinks they must also report to me, or to her. Worse still, her sons no longer respect me, as they did when I was younger and stronger. When they were young and wilful children, I had them across my knee often enough. But now Leo and Marcus are mature, full grown, and known as men not to be crossed. They both avoid me now, since they know I would give them advice, and it makes me furious that they do not wish to hear it. At least my daughter lets me know what transpires, every now and then. Though lately, she keeps me apart from my business completely. That irks me. And when I ask her to invite some official or merchant I have known, she promises to do so, but they never come. Sometimes she has forgotten, sometimes there are other excuses. I grow tired of hearing them. Theodora has worn me down with her silent refusals, as her mother once tried to do, but failed.'

He sniffs the air, and then reaches for his stick, to

nudge her. The talk of his cargo boats has reminded him. 'You may light the incense, now.'

She sighs quietly to herself, gets up, and does so. He pats the bed again, and again she slides back down against the wall, a little closer, but still out of reach.

'It makes me laugh, when I am not cantankerous, and I remember what a dutiful daughter she used to be. So eager to please her daddy, and so respectful. Ha! What has become of that child now? What has become of my world? My daughter, my little Theodora, what has she become? Once such a delicate and pretty little child, as light as the feather of a swallow, I would pick her up and throw her in the air while she squealed her delight aloud. As a tiny infant we nearly lost her to a fever. Afterwards, she attached herself like a limpet upon me. I did not mind; her body seemed so light that sometimes I had her with me much of my day. She watched me at my work and learned my business even from an early age. That must be why she became so good at it. Another thing I remember; when other traders came to visit me, she would always climb right up upon me to show her possession of me, and would not get down until they had gone. She wanted to rule me then; now, she has finally got her way.

Yet now, of course, it would kill me to pick her up, and she would flatten me. Would she not? I should not have let her grow so fat, because soon she will be like me, unable to move. She eats a whole harvest of figs and nuts and honey each evening. You can smile, yes, but is it not true?'

The girl nods, and then hears footsteps out in the corridor. She stands up quickly, just as the door opens. She feels so tired, she can't think straight. But the old master swings his legs off the bed, raises his arm towards her, and prompts, 'Yes, I will come for my bath now. I am bathed and washed and pampered as Cleopatra was for Julius...'

The girl ducks under his arm gratefully, and helps him to stand. The head servant, Timon, nods thoughtfully, turns, and leaves them to it.

As she helps him along, the old master whispers in her ear, 'My daughter thinks I smell of time, of old age. Such is her own terror of time that she means to wash it out of me... would that she could! I will tell you a secret. Her nagging is so tedious that I find myself pissing a little here and there, just in order to annoy her, though not in my own room. That would be stupid...'

She giggles, enjoying this strange feeling. She can't remember the last time someone made her laugh.

'I was named after our great Emperor Basil, known to us as the Bulgar-slayer, who ruled when our Roman Empire was still the greatest in the world: before those murdering thieves from Venice sacked our beloved city of Constantine and so nearly destroyed our empire. Those damned Latin pilgrims, so-called Christians, bringers of chaos, should have come in Emperor Basil's time. He would never have trusted them, and would have given them the great mercy of a quick death.'

'Don't look so shocked. They were not so merciful, believe me. I never had to kill with my own hands, unlike my fearless brother Justin, the soldier, but I had something of that old Emperor in me. After I had hardened my heart and left my youth behind, I learned to be ruthless. In lawless times, you have to be, if you wish to survive. In business, too, either you or your rivals must suffer; one will win, and one will lose. You must become blind to their loss or learn to enjoy it. Winning has its cost; rivals become enemies. I learned to see who my enemies were, and how to deal with them. Remember this; the hand that strikes an enemy should be carefully hidden, so there is less danger of being struck in revenge. If you have to act against others, then do it when they least expect it.'

Gently, she lets him down onto the bench in the disrobing room. He continues talking while she undresses him, oblivious to everything but his audience.

'From an early age, I could bend men to my will by persuasion, which is a skill any trader must learn. Know what others desire, and flatter them as if they already possess it... they cannot resist. Later, I also learned to keep people in a little fear, so that my words would always be listened to...' His eyes twinkle, and he taps his nose.

'In public, I was careful to be seen as a supporter of the church. When people think that the angels are by your side, your horns and tail become invisible... yes, you can smile. How did I know this? I learned early that priests are all too human, and that to know their weakness is to know how they can be bought. Later, I saw how the darkest era of chaos and destruction was brought about by Godly men. I witnessed how murderers and thieves can wrap themselves in the garb of Holy men, and call what they do just.'

He shakes his head, then glances up to examine her face.

'My own sins are nothing by comparison. I became too used to controlling the lives of others, too good at using trickery and deception, too good at hardening my heart to the suffering of others. Maybe it is in my nature. One of the words for 'Emperor' is 'Basileus'... do you think I would have made a good Emperor? Ha! But that is truly not my wish – after all, if I had been Emperor, I am certain my dear family would have poisoned me by now. So perhaps my fate is not so harsh, after all...'

*   *   *

End Of Empire

Basil is sleeping, though he feels his face twitch as the cool air of early morning enters the room. Someone crosses the room and shakes him. He sniffs the aroma of bread and sweat, and feels his body being kneaded, gently.

He hears an unfamiliar voice speaking as if to a child, straining with an effort to remain clear and steady. 'Wake up, master, wake up. Your daughter has died.'

The owner of the voice shuffles away from the bed to the arched window and begins to pull both the shutters open, hooking them against the wall.

Basil hears himself breathing in short gasps, as if he is about to reply but has no breath to do it. He rubs his eyes and considers her words again, blinking and shaking his head as the daylight floods into the room, trying to make sense of their meaning. He pinches himself, feels the pain, grimaces, and heaves himself into a sitting position. He sees a stout, plain faced woman staring out of the window, as if she too is deep in thought. One of the kitchen servants, he remembers. Why on earth have they chosen her to tell me this, he wonders? Because she is both stupid and clumsy?

She seems to inspect herself, patting her apron to remove a smudge of flour.

'How did she die?'

The woman looks down at the floor, folds her arms, and turns toward him. 'They think she choked on the stone of an apricot, eating in her bed.' She turns away to adjust the drapes.

'Take me to see her.'

The woman considers how to respond. She shuffles back to the bedside, trying to look appropriately respectful, and mournful. 'That's not possible, master.' Her face is flat, expressionless.

He scowls and narrows his eyes, trying to guess what she means.

Her cheeks redden and she lowers her eyes, keeping her expression neutral. Perhaps she has been instructed not to say too much. After a long pause, she risks a glance up into his face again. He sees a flash of panic.

She mutters, 'I am very sorry, master,' and begins to turn away.

His wiry, wrinkled arm darts out and grasps her hair. Before she can move, he twists it around his wrist and pulls. She yelps in pain and drops to one knee, her head pulled towards his, as he demands, 'Why not?'

She cries out again, but this time in anger, as she seems to remember her own strength. Her thick arms rapidly wrench his scrawny hand out of her hair. She stands up, backs away from him and mutters under her breath.

He hisses, 'Why not, you fish-faced cow?'

She shakes her head in exasperation and walks out.

He curses his own helplessness. One internal voice is crying, *no, no, this cannot be.* Another is whispering, *untimely, but perhaps also an apt end for my daughter.* He breathes deeply, and nods to himself, thinking, *Tyche has finally taken the last of my children.*

A minute later, he hears someone clearing their throat. He looks up to see the equally deadpan face of Timon, the head servant, in the doorway. Of course, he thinks. Timon chose her for the task to insult me, to show me how unimportant I have become in this house.

'I'm afraid your daughter has been dead for five days, sire. She is already buried.'

Basil guesses immediately why his daughter has been disposed of behind his back, so carefully and quietly. His grandsons Leo and Marcus have taken the opportunity to grasp their inheritance. He pictures them searching through his daughter's papers, while they kept him quietly out of the way on the terrace, or in his room. The lawyers would have known that she ran the business now.

Timon smiles briefly as he confirms this. 'You should know that ownership of all the property transferred to Theodora three years ago, and has now been transferred to her sons.'

'No doubt first she, and now they, paid the lawyers well. And a doctor too, I suppose, to swear that I was incapable.'

Timon's face breaks into a thin smile, again. 'She had already prepared papers, to say that everything passes to her sons on her death.'

Even if she had not, Basil thinks, I'm sure they drew them up themselves and, once again, paid the lawyer well. Now they control my business, and also my beautiful villa. Timon smiles far too much. Does my situation please him? Basil suddenly remembers an occasion when he had almost hung a much younger Timon upside down over a fire for his insolence, and deeply regrets that he did not. He starts to shout, cursing Timon for his disloyalty.

Timon face remains impassive as he waits for Basil to finish. Then he looks down his nose and strokes his chin, savouring the moment. 'You are no longer master of this house. Leo is the master. Be warned that he tolerates you, but he does not love you. I suggest if you wish to live comfortably a little longer, you should remember that.' He adds a thin smile and bows very low in mock homage. He turns his back and stalks out, leaving Basil brooding, muttering to himself for days, in a fog of helpless rage...

*   *   *

I had this villa built when I was a young man, and in this town it is unique. I chose a site that overlooks the bay, within sight of the harbour, so that I could watch my ships arrive. Somehow, like me, it has survived our troubled times intact, and not yet been burned to the ground. It can scarcely be seen even from the harbour below, thanks to the shape of the land around it, but its survival still amazes me. Although it has been enlarged, the best rooms are the original ones, opening at the rear onto a shaded garden and terrace. But it hides its true glory inside, does it not? That artist, Menas, decorated it for me with no expense spared. He came from a family of mosaic artists who had worked in royal palaces and cathedrals; I gave him the best materials we could find. At the peak of his powers, Menas poured his heart and soul into this work. I knew little about art, so he had complete freedom to express himself, unrestricted by normal conventions. My small villa does not look like a palace on the outside, but it has mosaics unlike anything you have seen, or will ever see again. Seventy years after I first saw them, they still take my breath away. Now, they have been taken from me...

Even in death my daughter harries me repeatedly, ferrying herself into my dreams, paying me back for my hardened heart in the face of her pleading. At first she talks to me calmly, and respectfully, as a slim young woman. She begins by sitting down and talking about her life before I refused her, telling me how much she has sacrificed for me. She talks at such length that I notice her growing older and stouter, until she reaches the age when I refused to let her re-marry. Then, she stands up and her tone becomes loud, bitter and angry. She complains, 'Father, my father, why did you hurt me so? What did I ever do to hurt you? I was your friend, the one who always defended you when others complained ...even my mother...' She looks down, as if pained by the memory of taking my side, and pauses. Then she looks me in the eyes, 'Now I hate you; you have become so mean and selfish...you are cruel to my children... but even so, I never dreamed you would hurt me so much, my own father. Now I cannot help myself from hating you, and sometimes I truly want to poison you...'

She grows fatter and her hair grows grey while I listen; her voice lowers again, and fills with contempt and disgust. 'You stink of piss and rot, old man, why won't you die? Why are you so awkward and demanding? How did you become so bitter?' She turns around, walks away a few paces, and then returns. At the end of the dream, she stands over me, laughing, and her ample folds of fat ripple as she says, 'Look at you now, father. Get up and walk, why don't you? Go to see the lawyers and claim your villa back, why don't you? Tell them how I tricked you, why don't you?' Then, I awake.

Sometimes, in a different dream, I watch her smiling at me and silently eating, eating; slowly fattening and becoming bloated. I know that she smiles at my expense. In her mind, she gloats about my helplessness. Then her face, still smiling, but now red and puffy, approaches mine as her enormous body waddles towards me. She begins to look puzzled, and gasps for air. Her face turns purple and her mouth tries to form silent words, gasping like a fish out of water. In this dream, I must watch her choking to death. I know that I am the cause of it, but I can only watch, helpless. If she coughs the blockage out, I will be sprayed with poison and bitter bile; if not, she will silently die and fall upon me so that her body weight will gradually crush the life out of me. As she begins to retch or to fall, I wake in a cold sweat, and realise that she is still paying me back, even in death...

* * *

But life still remains in this old dog, praise to Aphrodite. Since my daughter's death my life has not changed too much, except that the women slaves refuse to do my bidding, when I wish them to pleasure me. Even those once afraid of me refuse, and they know that I have no real power over them now. I have to pay them to do it, and far too well, with what little money I have left in my room. You may laugh, but this is a dreadful loss for me, since I rely on them for all my needs. Losing control of your own body is not so bad, if you can still control the bodies of others.

Some refuse no matter how much I offer to pay, like my poor little donkey. But one woman seems to like me well enough, despite my many faults. My comfort comes from the large and cheerful woman from Africa, one of the housekeepers, not afraid to say what she thinks. She moves slowly, deliberately and with great watchfulness. She never did fear me, nor does she find me repulsive. I do not mind if she sucks me dry, and empties my purse, because she also brings me the great gift of laughter. She may not be young or attractive herself but her warm, soft, and rounded body smells like the earth on a hot day. She feels exactly like the great earth mother when she helps me to lie on her, when I am most happy to be swallowed alive within the depths of her ample body. Most important, I can also make her laugh – I said to her, the last time, 'Truly, this would be the best way to die. You can kill me anytime.' So I bounced up and down upon her laughter like a cork upon the sea.

Another time, I told her, 'If I had known a few years ago what you were like, I would have married you while I could.'

She looked at me in mock disbelief, looked around her as if there are listeners, and whispered, 'It's a bit late now, Basil. Maybe when I was younger.'

At this we both collapsed, and cried with laughter. Since then, I have tried several times to persuade her that if she helps me escape, I will marry her, but she continues to laugh at me, chiding me for teasing her. For once, I wish that she would take me seriously.

At least I can still demand food and wine from the other slaves, and I have access to the terrace and the garden, and books from my library. I have discovered that Leo uses my villa as a place to entertain others, occasionally. I can tell by the preparations when this is about to occur. Each time, great activity fills the kitchen during the afternoon. Then they carry me to my room, well before any guests arrive. The door shuts, the lock turns, and a male slave sits outside the door. On the last occasion, I knocked and demanded some food from the feast.

'Be quiet.'

I started to make more noise; the door opened, and the slave smiled knowingly as he showed me the ropes and the cloth he had ready.

I nodded, and stayed quiet. After he had gone, I struggled to the door on my own legs and listened, remembering my daughter's goading...

Leo intends to move his family into my house at some later, unspecified date. So now I use my times of solitude to try to walk about, to make my legs a little stronger. With a few weeks of exercise, I find I can walk again, though painfully and slowly. See? My daughter's challenges in my dreams serve a purpose. Perhaps, in her own angry way, she helps me now from her grave. Meanwhile, I am waiting for the day when both Leo and Timon are absent...

The day arrives... late in the afternoon, the slaves

carry me into the garden and place me under the shade of a large fig tree. They bring me grapes and a copy of Pliny the Younger, and I tell them to leave me in peace, knowing how much this will please them. My garden has a back gate, and that afternoon I struggle towards it, having after much searching found the key that I hid many years before, in the days when I used to go out secretly that way to meet other men's wives. I giggle at these memories while I struggle along the path, stick in hand.

I make my way like a snail to the gate. My feeble and shaking hand feels as if it has snapped as the key turns, but this is only the noise of the lock. Are they deaf? My heart hammers, but no one appears. I open the gate, close it carefully behind me, and set off to make my way around to the front of the house and onto the road. It takes me an age to reach this point, and I have to pause for breath again. While I recover, certain memories tempt me to turn right, to go to the brothel, where I always had credit, but after much argument with myself I turn left. Manuel the lawyer's house is closer, and I will have no pleasure at the brothel if I am limp and exhausted by the journey there. Manuel remains the most honest man in the town. In the past, I despised him for this stubbornness. Now, I have need of it. Twice more, I have to stop and rest. I look around, but no one is following.

After what seems an eternity, I gradually approach Manuel's house. Stone lions, in true Lycian fashion, flank the gates. I pause in the shade, a final rest to catch my breath, and lean my head upon the cool stone. When I have recovered, I look up to see a hanging rope, leading up to a bell over the gate. What an ideal welcome.

I reach out to pull it, but a steely grip takes my arm and guides it away, turning me around, to see Timon's twisted face smiling down upon me. He holds my book in his other hand and brings his face closer, speaking with mocking deference while I smell his foul breath.

'Good evening, my former master. I think you must have forgotten this, and quite a few other things, this evening.'

Timon waves the book, and four slaves run up and bundle me into a sedan chair, slipping ropes around my ankles and wrists.

I start to open my mouth, but a rag is stuffed into it, and another tied around my mouth before I can spit it out.

Someone in the lawyer's house watches from a window, though my blurred eyes cannot make out who it is. My hopes rise for an instant, until I realise that I will appear to be just a senile old man gone wandering, being helped by faithful servants. So near, but my opportunity has slipped out of my hands. Will Tyche, my goddess of fortune, grant me another?

* * *

After his attempt to escape, the slaves watch Basil closely. That night, he cowers in the corner of his room, convinced that Leo will have him strangled, but to his surprise his scrawny neck remains intact the next day. Moreover, they still allow him to go out onto the terrace and into the garden, which really astonishes him. Then, he realises that Timon probably fears Leo's rage far too much to tell him what has occurred...

But now he knows that Timon watches his every move, and besides, he does not have another key. His efforts to buy one, by tempting the slaves with promises of riches and freedom, fall on deaf ears. Timon has no doubt prepared them, and they all have the courage of rabbits. He also has no coins left in his room, having spent them all, and nothing else of value. He curses his previous wastefulness and lust. Worse still, the African housekeeper no longer attends to him; she has been moved to another house. She must have told someone what he has said. His situation seems hopeless; Theodora's laughter echoes in his dreams.

Leo moves his family into the house, and things change. Work keeps the servants and slaves much busier; they cannot watch him so much. Leo and his wife avoid him, so that on many occasions he may not leave his room while they occupy the terrace or garden. But they leave the house often enough and they have two children, who occasionally venture into the garden after their tutor has given them their lessons. The boy, a morose looking child, like his father, does not even seem to notice Basil. His sister is the one that gives him hope: a pretty young girl, she looks self-conscious and moves awkwardly. Basil senses that she is just the right age, curious about her budding adulthood and yet still easily influenced. He begins to notice the girl observing him whenever he reads on the terrace.

He carefully waits until she begins to come closer. He makes sure the slaves leave him with sweet dates and apricots, and leaves them out in view. When he sees her watching, he simply smiles and gestures toward the fruit. The first couple of times she shakes her head and blushes, transfixed. Basil shrugs a little, smiles, and then eats one himself, to show that she has no reason to fear. But she slips away each time, and weeks become months.

One day, after he has given up waiting for her, he slips into a doze. He awakes to find her at the table, staring at his face and nibbling a date, her head on one side as she studies him. He pinches himself. It is not a dream.

'Hello,' he says.

She says nothing, but continues to chew and stare at his face.

'I am your great-grandfather.'

A long pause, and then she nods at last.

Encouraged, he goes on, 'My name is Basil.' He thinks carefully. 'This used to be my house, but your father lets me live here now.'

She swallows what she is eating and then speaks with the frankness of youth. 'I know. My father doesn't like you. He thinks you're crazy. He says you talk to the walls.'

Basil slowly nods, smiling and murmuring an acknowledgement.

'I'm Sophia,' she continues. 'I'm not supposed to come near you, but I wanted to see what you look like. You don't look like him at all.'

He thinks carefully again. 'No, I don't. Maybe I did

a bit when I was younger, but not now. I was always thinner than him, too. But I'm not crazy, just old. Do you remember Theodora?' She nods. 'When your grandmother was a little girl, she was very pretty, like you.' He watches her blush with pleasure, and then she looks anxiously at the bowl of fruit. 'Don't worry,' he adds, 'Theodora didn't get fat until she was old. And that was only because she ate ten bowls like this every day, with nuts and honey.'

She giggles, but turns to go.

'Wait,' he begins, wondering how to make her come back without scaring her off. 'I can tell you more about Theodora, anytime.' Her scornful glance tells him this is not enough, as she turns to walk away. Then, it comes to him. 'Or I can tell you a true story about Frankish pirates, and the treasure that my wife Eirene and I hid from the Franks. And where it is still hidden.'

Sophia stops in her tracks and turns to look back, a curious expression on her face. She nods in acknowledgment and announces, 'I have to go now. You can tell me about that later.'

A short speech, but spoken very firmly. To Basil, it has the sound of a decision made. He knows at that moment that eventually he will have her in his power. Given time and opportunity, he feels sure he can persuade her.

A week later she comes back, and after that, every four or five days. She seems to know when she will be called back into the house and anticipates it, making her visits sometimes short, but never interrupted. Her confidence in her own knowledge and ability verges on arrogance. She seems used to her own way and sure of her good looks. She has inherited some of her grandfather Simeon's fair colouring, with brown hair that turns fair under the summer sun; a look that turns heads in a crowd, much sought after. She looks thin but athletic, with graceful legs that have grown too fast for her body.

At first Basil keeps her interest with stories of his younger days, embellished a little to make her laugh, and he makes up others to keep her smiling. At times she wrinkles her nose to show when she feels bored or puzzled, but he keeps the story of the treasure back, for later. 'When I know that I can trust you,' he says, whenever she asks about it.

He finds ways to draw her closer, speaking softly and feigning deafness in one ear. He knows that trust is a fragile plant, watered by affection and gentle touch. He starts by patting her back as she arrives and leaves, and gradually she grows less tense and sits closer. Then he leans towards her and their shoulders touch, when he whispers in her ear, or pats her arm to emphasise a point. He cannot resist unnatural thoughts on some of these occasions, as she draws closer to listen, with such eagerness and anticipation shining in her eyes. He tells himself, my enforced celibacy does me no good at all. Sometimes, he even forgets his place in his story, looking at her in confusion, and has to be reminded what he has just told her. She does not realise why, of course; she merely takes it as a sign of his age and helplessness.

When Sophia begins to sit right up close to him, without any encouragement, he knows their little plant is almost in bloom. The time has come. So that afternoon he tells her how Eirene and he, trapped by the Frankish pirate raid, divided their gold coin and jewels, and hid these two hoards separately. He spares her the worst details of what followed, but tells Sophia the conclusion – that with God's (or the devil's) help they both survived. He tells her how, so relieved to be alive, Eirene took it into her head that they should leave her part of the treasure hidden, so that if some other disaster strikes without warning in future, they will never be destitute. And he tells Sophia that they never needed to dig it up again...

He does not divulge that, for years, Eirene would not tell him where she had hidden her part of their fortune. He does not tell Sophia that he suspected Eirene had secretly given it away. Nor does he tell Sophia of his own growing frustration and rage, when he needed money for the business; of the half-hearted beatings that Eirene endured in silence. Her stubbornness eventually convinced him that her part of the treasure had gone forever, leaving an angry silence between them, broken only by Eirene's deathbed confession.

Sophia considers his story carefully, and then, with disarming directness, asks, 'So what are you going to do about it now, great-grandfather? Leave it there forever?'

He scratches his head and plays dumb. 'I don't know, Sophia. What can I do? I'm alone. No one likes me. They won't let me go out, even if I could walk. I just don't know who to trust.' Then he pretends to notice her, and smiles.

She grins and looks at him with her dark, knowing eyes, wide open and glistening slightly. They look like pools of dark cool water, in the shade from the August sun. He wants to go swimming; but no, he tells himself, not here, not now. Then she whispers, 'You know you can trust me, great-grandfather.'

He savours the moment for a while, strokes her arm and her hair. Her persuasion is also his opportunity. 'You're right. I think I can, Sophia. I will tell you where it is, but not yet. First, you must do something for me. I just want to walk outside in the street, and go down to the sea once more before I die. You must get me a key to my room, and to the garden gate, and then I will tell you.'

She looks at him, long and hard, weighing him up. He can see her thinking that he is, after all, in no state to go digging for treasure myself. A door opens from the house. Timon's voice calls out, and she quickly ducks down out of sight. 'All right,' she whispers, as she slips away. 'I have to go now.'

* * *

For two weeks Timon keeps me a prisoner in my room, while my fretting voices grow louder and louder each day that I am confined. The slaves dangle hope before me, maybe tomorrow, maybe tomorrow; but I fear the silent noose, imagining that Timon has been spying on us both. Has he reported my conversations with young Sophia to his new master? I curse him and spend long days imagining what I would do to him, should I ever regain my power. A tall, thin man, Timon has fleshy lips the colour of dates: I imagine stretching him to make him taller still, before hanging him out in the sun to dry.

I need not have worried. God had simply blessed Sophia's mother with a summer fever, and since she has the habit of monopolising the terrace for her recuperation, and she loves her illnesses, this takes some little time. One afternoon I find myself back in the shade of the plane tree, my heart pounding with anticipation, like a young man awaiting his bride. The glaring August sun dazzles my eyes while the sweat trickles down my back even in the shade. The slaves do not offer to fan me, and disappear inside. I mutter a little but feel secretly glad, as I want no witnesses.

Minutes stretch into hours. Just as the last of my hope evaporates, Sophia appears beside me, smiling. 'How are you, great-grandfather?'

I put on an appearance of doziness, as if I have just awoken. 'Oh, I am well. Enjoying the air.'

She sits down next to me. I embrace her, and offer her fruit, which she refuses with a smile. I let her chatter, waiting until she raises the subject, which I know she will. Perhaps she feels too anxious, for she tries to seem casual, taking a long time to get to the point. And she seems openly flirtatious, which makes me realise that this young girl is practising her skills at getting what she wants. When I begin to stroke her back she purrs like a cat, pushing back and half-closing her eyes. Is that innocence, or not, I think? I have to tell myself to be patient, and stop thinking about her in that way.

'Have you decided whether to tell me yet?' she asks.

I look at her and smile but I say nothing, as if considering, so that she feels a need to say more. I want to hear what she has to offer.

She blurts out, 'I have the keys here.' She fishes into her tunic and brings out a small bundle wrapped in cloth. She looks at once both anxious and triumphant, clutching my prize in both hands.

I want to kiss her, and I let myself do so, to show my pleasure. 'Of course I will tell you, Sophia. I will tell you now in words, and later I will also draw you a map to ensure that you will not forget.' But I cannot bring myself to violate Eirene's spirit; so I tell Sophia exactly where, long ago, I hid my part of our hoard. Besides, I might yet need Eirene's part myself, for the lawyer. She listens carefully, repeating every word I say, so that she will remember. I have to hide my smile, as I imagine her searching. At least when she does find that place, she will find the box that I left emptied there, after retrieving it. Hopefully, she will believe that I have spoken the truth, but that someone else has got there first. In my own mind, I do not really feel that I am cheating her. If I do regain my fortune I will certainly repay her tenfold, compared to what Eirene left for Tyche.

Just as I finish my story, and lean back to observe her, I hear a door open from the house. My heart sinks. Even with my poor eyesight, I can tell that it is Leo. He is looking in our direction. Fortunately for me, I am now leaning back and not touching her. I feel a flood of relief, but Leo still looks like thunder as he strides towards us.

Sophia jumps up, alarm etched on her brow, and immediately begins to walk away. She still has the keys, and in my mind I begin to curse her for the clever little whore that she seems to be, at that moment. Then I see her put her arms behind her back, and unseen by Leo, she throws the cloth bundle back toward me. It lands on the ground, in plain view, two paces from my feet.

My freedom lies so near, yet so far away. I watch as Leo stops, waiting for his daughter to go to him. He hisses a long, withering condemnation into her ears and then gestures for her to go into the house. I try to take advantage by twice dragging at the little bundle with my stick, to bring it closer, but each time I miss. Now, she leaves. I miss again. He will deal with her later, I suppose.

Leo strides over towards me and stands ten paces away with his arms on his hips, looking down at me. For once, I am glad that I revolt him so much that he does not come closer.

I try hard not to look down at the ground while he speaks.

'You are not to speak to my daughter, or you will

never see the light of day again. Do you understand me, old man?'

I nod. I am thinking desperately how to distract him, but my brain swims in glue. His eyes drop, and he looks curiously at the small patch of cloth. My heart sinks into my feet.

My brain whispers to me – it seems a poor plan, but I struggle to my feet, as if in mortal fear, and cry out, 'Don't kill me, please. Have mercy.'

He looks at my face, clearly amused at my fear, and laughs at me. Then he spits, to show his contempt. 'Just stay away from – from both my children.'

Distracted by the thought of his son, he wheels away and snaps his fingers for the slaves behind him to gather me up and return me to my prison. My bones are old and brittle, but I have no time to lose. I step forward, and sink to the floor as if in supplication, and the breath is knocked out of me. He turns around and laughs at me again. But under my gasping chest, my clawing fingers grasp the precious bundle. I am down on my knees, winded, with my face in the dirt, cowed before him at his feet. He has no idea that I have beaten him.

In my room that night, I wait until silence descends in the darkest hour of night, when even the slaves must sleep. I recognise the garden gate key, since I knew it well. The other one must be for my room. I rub this key with some olive oil kept back from my supper, slip it into the lock, and turn it.

It sticks. No matter how I try, it will not work. Ah, little Sophia. How I curse you this night, and the next, though it does occur to me that at least one person in this nest of vipers has inherited my wits.

* * *

Only when the cool of autumn arrives, does Leo allow the old man freedom to cross the threshold of his room again to bathe or take the air. Another season gone, when Basil knows he has precious few left to spend. He guesses that Leo is demonstrating what life will be like if he disobeys him again. When at last Basil is allowed outside, he sees no sign of Sophia for three weeks. He begins to worry that she has already dug up the empty box, and now avoids him.

Yet once again she appears as if by magic, just as he has given up hope. Or rather, her voice appears. One day as he sits on the terrace he hears her whispering his name. He turns, looking around to try to find the source of her voice. He sees her beckoning from one corner of the garden, from a space in the middle of several oleander bushes. She points at the ground there. A good area of shade falls there in the afternoon, and the place cannot be seen from the entrances to the house. He understands, and nods. She disappears.

Thereafter, he asks the slaves to take him there in his chair whenever he goes outside. A week later, she slips out from behind one of the bushes, skips over to his side, embraces him, and sits at his feet. Her eyes sparkle as she smiles at him.

'Have you found the treasure?'

She shakes her head and smiles again. 'No Great-Grandfather, not yet; I'm keeping that for later. Besides, it would be too difficult to do on my own. No, I'm happy because...' she looks around us conspiratorially '...a boy sent me a love poem.'

She goes on to tell Basil his name, about his family, and all manner of facts that he knows will not impress Leo at all. In fact she babbles so incessantly that he struggles to find a pause to speak to her. There is nothing so irritating as a young girl's infatuation, except perhaps that of a boy... he struggles to keep his temper. But he has to silence her somehow, as he fears her prattle will be overheard before he can correct her mistake, if that is what it was. She seems blithely and completely unaware that he might be dissatisfied.

He speaks to her a little sharply, in the end, but keeps his temper. 'Listen to me, please, Sophia. You gave me the wrong key. This is not for my room.'

She looks surprised and takes the useless article from him, inspecting it closely and biting her lip. 'Sorry. I thought this was it, really.'

He sighs. Her manner convinces him. 'I believe you,

Sophia. But I need the right one. And be careful. Your father must not know.'

She looks at him as if he is very stupid. 'I know that.' Then she looks around, as if sensing danger, and gets up, as if to punish him by leaving. Has he offended her? He starts to ask her to stay longer, but she has already gone.

He need not have worried. Events are conspiring to drive her in his direction. One week later she appears again, this time looking sad and sulky. 'My father found out about the poem. He's banned me from seeing him.' She sniffles and sobs as she tells him this, a curious mixture of helplessness and rage against parental authority.

He pats her back, and then rubs it, as she likes him to do. She sits on the arm of his chair and rocks a little while he does this. He lets her anger boil for a little while, then waits until it cools enough for him to ask about the key.

Her eyes narrow and she grits her teeth, making him feel anxious, but it seems she is just enjoying her moment of triumph over her father. She slowly reaches inside her gown and brings out a key, clutching it in her fist as she looks at him, grinning with success.

In his joy he embraces her, and she puts her arm around his shoulder. He tells her she is a great joy to him. She hugs him back, saying with some venom that he (her father) never cuddles her anymore, not for years. She clings to the old man for a long time. They both drift into that place of great contentment, which comes upon a man or a woman (or indeed even a young girl) when they forget themselves in the comfort of another.

Sadly, this moment must end. Basil has a curious sense of wondering how he has got to this place, as he realises that his face is now pressed into her scented little breasts, and gently pulls back from this little heaven. And he swears to himself that he has no idea how his hand has come to be under her robe, or what it has been doing there. Just as, in fact, he has no idea how Leo has managed to creep up on them so silently.

End Of Empire

After a long pause the silence is broken by a horrifying sound. It is not so much the crack of the blow as Leo strikes his daughter, or her cry of fear and pain, that horrifies him – it is the noise of metal on stone as that precious key bounces across the path, watched by Leo's cold and unforgiving eyes.

*　　*　　*

Purgatory

When Leo discovers Basil embracing his daughter, his shock and fury almost overwhelm him. Had he had a weapon in his hands, he would certainly have killed the old man on the spot. Fortunately, his concern for his daughter allows him to defer this pleasure. And his curiosity has been aroused by the key that fell to the floor. He determines to find out exactly what has been going on. Such is his daughter's fear of retribution, and perhaps guilt too, that she does not need much persuasion...

By now his anger has cooled, replaced by a desire to make the old man suffer, slowly. He decides to let the old man spend a sleepless night waiting to be killed, first.

The next morning, he summons Timon and gives him instructions. Then he follows Timon to Basil's room and watches from the door.

While other servants remove the furniture and carpets, Timon ties Basil's hands together carefully. He fixes a hook into a beam across the ceiling; neither man speaks. Timon then helps him to stand, feeds the rope through the hook, and pulls until the old man is suspended from the ceiling, as if he were reaching upward, in such a way that he can only just support his weight on the front of his feet. After less than an hour Basil's old, wasted legs lose what puny strength they have. Now, he can either suffer agonising cramp in his legs or take the weight on his wrists, which soon become equally painful.

Every hour or so, Leo returns to watch. Once he is sure that Basil is merely suffering, and not yet dying, Leo orders Timon to use the whip – not too hard, not enough to break the skin, but a lash here on his back, and another there on the soles of his feet. Leo enjoys this entertainment – and he makes Sophia watch too, as a lesson to her. She sighs and pretends to be bored, though Leo can see her silently gritting her teeth.

Every time they whip him, Basil screams and loses all his breath, and it takes him longer and longer to get it back. He loses control of his bladder and bowels, so that Timon has to send the slave girl to wash him down. For the body of an old man, this spectacle becomes a slow crucifixion, exactly as Leo had hoped.

Now, Sophia begins to cry; he sends her away. Even Leo is beginning to have second thoughts. Servants will gossip, after all. And of course Sophia tells her mother, who comes to confront Leo...

'For God's sake, husband, stop this before the old man dies, so you do not taint your own soul. Yes, the old man is wicked, but leave his punishment to God. This whole business is appalling, especially his screaming and wailing, and the smell, not to mention Sophia's distress. Why don't you just lock him in that storeroom in the cellar? After all, out of sight, out of mind...'

*   *   *

Two days later a barefoot girl opens the cellar door, holding up an oil lamp to inspect the figure lying in the bed. She carries a bowl of water, which she sets upon the table. She hears a feeble groan as she sets the lamp upon the ledge above the bed. She asks, 'Water?'

The noise suggests assent, so she lifts his head and places the cup to his lips. He sips noisily, part of it spilling out of his mouth, until the cup is empty. Then she carefully bathes his wounds. His eyes slowly begin to follow her actions. Every so often, she hears a noise, a muted animal sound, and she glances at his face. She sees his mouth open and shut, open and shut, wordlessly. 'Hush,' she tells him, 'don't talk now. Save your strength. I'll bring you some broth later.'

In Basil's mind, he is telling her a story, and she is listening. The beating has unchained the voice in his mind, the one part of him that can be free; he will hold on to an image of this girl for company, as his listener...

*   *   *

While I hung there, drifting in and out of my body, the life slowly dribbling out of my mouth and my arse, Leo came in to study me. I began to recognise his true form – a short, dark, stocky body with dark hair and bushy eyebrows, muscular like my brother, but much smaller – as an enormous crow. I could tell that he was waiting hungrily for me to die, waiting to feast upon my eyes, as crows do. I tried desperately to stay awake, to keep looking at him, to save my eyes. I remember him talking to me at some point, telling me I deserved this punishment for the lives I had spoiled by my selfishness and greed. I tried to force myself to listen, but everything went black. The next thing I felt was a bucket of cold water thrown over me, followed by the sound of Leo's reluctant voice, 'Cut him down.'

My fragile bones are now riddled with hidden cracks. My flesh withers, and my twisted wrists will certainly never turn a key again. Maybe I should have been less strict with Leo when he was a boy, and he might have treated me less harshly. I suspect it was not my beatings – after all, that is common for wilful children – but the way I took his playmate Helena from him, that gave him all this hatred for me.

From this pretty little seed, Helena, all of Leo's bile sprouted. Leo spent much of his childhood playing and learning alongside her, before and after the death of his father, Simeon of Kadianda. Simeon had known Helena's family well – her father, a childhood friend of his, later became the governor of Makri. Because Leo and Helena both had the same tutor, they took many of their lessons together; in play they were inseparable. Theodora and Simeon had hopes of a very profitable match between them, since a governor's relatives pay no taxes.

But this hope died at the same time as Simeon. I remember visiting my daughter a week after Simeon's funeral; the house felt like a shroud. And yet, even in the midst of their own grief, I found Theodora and Leo talking earnestly to a sobbing Helena. They noticed me and stopped talking, while tears continued to trickle down the girl's face. My daughter stood up and walked over to me, her eyes brimming, gesturing for me to follow her into the next room. I did so.

'What is it?' I asked. 'Has someone else died?'

Theodora swallowed and bit her lip. 'It's almost as bad. Helena's father, he's lost everything; he took the wrong side.'

'What do you mean?'

'The new Emperor, Basil, the succession; he declared his allegiance too early. It's calamitous – everything they own has been confiscated. They have nothing left now. What are they to do?'

Luckily for her family, Theodora had become fond of the girl. She allowed her to continue to sit in Leo's lessons – as a favour to the family, and to Leo. This charity continued for several years, even after Theodora and I brought our families together. I watched Leo and Helena play and grow together, and I watched Theodora send money and food to Helena's family. Although marriage to Leo was now out of the question, Helena's life was now entwined with ours, and I had begun to consider whether we could employ her in some way. One day her eyes caught mine as she leaned over, setting a table with plates. She smiled and then blushed, and I felt my body stir. I looked again. She had blossomed into a young woman, with a ready smile, long dark hair, and the most wonderfully pointed breasts.

I was approaching my sixty-fifth year; Eirene had become a distant memory, and I had given up chasing other men's wives. I did not wish to marry again – but I wanted a concubine, one who would not be any trouble for me. Helena seemed the perfect age, and in looks she reminded me of my first wife. Her family's loss, I realised, was also my unexpected good fortune.

By now, her father owed a lot of money. If you must choose a wolf, they say, choose a tame wolf. I quietly encouraged the others to call in their debts. Then I went to her parents and bought Helena from them. Of course, we did not call it that. Such ancient and common remedies must be dressed in finer clothes. I cleared all their debts, and set Helena up in a house nearby. Her parents accepted my help with relief. No doubt they hoped that I might become so fond of Helena that I would marry her, eventually.

Despite all her youth and beauty, her education and her wits, that temptation rarely crossed my mind. She would read my books to me – whatever I chose. She could act, and speak as a poet, a philosopher, a general, or even a fishwife in a comic play. She learned how to massage my old body well enough, and how to satisfy my bodily needs too. Yes, she became good at that. But I suppose Helena always knew too well that her parents depended upon my help. So she deferred too much, and seemed terrified that she might offend me. She kept any spirit of her own hidden from me, and whatever is withheld cannot be savoured. If she had shown me some of her spirit, argued, fought a little – for I know she had brains, and could use them – I might not have lost interest. But I did not want a doormat; that can be bought at the brothel, in different shapes and sizes. Her passivity felt to me like another empty soul and that brought out the worst in me. Even when I mistreated her, she never objected or complained.

After six years I grew so bored with her that I passed her on to another merchant as part of a trade. After me, Helena took the role of concubine to two other men, and so acquired two more houses with which to support her family. So, perhaps Helena did use her brains after all, by creating boredom for me. Ultimately, she set up her own high-class house of pleasure. Because of her education and good taste, she has done well.

But I still remember the expression on young Leo's face when his mother told him my plans; horror at first, then as he left the room, a look black as thunder. She had been his companion for years. After this event, Leo began to avoid me. Perhaps the poor boy had clung on to the idea that she would be his. If so, he must have been consumed with jealousy. I suppose, deep down, I knew this. But my arrangement had become necessary for everyone.

Well, Leo could certainly have Helena now, today, anytime, if he wishes it. Indeed he must have had her at some time, since most of Makri has had that pleasure. But that does not help him to forget or to forgive. I fear that this loss of this youthful playmate hardened his heart. To me, Leo will always remain a sour faced and sulky boy. But I wonder, has someone also told him what led to his father's murder?

* * *

Since Leo had me whipped, I have started to dream of his father, Simeon of Kadianda. In the first dream, my daughter Theodora accompanied Simeon. They came together as man and wife to speak to me about Leo, as if he were still a boy. They came as visitors to my house, into my great library, as they would have done, years ago.

And yet, in my dream I also understood that Leo had become a man – and they talked as if they knew this too. Simeon began, 'We have come to ask a favour of you, as parents...' My daughter interjected, '...and as your daughter.'

They paused and smiled. Somehow, I knew they had come back from the spirit world. They looked none the worse for it, however.

Simeon continued, 'For the sake of young Sophia, as well as ourselves, we need you to forgive Leo for what he has done to you.'

I considered their request. It surprised me; I had expected Simeon to ask for his share of our worldly wealth to be returned to him. Then it occurred to me – that would not be of much use to him now.

Theodora added, 'Your forgiveness will help Leo join us in our world, when his time comes.'

Clearly, they knew everything that had happened recently. In this dream, somehow Leo existed as both boy and man, but I existed only as an old man. So whatever I said, it would make no difference to me, now. I cleared my throat and told them, 'I might well have done the same to Leo, had the tables been turned. At least he let me live, so I bear him no malice now. Is that forgiveness?'

This statement seemed to satisfy them. They left, and I found myself remembering the events that led to Simeon's death.

* * *

I had seen fifty-five summers come and go, but many women still found me, or my power and money, attractive. My grief at the loss of my wife Eirene had passed: mentally, if not physically, I felt at the peak of my strength. Lean and muscular, with a thick head of hair turning silver, my confidence was tempered with experience. Simeon and I had, with much endeavour, become the two most powerful merchants in Lycia. United by Simeon's marriage to Theodora, my former rival worked with me to keep costs low and prices high.

My ships plied the sea routes. I knew them well, and had many ships with good captains. Pirate fleets, from Norman Sicily and other Latin kingdoms of the Franks, posed the danger. But I had an invaluable contact with Godfray of Kos, the Frank with whom I traded goods and information; we warned each other of impending raids by the other side. I had earned enough wealth to buy vast tracts of land. By joining the governor's council, I also paid minimal taxes.

Simeon preferred to trade overland, with the Turks in the east of Anatolia. They took their share of his profit, but the overland routes had less risk. Most Turks, nomadic farmers, only posed a danger if foolish travellers ate one of their animals; it was far better to go hungry. Occasionally a small band of warriors might threaten, but an armed escort would usually frighten them off. The Tartar hordes were keeping most of the Turkish army far too busy on their eastern frontier.

Simeon and I had a rival, however. Nicetas had the energy of youth and he often travelled overland himself to find new business, especially for silk, incense and spices. As the silk roads now crossed a war zone, these were in short supply. Simeon and I had more wealth, but Nicetas' slowly gained influence and strength, since he would undercut our prices whenever he could. But his travels left his wife Mary alone (and no doubt bored) and I had heard Nicetas boast about her prettiness. So I aimed to take full advantage: during this period in my life, other men's wives had become my trophies.

Normally I regarded these encounters as a playful game of chance: outcome uncertain, but fun to try. In Mary's case, the smouldering rivalry with my upstart rival had flared my desire into a perverse compulsion. I had to bed this woman. I waited until Nicetas left the area and called at his house, pretending to look for him on a matter of business...

Nicetas's wife was small, but rounded and voluptuous; not beautiful, but ripe and blooming. As she approached the door, a servant whispered in her ear. She seemed a little flustered and I supposed that she rarely had the company of other men.

'He isn't here?' My voice expressed surprise and disappointment. She knew who I was, but I had dressed casually, and had no escort. I wore practical, working shoes, a plain tunic, and my thick silver hair was, if anything, a little unkempt. I paused for a few moments, as if uncertain. 'Perhaps, if you don't mind, that is, can you pass some ideas on to your husband?'

A look of surprise crossed her face. She hesitated a moment, and then nodded. Her eyes studied my face, searching for my intentions.

I smiled, looking down for a moment as if in reflection, and then met her gaze again. 'I am glad to hear it. When my wife was alive, I often discussed my business with her, and sought her advice.' There was some truth in that, but I also knew how to flatter a woman: by comparing her to what must be most favoured.

Mary nodded, and half a smile now played upon her lips. I waited, patiently, and glanced along the street. She hesitated for another moment, but then opened her door wide, offering him the customary hospitality – water, bread and fruit. I nodded my acceptance, noticing how the upper part of her cheeks turned slightly pink. I was beginning to sense her attractions.

I pretended to take Mary into my confidence, suggesting ways that Nicetas and I could work as partners, not rivals. While I spoke, she listened carefully, and her eyes seemed to study my hands, occasionally glancing up to catch my expression.

When I had finished talking, she smiled warmly, with her head inclined to one side. 'I'm sure my husband will be delighted to hear of your offers. But I must warn you he is by nature very independent. So I really can't predict what he will do. I hope you won't find that too disappointing, but I hope you prefer me to be honest with you. Is that so?'

Her expression conveyed the combination of hope and puzzlement so perfectly that I laughed out loud. I had not expected to call on such a skilled diplomat.

Once the ice had been broken in this way, we both spoke openly and with growing humour about the other notables of Makri. She knew how to laugh, too.

Time slipped by, in her company. She made no move to end the conversation until at least two hours have passed. It seemed innocent enough, but I knew the company of anyone but her husband must be a rare treat for her. And I assumed that men, including Nicetas, rarely made her feel valued as an equal. Later, I was less sure about that – in that household, perhaps she was the driving force. But she seemed to see his visit as a sign that she and her husband stood on the threshold, ready to join the elite of Makri.

A few days later, I invited her to my warehouse to show her some of my rarest silk cloth and rugs. I asked for her opinions and encouraged her to speak freely and once again we enjoyed a long conversation. I behaved very correctly, before suggesting that she might like to come to view some of the mosaics in my house. I knew she must have heard of them.

She looked hesitantly at the floor. 'I'm sure it would be interesting. But perhaps it would not be wise. You know what gossip is, what lack of respect there is for a woman alone. Please do not be offended; I would love to see them. But I think I must refuse, and wait upon my husband's return.'

I sensed that she felt in two minds. 'I promise that you already have great respect from me. My invitation reflects a matter of simple friendship, to show you the best artwork in this district. You and your husband are more respected than you think in this town. Only the callow and ignorant would think such slander. Don't allow stupid people to cause a problem.'

She glanced up into my eyes for a long moment, and then averted her eyes. A faint smile seemed to play upon her lips. Then, she nodded her assent.

*   *   *

One side of my dining room opens onto a balcony, above a terrace that looks out towards the sea and the mountains across the bay. Opposite the balcony on the long, decorated wall, male and female dancers perform in fine, flowing robes, stretching gracefully up to the heavens or leaping in mid-air, with a background of gold representing the heavenly sky. To one side of the dancers, smiling musicians admire the dance while they play a variety of instruments. On the other side, conjurers and snake charmers wait and practise, and one man breathes a long stream of fire into the air towards the dancers. Overlooking the dining table, two royal feasts adorn the side walls, for which all these dancers seem to perform, defining a carefree mood.

On one side, Solomon and a beautiful, slender, coal black Sheba lie facing each other upon two silken, jewelled couches, set upon a raised dais. Splayed limbs stretch languidly out toward each other, fingers play along the edges of robes, and their eyes seem locked together. It does not look as if their minds are on the food being set before them.

On the other wall, Cleopatra and Julius captivate each other in the middle of their feast. Surrounded by partly eaten delicacies and meats, both are laughing in a moment of playful union as she leans over him, about to feed him with a date – while he dangles a fig out towards her, his arm bent as if teasing her with the offer. Their eyes have a peculiar quality, somehow gazing upon each other but also looking out of the wall at the people who view them.

When you eat in this room, you seem to be caught in a timeless scene, feasting with the gods. When the sun sinks outside the balcony and plays upon the walls, the whole room glows with fire and gold, and the dancers come alive.

I knew that something about great art, like poetry, could melt a woman's heart. Or if not her heart, her morals. Those lifelike scenes, emblazoned upon my wall in bright colours against a background of gold, reflected in the soft light of the lamps, overwhelmed any person who had never seen a great mosaic before. I was not surprised to find that even Mary, of all people, became speechless, moving around the room, exclaiming repeatedly, 'Oh ...oh my...oh, my word.' She could not sit down, wanting to view them from every angle.

Those eyes – Solomon and Sheba, and Julius and Cleopatra – continued to look down on Mary as she ate and drank good, strong wine to celebrate our new friendship. Later, after we had eaten, she told me that she had never seen anything to compare. I was beginning to feel intrigued, and a little aroused, by her ability to show her pleasure so openly.

'There are more, if you would like to view them.'

'More?'

'Yes. And equally good...'

'They amaze me. They make me feel young again, as when you see things for the first time. I haven't felt like that for years. I would love to see more.' She looked down at the floor, as she revealed to me her longing for moments without worldly responsibilities. I knew she was already mine, at that moment.

I chuckled with approval. 'That's marvellous, that they stir such pleasure within you. It can be so wonderful to feel like a child sometimes, can't it? A rare and special pleasure.'

Mary smiled and nodded her assent. A long look passed between us.

I led her to see the other rooms. She danced from one foot to the other, running on ahead in her eagerness. I followed, enjoying her display, feeling my anticipation grow. The last, and greatest, mosaic adorns my bedroom walls. At first Mary did not realise where she has ventured; but once arrived, her eyes could not tear themselves away, while her hands begin to touch and stroke her own hair. I knew the bedroom mosaic would fill a stone with passion. It had never yet failed to put a woman into the right mood. I often wondered, did Menas intend this or was he simply caught up and absorbed by his own fervour?

Mary took a step backwards. Her hair brushed my face and our arms bumped as she turned to murmur an apology, breathing rapidly. I could feel my own arousal stiffening, as I caught her wrist. She hesitated, but did not resist. With one hand I pulled her slowly and deliberately towards me; with the other I stroked her wrist and told her, 'Just let yourself be young again.' Then I kissed her lips. She did not move away, and began to kiss me back.

I whispered, touching her breast, 'This will become part of our own sweet bargain, don't you think? I am yours. So you might as well allow yourself a little pleasure, a little girlish wickedness, and enjoy me.' I lifted her robe, slipping my hand inside. She inhaled deeply and bit her lip, but her own hand moved down to explore my body in response. I added, 'I hope you enjoy a man who drives a hard bargain, for this bargain is already very hard...'

She breathed out quiet laughter as her hand sought confirmation of my boast and closed gently around me, while her other arm draped itself around my back. Then she lifted her mouth and slowly licked my ear, before breathing into it, 'Every girl has a soft, soft spot for a bargain like this...' Thus invited, I found it; she gasped quietly, and murmured approval...

Mary did indeed enjoy our sweet bargain; soon she was crying out to the heavens. Afterwards, she had a mild attack of guilt, turning to ask the wall, 'Oh God, what have I done?'

I patted her rump. 'God does not reside in my wall. If He did, however, He would tell you that He just observed you rediscovering a great pleasure, and that He knows your husband is no saint either, on his travels.'

She turned and smiles before adopting a sweet and innocent expression, 'You terrible, terrible man.'

Thereafter when we met, her enjoyment increased further – though I was too blind, too preoccupied with my business, to truly notice and to consider what this might mean. I broke the news to her that I would not see her again, shortly before her husband was due to return.

Mary looked puzzled, then began to cry, silently,

and turned her face away. This, I did not expect. How could I put an end to this? Instead of comforting her, or making excuses, I allowed my cruelty to take the reins.

'We've played our little game,' I told her. 'It's over. You know, I never had any intention of doing business with you, or your husband.' I behaved to her as if she was my rival, and not Nicetas.

I understand now that for Mary, to be used was one thing. To be treated like a fool, and tossed away, was quite another. She got to her feet, wiped away her tears, and turned upon me. Her eyes narrowed, and then blazed with anger. 'I knew that. That was not important to me. But is that all I was to you – a little game?' She stared back at me, her eyes blazing. 'In that case, you should be careful whom you play with.' Then, she stalked out, without a backward glance.

I had created an enemy by misusing my own good fortune. I did not think that Mary would tell her husband about the affair, but she did. And of course, she told Nicetas that I had forced her; that having been enticed to visit my home she had submitted, unwillingly, helpless to resist me in my own house. Soon after Nicetas had returned, one of my local men quietly warned me that Nicetas had sworn to kill me. A little horseplay had now become a deadly war...

For the next two years I kept my bodyguards close and my plans secret, but a life lived in a fog of fear wore me down. I realised this game had only two endings. In business, Nicetas took every opportunity to undercut me. I feigned indifference, but waited patiently for my opportunity. It came when Nicetas tried to do a secret deal with Simeon, hoping to force a wedge between us.

Simeon kept no secrets from me. One evening he called by, to explain. 'Look, Basil, Nicetas plans to bring a large cargo of incense and spices overland, in which I have a half share. He didn't want you to know – but I don't want to make an enemy of you, so I am offering to let you have half of my interest. There will be plenty of profit for both of us.'

I nodded, and asked about the costs. Then, I

pretended to ask about the risks. 'Which route is he using? Is it safe?'

To my surprise, Nicetas had told Simeon his exact route through the mountains – perhaps Simeon demanded to know it, or he gave Nicetas advice.

We shared some wine while I pretended to think it over. Then, I declined the offer. 'I have enough cargo of my own on its way. Besides, I trust the sea, and he made the offer to you, not to me.' I feigned polite indifference; Simeon seemed ignorant of the feud.

The next day I sent my greetings to Godfray of Kos on his pirate-infested island, only two days sail away. Within my sealed message for Godfray was information about the cargo, its probable route, and its owner.

The Franks took three shiploads of men, landed in a quiet bay, and journeyed into the mountain passes. There they waited for the caravan, and fell upon it at dusk. Normally, the Franks took captives for ransom; especially leaders, captains, and well-dressed men. So it was no surprise when the Franks lined their captives up, asked for names, and asked who could pay a ransom. Nicetas told them his name, insisting he could pay, repeating his name. A tall, red-haired Frank stepped up behind him and split his head apart, with an axe. The other captives were taken away to be sold as slaves. But a few men had escaped into the shadows, and later reported what they had seen and heard.

I had realised that Mary's suspicions might fall on Simeon. I warned Simeon to take care. But later, I realised that Simeon seemed too preoccupied with his own losses to listen to my warning. Perhaps on that fateful night, Simeon visited Mary to pass on his sympathy – that would have been typical of his directness. He certainly went alone. If so, his visit must have felt like salt in a wound, and became Mary's chance for revenge. Simeon's body was found in the street the next morning, his throat cut.

It hurt me to see my daughter grieve so badly. It was generally assumed that Simeon, in his expensive clothes, had fallen victim to a simple street robbery. But when I discovered that Mary and her children had left in a hurry, supposedly for Nicaea, the day after Simeon's death, the pattern of events fell into place. I sent two of my Cumans in an attempt to find Mary and strangle her, but she had covered her tracks well. Good riddance. Out of all this trouble emerged more unexpected good fortune. A few months later, I quietly bought most of that cargo from Godfray at a very good price. Not only had I got rid of an enemy, I now had a complete monopoly on the local trade – which I would use in the years that followed to grow more of the great wealth that Leo now enjoys...

*   *   *

My dreams swell with the dead so often now that it seems as if these ghosts constantly arrive and depart whenever I move in and out of sleep. It troubles me. They say that when you constantly dream of the dead, this signifies your own approaching death. At the moment, I cannot rid myself of an older Simeon. He constantly comes to sit by my bed and watches me, not saying a word. He dresses in silk, as he always did, and smells of incense. He comes so regularly that it has become strange when I wake up to find him gone. I would not mind, but this Simeon looks just like his corpse when they found him in the street.

I know I should never have let Mary down so harshly. Had I wisdom, I would have continued to see her, to keep her sweet, and quiet. I should have enjoyed Mary occasionally and kept watch on Nicetas through her eyes. But I refused Tyche's gift and my foolish, misdirected cruelty turned the milk and honey of her passion sour, bitter, and poisonous.

I cannot abide this silence from Simeon. I would rather that he berate me and blame me for what happened, and not just sit there without speaking. When I tell him this, he just points at his throat, showing me where the source of his voice has been neatly sliced in two. Perhaps he is trying to give me a warning; after all, I did try to warn him. His silent vigil is most eloquent.

*   *   *

203

Tyche's Cave

The girl moves silently into the corridor, cradling a wooden bowl and spoon against her chest with one hand, balancing an oil lamp in the other. On her left, bright shafts of sunlight penetrate stone arches and embroidered curtains, warming her calves, but she turns her head, her eyes avoiding the glare. As she steps from the cool of white marble onto silk rugs, they seem to caress the soles of her feet. Her eyes are drawn to the mosaic that covers the walled side of the corridor, her focus flickering along the design as she moves, looking for the birds amidst the leafy branches.

In the centre of this design a heavy drape hangs, masking an entrance to the underworld. She pauses there and inhales deeply, trying to fix the comforting aromas of incense and perfume, the smells of the main house, within her lungs. Then she pirouettes, pushing the drape to one side with her hip, and slips through the aperture behind it, her slight body brushing against the cool stone within. As the drape falls back into place, the world of light and luxury vanishes.

She raises the lamp, peering forward and down into the gloom, sniffing at the stale, damp, musty air. Stone steps, roughly hewn, descend into the rock under the house. She sighs, grits her teeth, and feels her way carefully down, reluctantly pursuing a small void of increasing darkness. Where the steps end, the narrow corridor divides – a sharply cut, narrow passage curves to the left and a rougher, wider corridor opens off to the right. She turns left; a dozen steps later, a wooden door flickers into view. A few steps more, and her lamplight glints on metal hinges, outlining a spider's careful tapestry above her head. She pauses here – a whiff of human decay and despair seems to slither out from under the rough wooden door, assaulting her throat. Her bare feet sense the coldness of the rock; her toes curl.

She shivers, sets the bowl of cold soup down and reaches to grasp the iron bolt – then frowns when she sees it is already released. Her heart stops. Did she forget, this morning? She closes her eyes and prays to God that no one has been down here, so that she may escape a beating. She sucks in another deep breath, and pushes the door open. A rancid stench, not quite solid, rolls over her. It causes her to flinch, increasing the violence of her urge to step away, to flee to the light above.

Against the far wall, covered by a single rough woollen blanket, a shapeless figure lies prone on a small cot. The old man's body lies still and silent, but he is clearly awake. Two eyes glitter as she approaches and then, as recognition dawns, they regard her with curiosity. He speaks softly, his voice a little slurred, devoid of his usual precision. 'Ah, so you come now... my little treasure. Has Timon sent you... to be my last request?'

The girl shakes her head at his nonsense. She feels far too exhausted for this today and sighs as she places the lamp on the ledge above the cot. *At least he seems here in this world today*, she thinks. 'I've brought your food...'

She stops, puzzled, noticing a jug and bowl upon the floor in the corner. She shrugs, sets down her bowl and pulls back the blanket; now she sees that the old man's hands are bound together, the same rope looped around his waist to immobilise him. She drops the blanket, wringing one hand with the other, biting her lip. *Has he tried to escape again, and been caught? If so, I will surely be whipped again.* Her face remains a mask, but her shoulders contract, and she whimpers.

Amidst his matted, patchy hair and whiskers, his eyes watch her, studying her reaction. He nods slowly, and then speaks again. 'Don't worry. Timon brought the wine here for me. You'll not be punished... at least, not for this...'

She nods and breathes a deep sigh of relief, only to cough the foul air out. Can she believe him? *This is just how he used to sound, before they put him in the cellar. But now, he cannot promise me anything. Can he?* She steps forward to examine his face at close quarters, searching for signs of deceit. Eventually, she shrugs and pulls his light, bony body upright, balancing him against the wall. He smiles again and when he speaks, she hears a tone of authority mixed with resignation.

'Let me explain, my little treasure. You know what I am now: an old, helpless husk. But once I was Basil of Makri, a Roman, a merchant who traded with wealth beyond the dreams of most men – and also with lives and souls, even of those whom I loved. I survived fire, war, storms and pirates. At least, once I was such a man... now, through lack of foresight, I find myself a prisoner here in my own home. I trusted my family too much – and they have repaid me by shutting me away. Is this not true?' His eyes fix upon the jug, and his voice urges her. 'More wine... I must have more...'

She does as he bids, though her mind is still racing. *No one has dared bring him wine since they locked him down here, in this miserable storeroom – so why should Timon, now, of all people?* She pours the wine from the jug into the bowl. It smells rich, not even watered.

He snorts with amusement as he watches her face. 'Ha! You do well to sniff it, my little treasure, before you taste. It is good wine, granted. But the potion within it is not for you, unless you wish to sleep like the dead. Timon tells me it is a sleeping draught.' He grimaces. 'I have no reason to disbelieve him. But he hasn't given me enough – the fool tied my hands first, and only then realised he would have to feed the wine to me. And you know how little patience he has. Come, let me sup.'

She hesitates for a moment, then lifts the bowl to his lips. Basil slurps and sucks, naked greed on his face, wine spilling out around his chin. She waits until he finishes, lowers the bowl, and wipes his chin with the blanket. He tips his head back, licks his lips, and rolls his tongue around his mouth, searching for the last remnants of the wine, before gulping some air. While he struggles to catch his breath again, she studies him, searching for some further clue. She watches him half-close his eyes and emit three deep, shuddering sighs.

'Listen to me.' His voice comes in short gasps, breathing and talking to the girl at the same time. 'Timon will return soon, to finish me off. This... this is his way.

The wine is a kindness, a blessing. It makes it easier... for both of us. He'll return later with a silk rope, or suchlike. Something that leaves no mark.' He meets her eyes briefly and looks away again, staring at the floor. 'Don't let my last vision of this world be the pleasure on his face. I would rather dream my way into the next world, even if my dreams do fill with vengeful spirits...'

She stares at his face as he sits there, for a long time, looking down. Both remain silent, locked within their own fears, until he speaks again.

'Give me more.'

The girl obeys. This time he guzzles more slowly, deliberately, savouring his own last supper. With each swallow now, she watches liquid pulse gently from the corners of his mouth. His actions seem slower, less coordinated, as the deep red wine and the potion within it seep through his veins, filling him with a pensive weariness, drifting in like fog. As she tips the bowl for him to drain, the last few drops bleed from his mouth and dribble down his scrawny throat, following paths formed by wrinkles and blue veins. She tries to beat down the horror and fear that is rising within her. This time, she cannot wipe his mouth. She is frozen.

He catches his breath, and lifts his head to look at her. 'Listen to me, my little slave. You must not remain in this house. You know too much. If they think that you may talk, they will silence you.' His eyelids are drooping now, but he sighs and continues. 'You... you gave me kindness when no one else would, so listen carefully. When you leave here, don't try to take the main roads – that is how runaways are caught. You must hide yourself where no-one will look. Go over the pass above the town... onto the peninsula, to the village near the ruins of Karmylessos. Look for a family in that village. Any family with old ones: the older the better. Tell the old ones you were a friend to Basil of Makri, the husband of Eirene. In that village, they will shelter you. And ask the old ones to show you the path to the ancient shrine... to the goddess of fortune, Tyche. Someone will know the way...'

He closes his eyes for a second. Then his head

twitches, twice, until the eyes half open and meet her own. 'Go to the shrine. At the mouth of the cave, under a layer of flat stones, you will find an ancient well. Look within it. You should find gold there, enough to start your life again. My wife hid it there, many years ago. You have been my last treasure, so you shall have my first...' He sighs, closes his eyes again. Then he slumps back, mumbling, 'Be careful, though. Respect Tyche, or she will play a trick upon you. As she did to me...'

She sits, stunned and paralysed, feeling her stomach churn while she watches his body surrender to sleep. Her mind races, comparing his words to everything she already knows about this house, this family. Can she trust him? His slack, inert form begins to slide sideways and down. She moves to catch him and pulls his body across the cot. She forces herself to think, to plan. 'A curse upon this house,' she mutters... then shakes her head, remembering that this particular house has no need of curses.

That thought spurs her, and she shakes herself like a dog. She wipes his body and the drinking bowl clean, replaces the blanket, and checks that she will leave the room much as it was before she entered. Only when she shuts and bolts the door, does her body permit her to make haste, to flee. At the top of the steps, she pushes the heavy curtain aside and rushes into the blinding light, sucking life into her lungs at last.

She almost blunders into the cadaverous figure waiting there.

'Did he refuse his food?'

Timon's dark eyes examine her and the bowl of soup she carries, just as a cat observes a bird. He has a pillow tucked under one arm. She cannot speak.

'Well?'

'No... no... he was asleep. I could not rouse him.' The words spill out without thought; she floods with relief at what she hears herself saying.

'Well, perhaps I shall go and see him now. You may leave. Go and help in the kitchen.'

She swallows, ridding her mouth of the taste of

rising bile, for a moment at least. 'Yes. Thank you, master.'

*   *   *

Three days later the same girl slips on a loose rock, stumbles, and halts; grasping the moment of respite in a patch of shade, she wafts air under her face to cool the sheen of perspiration lightening her olive skin. She peers down and studies the twisting descent for a moment, frowns, and allows a deep sigh to escape. Then she lifts her gaze, welcoming the distraction of the ruined churches dominating the ancient island city, a mile distant across a narrow strait of sea far below.

Dark curly hair, cropped short, frames a pale, hollow cheeked, hungry face. She can pass for a boy, if she needs to. She wears a loose robe, worn, torn and patched; her sandals have been crudely repaired with the same thin rope that she uses as a belt. A small cloth bundle containing her worldly possessions hangs over her shoulder. This path is becoming impossibly steep – but having stumbled upon it, and followed it this far, why not a few steps further? She restarts her descent, picking her way carefully down the crumbling slope.

The path hairpins down, then cuts sideways onto a narrow, descending ledge; emerging onto a platform of land, dotted with the stumps of dead olive trees. The jagged outcrop above throws a dark shadow down, veiling a shallow cave; within it, layers of yellow, brown and grey rock twist up, around and over, creating an outlandish vision of receding archways, a twisted gateway leading into the underworld.

This must be the place.

As this thought dawns, a gust of wind that seems to contain a presence almost knocks her off her feet. Abruptly, she feels as if she has stepped upon the body of a slumbering giant, and feels herself holding her breath while it twitches, coughs, and opens one eye. She hears herself muttering in Coptic, her native tongue, 'God is gracious'. She crosses herself too, for good measure and resists an urge to drop to her knees.

No, you must stop acting like a slave.

But then she hears her own voice again, whispering, 'Tyche, if you can hear me, grant me good fortune.'

The moment passes. She glances at the stumps of the dead olive trees, and looks beyond them to the rubble of the island city, sacked by pirates centuries before. *You couldn't protect Karmylessos, though, could you, or its people? So, where is your sacred well, filled in by the Christian priests?* She looks around. Under the cliff, at the mouth of the cave, in the centre of this once-holy olive grove, the ground is covered with flat stones. She steps forward and pulls up her sleeves, frowning at the faint red scars that criss-cross her arms. She begins to move the stones away one by one, gradually uncovering a small, low, circular wall. It looks tiny, as if it were built by children.

She shrugs and begins to remove the stones and rocks from inside it, slowly revealing the well below. The effort makes her feel faint. Soon, she has to take a rest. *Am I wasting my time? Maybe the old man was mad, after all, and his stories were fantasy, or deceit.* She frowns and forces herself to work again, refusing her doubts. *I have nothing to lose, nothing – and the people here, on this peninsula, they still respect the old man. They sheltered me, and gave me food, at the mention of his name.*

Reaching deep into the hole, her fingers touch something that yields; something other than stone.

She leans further, until her body feels almost entombed, and one by one pulls out half a dozen more rocks. She uncovers a dry, stiff, slightly yielding object. She hopes it is not a dead animal. At last she frees it and pulls herself out, dragging a flattened, compressed, mummified leather bag. She swallows; it feels much heavier than leather. As it cracks and bends in her hands she feels objects move within its flattened folds. She carefully wrenches the neck open, causing fragments of the drawstring to drop away, and tips the contents out, into the light of day.

Her hand clamps over her mouth. She hardly dares to breathe, in case the goddess Tyche takes this day back, and returns her life to its previous condition. After a while she blinks, and begins to breathe again. *What else am I holding inside?* Slowly, she shakes her head and begins to laugh quietly to herself, as a flood of sensations release into her veins. *My name, Zahra, is a flower. My life has flowered at last. They thought I was stupid. They told me not to waste my time listening to him. They told me he was crazy, senile, wicked, not to be trusted. When I helped him, they punished me, and then laughed at me. That's what you get, they said, for listening to him. See how much trouble he is?*

Who is laughing now? My mother and I were both born as slaves, but that old man gave me the will to escape. His stories told me of his own choices, between good and evil, and how we become what we choose. He boasted of his bad choices, at first – later, I realised that within his boasting, often a confession dwelled. She starts, with a sudden realisation. *When I first listened to his stories – that was when he started to call me his hidden treasure...*

As she sits and gazes at her unexpected good fortune, coins and gems glinting dully in the sun, Zahra also remembers the goddess. She picks out two large gold coins and drops them back into the leather bag. She carefully places it back into the well, gives thanks, and solemnly promises the goddess to use her gift wisely. She wraps the other coins and the jewellery carefully within her own cloth bundle, and then refills the well with rocks. She covers it up, replacing the flat stones. As she turns to leave, she has an image of a giant sinking to earth in her mind, settling down to slumber once again.

*   *   *

Acknowledgements

For everyone who helped me, heartfelt thanks: especially my wife Sheila, who always encourages and supports my scribbling, and Cengiz and Ayse for giving me the inspiration for this book.

Generally, thanks to all of my ex-patients for teaching me about life, and to the many Roman historians who have collected accounts of experiences relevant to the turbulent era of this novel. Particular thanks are due to Donald Queller and the late Thomas Madden whose vivid history of the fourth crusade captured so much human detail, and Michael Angold for his helpful comments and advice about my story.

On the technical side, thanks to Oya Aynur Şirinöz who created the artwork on the cover, and Tom Bromley for his editing.

Author's plea

A polite request; every author writes to be read... if you enjoyed this book, please tell other people about it; either by word of mouth or by reviewing it on websites such as Goodreads or Amazon. Better still, pass it on or use it as a gift for people with similar tastes...